# THE SONG OF O'SULLIVAN'S CHAIN

Bruce Sudds

AOS Publishing, 2023

Copyright © 2023

Bruce Sudds



ISBN: 978-1-990496-40-0

Cover Design: Jessica James

Visit AOS Publishing's website:
www.aospublishing.com

This book is dedicated to my family and the community
I am fortunate enough to call my own.

"They [the Irish] hate our free and fertile isle. They hate our order, our civilisation, our enterprising industry, our sustained courage, our decorous liberty, and our pure religion. This wild, reckless, indolent, uncertain and superstitious race have no sympathy with the English character. Their fair ideal of human felicity is an alteration of clannish brawls and coarse idolatry. Their history describes an unbroken circle of bigotry and blood."

—British prime minister Benjamin Disraeli, 1836


"Quarantine"
by Eavan Boland

In the worst hour of the worst season
    of the worst year of a whole people
a man set out from the workhouse with his wife.
He was walking—they were both walking—north.

She was sick with famine fever and could not keep up.
    He lifted her and put her on his back.
He walked like that west and west and north.
Until at nightfall under freezing stars they arrived.

In the morning they were both found dead.
    Of cold. Of hunger. Of the toxins of a whole history.
But her feet were held against his breastbone.
The last heat of his flesh was his last gift to her.

Let no love poem ever come to this threshold.
    There is no place here for the inexact
praise of the easy graces and sensuality of the body.
There is only time for this merciless inventory:

Their death together in the winter of 1847.
    Also what they suffered. How they lived.
And what there is between a man and woman.
And in which darkness it can best be proved.

"[The Irish are] as great a curse . . . as were the locusts to the land of Egypt."

—George Brown, Canadian member of parliament
and founder of *The Globe and Mail*, 1856

*from* "Grosse Isle"
by Al Purdy

Look stranger
see your own face reflected in the river
stumble up from the stinking hold
blinded by sunlight and into the leaky dinghy
only half-hearing the sailors taunting you
                    "Shanty Irish! Shanty Irish!"
gulp the freshening wind and pinch yourself
trying to understand if the world is a real place
stumble again and fall when you reach the shore
and bless this poisoned earth
but stranger no longer
for this is home

# Contents

# 1. The Song of Spirits

### June 19, 1998—Grand Island, Ontario

"You have to understand that we live in a land that holds the memories of mountains and their demanding spirits," my great-grandfather, Michael O'Sullivan, said to me as he was leaving this world, in his 108th year. I sat beside the bed in the ancestral home of my father's family on Grand Island, across from Kingston, Ontario, as he said those words.

"That's where we begin," he added, and lifted his hand towards me. I met the hand and held it in my own. It was large and still had the strength I had known as a child. I had returned to the island, the place where I spent my summers as a kid, to be with him. And when he spoke, I felt as though my soul was being fed a little. I didn't realize how hungry I was until these words were set before me. It was like the day when I was a child wandering the woods near his home and found a sole apple tree. Though it was autumn and the forest was ablaze in fall colours, the flavour of a sweet apple was the rare, unexpected gift that has stayed with me. Was it wrong of me to take from this man who was passing? I didn't think so. And *passing* seemed to be the correct word for it. I could feel a transfer of something nearly material.

"There were incidents and notable individuals long before me and the lighthouse I kept. But you should understand that we are the children of this place. Just as our family was in Ireland."

I needed to hear what he said, maybe more than anyone in my family. I was at a crossroads in my life, and being here, with my great-grandfather and the rest of my family, seemed to be the right place for me. I knew the answers as to what came next for me, would emerge here . . .

"Do you recall the stories I told you as a boy? You and your cousin? I thought you would. There are spaces on the earth that are touched by spirit. Just as some people are imbued with the same. Some around here—Irish, of course—say that fairies came with us from the old country. But there's no way they would board those coffin ships, with their stinking injustice and death. No, there were spirits here, and we are a people who are willing to hear them. Just as they say the same in Ireland in the old tales. When I read them, they remind me they are here as well. That they are present here came to me, in parts, over my lifetime. And those same creatures will make demands of us. No different than the spirits in Ireland.

"The story of it that comes to me, just before I fall asleep, goes like this: Before there was Lake Ontario or the mighty St. Lawrence River pouring into the Atlantic Ocean, there were great mountains just north of here, and on those peaks were creatures not human. They dwelt above the clouds on these soaring peaks. Feeding on the mist that wrapped around the summits. They sipped it at their leisure. And floated, not walked. They had a language, but to us it would be called song.

"When the great glaciers were hurled from the north to the south, they were slowed in their progress by these spirits, trying to protect their home. In time, the creatures were defeated and destroyed by the cold walls of ice. The glaciers, as you know, made slow progress, but progress nonetheless, and toppled these great mountains.

"Time passed, and the ice finally melted, and the bodies of these spirits were left strewn in the waters of the melted ice. And that water flowed down here. Lake Ontario was created with the bodies of the spirits at the bottom of the waters and beneath the soils of the islands in the lakes and St. Lawrence River. So the waters, and the islands especially, are infused with the spirit of these creatures, who, if you listen, will guide you.

"If they ask, that's why you can say we're wily micks who still refuse to be formed into something other than what the spirits demand. That is what forms us if we allow it. Like the reshaped shoreline after the storm."

# 2. A Lighthouse

October 11, 1927—Kingston, Ontario


"You'll never raise your light up there," Bert Hazelton pronounced.

Michael O'Sullivan bit down on nothing at all. He looked past Bert, because he knew that if the man could see his face, he would catch the disdain that Michael struggled to hide.

*I know I'm tired, but he is still a haughty customer. Calls me in to meet him and doesn't even get a room. Just standing in the lobby of City Hall like a brush salesman. But I need to get this done. There's no rest until I get this done. He looks rested, though, doesn't he? And hands as soft as a cloud when he finally shook mine. I had to leave my mitt out there for too long. He could be a worker, pretty tall and broad, but you can tell he's a generation away from that. Now he hires workers. Pale skinned from not being outside and that cropped blond hair. His mirror at home is likely exhausted at him preening in it, getting his hair just right.*

"Well, Mick, it's your decision to make, how to get it up there, I suppose," Bert said. *I've offended the man. And he does seem capable. Respected by many. And a big fella. Every part the Mick, with that wild, thick hair, pointed chin, and mischief about him. So much mischief with these people.*

"Right. 'Tis." *He's retreating now. Just get it done. You know you have to get it off that shoal they call an island. . . Do I? Do I know that? It was just a goddamn dream. Sorry, dreams. Over and over again. . . And voices. The damn voices. They'd think I was crazy if they knew. They would take away my post as the keeper. Lock me up in the pen here. And they'd be right to do so, maybe. And that's why I can't talk to anyone about it. Even the priest.*

*And him calling me Mick. Only my family and close friends call me Mick. That's the thing, isn't it, with being named Michael and being Irish? The obvious nickname is Mick, but it's also one of the curses that are used against me and my kind. It's how he says it. Like he's spitting it from his gob. But he's got the contract. Swallow it up and get it done, Mick. I guess I can't hide that I'm Irish. Even if I changed my name. And I wouldn't, would I?*

*He doesn't know what he's talking about anyway. He barely knows the waters or a craft, let alone lighthouses. He's just a mill owner from miles north of the drink. As was his father. And his dad, they say, farmed. The whole clan of them escaped, generations back, from down in the Hudson Valley, before the Yanks drove 'em out for being a bunch of king-lovers.*

*And I served in the war. Volunteered even. They wanted fishermen home, catching food for people, but I didn't feel it was right. So I served, didn't I? It was at the end of the affair, but I fought, though.*

"I just don't think you can pull the lighthouse up the slope with a team of horses."

*That's it. I've had it.* "You're right. I'll do it with the one."

Bert just shook his head. "When will you do it? I've gotta see this. Well, I need to see that the job is done completely."

"The ice is gonna set thick enough, to be sure, by the second week of January. It always does. I'll get it done then."

"Let me know the day, and I'll have to come out to see it."

"Grand. But I'm sorry if this is the best you know of a good time, Bert."

"It isn't, Mick. It's my duty."

"Call it what you will, then."

With that, Michael turned and made his way out of the lobby of City Hall.

*Isn't it rough enough that I have to do this errand? A fool's errand, likely, but I have to put up with this stiff royalist? He's not even a full Brit. I think he's half a Dutchman. Wooden shoes and all. I've come all the way to the mainland just to listen to this?*

Michael quickly made his way from City Hall to the ferry docks. *I don't want to risk the voices here on the mainland.*

He was tired. The dreams were continuous and demanding. The voices, when he was alone outdoors, were jarring. They would frighten him.

*I like fishing. I like the water. I didn't mind being a lighthouse keeper. It's easy enough. I come to this island—well, this pile of rocks, this spit here by the shoal beneath—each morning and on the way home. Turn it off in the morning, turn it on in the evening. And it's a nice spot to read a book. Quiet, isn't it? Any fool could do it. Even Hazelton, if he knew how to navigate a craft.*

With that thought, Michael laughed.

The lighthouse stood on tiny Day Island. An oval landmass in the lake, about 280 yards long. It was only about a third of a mile from Grand Island, and before the light had been placed on it the shoals that surrounded it had been the ruin of many ships. The original light was replaced in 1900 by the current configuration. A report by the "Superintendent of lights above Montreal" at the time described the light thus:

Latitude North: 44 11 30
Longitude West: 44 9 20 (1871 76 33 0)
No. of Lights: One, Fixed or Steady
Colour of Light: Red
Miles Seen in Clear Weather: 6
Lighthouse: Square, Wood
Height of Building from Base to Vane: 39 feet
Year Lighted: 1858 (former) 1900 (current)
Character of Illuminating Apparatus: Diatropic of the 7th order.

*Why do I have to be a lighthouse keeper and now a mover? I just want to be left alone in my skiff. Well, I'm almost not one. If they change their mind, if they won't agree to move it, I told them I was done with them and the job. That should push them. There's no one left out here to do the job. It would be too much of a burden for anyone else, travelling all that way to the island, when it's just across a bit of a channel from my home.*

*But I have to get it done or I'll never sleep again. The dreams. Over and over again. Massive walls of ice lurching down Lake Ontario from the west. Like the glaciers that formed the land thousands of years ago. But this time moving fast, tall as mountains. White or clear, cold and malevolent. And that creature out there. A man? Somehow familiar, but I couldn't get a good look at him. Did he have wings? But he couldn't fly from the icy onslaught. I guess this is dread. Like when we arrived at Passchendaele in '17. It's like the ice could destroy the entire world. And each time, the lighthouse appeared as the object standing between myself and the advance. I can't speak of dreams to Hazelton or anyone else. Not even Sarah. They'd all think I'm off with the spirits.*

*And then the whisperings. Almost always when I'm alone, outdoors. As though the words were travelling on the wind. A message sent from some mischievous creature riding on a westerly, to be sure. Always warning of the troubles to that winged creature. And when I try to hide from them, reading the old books in the study, they find me when I pause and lift my eyes from the page.*

*Speaking to Father O'Reilly had no medicine in it, did it? He only has room for his one god and his son. I have room for more. They push out his gods, don't they? Jesus doesn't speak to me here. No, it's the spirits of the land and water. I'm sure of it. Demanding buggers that they are.*

He remembered his father speaking of problems a neighbour had at his farm. The new house was built and then windows broke and cupboards slammed in the wee hours. The spirits, the *sidhe*, he said the neighbour, Scott, called them, might have known this place as their own and they disturbed them. Scott had gone to the smithy in town to borrow every piece of iron he could, from chains to anvils, and placed them around the house to drive out the vexed creatures. It worked, he said. They hate the iron.

*But what will I do? Wrap my foolish head in an iron cap? But maybe the lighthouse?*

He had a metal chain, inherited from his father. About ten feet long. And a few other devices salvaged from his farm and from those nearby—a hay rake, a thresher, discarded—that he disassembled and placed around the building, along with parts of a plow. Sarah caught sight of him distributing the items in the yard around the house. At dinner she had questions.

"What sort of business are you up to, leaving machinery in the yard?"

"Oh, just something I thought I would try."

"Try do what?"

Michael was flustered and embarrassed.

"My God, woman, leave me be. Do I interfere in your day and tasks? I do not, do I?"

"I was curious, Michael."

"Well, that's a cat killer, isn't it?"

"Do I look like some cat to you, Michael O'Sullivan!"

"No, you don't, do you. I'm just sayin' is all."

"You're saying foolishness."

"Now you're on to something, Sarah, now you are."

*She's right. It's making no difference. I had just dropped that old piece of a plow beside the building. The last piece to form the iron circle. The wind kicked up and that voice came back on it with whisperings of the winged man in peril. And me, screaming at the wind, hurling the piece of metal at it. A madman. And I quit reading the old books of Ireland in case they were conjuring these spirits, didn't I? But it made no difference. It only left me missing the tales and telling myself the ones I could remember. There's no protecting me from myself, is there?*

So, with others, Michael spoke of the need for the lighthouse to come down for reasons of safety. Security. The iron-bound concrete caisson that the lighthouse had sat on was supported underwater by four square groynes built of oak timber and filled with rock. Michael found, and reported, that the groynes were deteriorating and urged the local authorities to move the tower to Grand Island. The island he called home. At Clear Point, on Grand Island, there stood a bluff about some thirty feet above the lake. In his dreams, he was standing there, on his neighbour's property, the Reeves farm, watching the walls of ice below him. He clearly had to move the lighthouse here.

*But why does it matter so much? So a few day sailors and merchants can move around the islands here? Anyone who knows anything keeps away from this part of the lake and stays close to the Kingston side on the mainland. Foolishness.*

His home on the island had always brought him great peace, but now that was shattered. The O'Sullivans had owned this land for nearly forty years. The fifty acres had been purchased by Michael's father, Seamus, and his wife, Bridget, in 1888. With the help of Seamus's father, Patrick.

The land for the lighthouse was purchased from the Reeves family just months before Michael's meeting with Bert Hazelton. He had also purchased the surrounding land so that his holdings were now ninety acres.

Seamus O'Sullivan had contracted local limestone to build the house, which was finished the same year he bought the land. Bridget had protested at the expense of stone over wood, but Seamus had told her that "if an Irishman is going to build a house here, it better be of stone, so there's not a chance all the royalists can call you shanty Irish." An addition was added when Michael was a child. Bridget liked to remind her husband that they would be using wood, so he better brace himself for taunts. Seamus found little humour in it.

The main barn and the machine shed were added in the first few years as well. The lighthouse was adjacent to the western edge of his property. As Michael was their only son, and Seamus was a pilot for boats travelling the St. Lawrence River, locals were hired to help with their herd of dairy cows.

The house had two large fireplaces. One in the dining room and another in the sitting room. Both were nearly six and a half feet tall at the openings and just as wide. Much of the furniture in the house had been handed down to Michael from his parents. The large oak dining table and chairs, the more recent mahogany chairs and loveseat, the wingback seat and footstool by the fire in the sitting room, the desk. And many of the photographs and paintings in the study were welcome reminders for him of his mother and father.

Seamus and Bridget had passed away nearly ten years before, during the Spanish flu outbreak. Seamus, they believe, contracted the illness piloting a ship out of Montreal. He had brought it back home, and he and Bridget succumbed to it over the next two months.

Michael had missed the notification about his parents' death as he was already returning to Canada after the armistice with Germany was signed. He was on the ferry, happy to be home, when Margy Best offered her condolences and was mortified to realize she was sharing news he had not yet heard.

When he arrived at the house, still in shock, he wandered the rooms for nearly two hours and could feel their presence while being devastated by their absence. The house and everything in it became his way of keeping them near to him in the years to come.

Michael loved everything about his home. The stone walls, the waters that greeted him, and the community of care that surrounded him. He always told his sons, "You're given the right amount of room to grow here. But no one goes it alone." It was true. The island's population was small enough, at roughly seven hundred people, that distinctions that occurred on the mainland, between rich and poor, Catholic and Protestant, were muted. Individuals were judged by their behaviour, their ability to take care of themselves and, when needed, care for others on the island. Their home on the island was "hard won," Michael's grandfather had said, when they were young. Patrick was the first off the boat from Ireland. A famine baby.

When he was a boy, Michael would ask his grandfather, Patrick, questions about their family and his life. Patrick would tell stories of his farm north of Thayendanegea and the people in the area. But when Michael pushed for stories of Patrick's parents and what it was like in Ireland and how they got here, Patrick would grow silent. In those dark silences, Michael would feel he had done something wrong and change the subject. He often wondered if the lack of answers he received as a child spurred him to read so much Irish history, mythology, and literature when he returned from the war.

Seamus, for his part, spoke to Michael of life on the farm but also of travelling up the St. Lawrence River with his mother and father on a summer holiday. He loved it. The myriad of unique islands. He made up his mind he wanted to be out there, and as a teenager he worked on fishing boats leaving from Thayendanegea. As he grew older, he apprenticed to be a pilot on the St. Lawrence, one of the few Irish Catholics to be doing so. Guiding ships down the mighty river, he loved seeing the grand homes of the older Protestant families on the waterfront and on the islands and decided that was for him.

His father was happy to sell the farm to help Seamus raise the money for the tract of land to build a home on Grand Island. He ensured that the new home had a bit of a farm as well.

"They loved this place," my great-grandfather told me. "It had been generations since our family had a home like this. You know, land we owned, a fine house and a working farm. None of it could be taken from us. A life with so little want . . ."

Finally, the day came in January for Michael to move the lighthouse. Bert took the ice highway from Kingston's harbour south towards Forest Island. Most travelled it by buggy or horse or even walked it, but Bert had one of the first cars in the area. It was a second-hand Model T, but it was a car nonetheless. And he was proud to drive it.

It was the end of the first week of January, and the ice road was clearly marked with discarded Christmas trees. Bits of garland and tinsel were still attached and glittered in the intermittent north wind. The world before him was a wash of white: snow-covered ice, a light grey sky, and humps of two pale, snowy islands ahead of him, with leafless, stone-coloured trees.

*If he doesn't get it up there today, he's going to have to figure out another way—at his own expense. He'll not get another bit of money out of me,* Bert Hazelton thought.

A hand-painted sign tied to a piece of lumber held up by a foot of frozen snow told him "Day Island," with an arrow marked, pointing to the right. Bert followed it. He could see Michael and his team of horses.

When he reached the island, he stopped his vehicle and stepped out. He counted six horses. A mix of Clydesdales and saddle horses. Michael had borrowed most of them from neighbours who could spare them for the day. Few were travelling in the winter and they didn't need to hook the horse to the buggy.

Bert stepped out of the car, smiled, and said, "I see you've come to your senses and are using a team of horses."

Michael looked down and grimaced. "Right."

Bert's gaze was pulled to the towering building. It had seemed so small from the mainland, but here in person it was imposing.

"I'll load it onto the timber skids here and we'll get across the ice," Michael said, gesturing to the great trees at his feet with the bark still on them that had been rendered limbless to serve the purpose.

"Okay," said Bert.

The lighthouse was still perched on the caisson supported by the timber groynes. Michael could slide the building onto the wooden sled he had formed and then pull it the three-quarters of a mile to Grand Island and its new home. To do so required a chain.

*The chain will have to be large and strong,* Michael thought, when he was considering his task. *Greater than anything I or my neighbours currently own. Big enough to circle the tower twice, to be sure, and then connect into the rigging on the horses. A great length of chain. And each link needs to be mighty. Not one can give way if I'm to accomplish the task.*

Michael stood still on the ice. He knew there would be no rest for him until he got this right, and there would be no room for error. He had staked his reputation on the need to move the lighthouse and was adamant about the location it had to call its new home. An error in the process of moving it would cause others to doubt him and put the entire project in jeopardy.

He hoped to quell his concerns by turning to the task before him.

"Can you give me a hand with the chain?" he asked Bert.

"You didn't bring no one?"

"Just you."

Bert sighed and took the chain in his hand. His wrist gave a little. He was shocked at the weight of it.

Michael smiled and his mind turned to the forging of the chain. He had gone to Shaughnessy, on neighbouring Cashell Island, for it. He explained the purpose and Jack Shaughnessy laughed and told him he had never forged such a piece of chain as this. "It will take us days and weeks to get it done. But there's a local outfit that's been pulling iron from just north of here, and I can work with their steel rods to form something, I'm sure."

Each link was more than five inches long and over an inch in thickness. Michael watched Jack and his son in the shop stoke the fires, drop the wrought iron into the flames, and then bend the metal into a scalding length, add it to the previous link of the chain, and forge weld it closed. Great sparks flew as the hammers came down on the metal to force the pieces together.

He was mesmerized, and unsure why this was the case. He had been in smithing shops in the past, but something about what was being done carried a great import for him. More than he expected. The Canadian Shield to the north was the base of ancient mountains, and this was where the iron was extracted. *Some of the toughest and oldest stone on the earth gave itself over to make this,* Michael thought.

And he thought of the dreams that followed that day. The sprites on the mountains, sipping mist from the air and battling the wall of ice that stole their homes and their lives and sent their bodies into the lake. He had woken from them sweaty and gasping for air.

*It's too much. Too much for one man's mind to bear. All of these dreams. It may drive me mad. What am I to do with this sort of information?* He would pull himself out of bed in the dark. *Better to continue to be tired than to face more of these sorts of dreams.*

Michael snapped back to the job at hand. He looked at Bert.

"They've all been collared," he told him. "Can you link the traces onto the form there?"

He had arranged the horses with one large Clydesdale as the lead and the rest paired in twos behind. At the rear of the team, he had fashioned a log into a gathering point for their lines, beyond which was his newly fashioned chain.

"Fine," Bert hollered to Michael, who had already moved on to the work of connecting the two ends of the chain to the device.

The round timber skids, each nearly ninety feet long each and twenty inches at the widest point, lay waiting before the building. Michael had looped the chain around the structure. He had run chains from the log behind the horses to the skids as well, so they moved along with the tower.

The horses stood quietly. Everything was done. Light snow fell, and the only sound was the breathing of the men and horses.

*I guess this is it,* Michael thought. He strode through the snow to the front of the team,

He placed a hand on the muzzle of his favourite of the animals. She was his own saddle horse. Bay, he called her. Of course, it was her colour, but he liked that *Bay* was close, in its sound, to *baby.* And he always had affection for her. She has calm, perseverant, and seemed to enjoy his company. In the quiet days of winter, with no fishing to do, he would often make an excuse to be in the barn with her, fixing something or other. Bay had heard of his troubles. The dreams and the plans for today. He needed to rely on her now.

*She's the greatest listener I've ever met,* he thought, and quietly laughed.

Michael moved to the front of the team. He looked to see Bert, back at the lighthouse, inspecting the chains.

"Okay, Bay, this is it. We gotta get across now." He placed his head on her muzzle. When he did, he realized how tired he was.

"Bert, I think we're ready."

"Fine."

Michael placed a hand on Bay's collar and calmly whispered, "Let's go, girl."

She took a few steps forward, and the other horses in the team felt her pull on the rigging, looked at her, and slowly moved with her. Michael continued his slow walk, and the chain jangled and grew taut. The towering building groaned, there was a pause, and it then scratched against the concrete slab it had stood on for years.

The distance to the new location was less than a mile as the crow flew, but their trek was no flight. They were on the north side of Day Island and would need to reach the north side of Grand Island. The shortest route would have been across the island itself. But the route of least resistance was along the ice. Which meant they had to circle the small island and then drive south to reach Grand Island. The ice road would be little help to them. They would intersect it for thirty feet or so.

The snow was deep, nearly three feet on the ice, and the day was cold. Getting on for minus four degrees Fahrenheit.

The horses were pulling and getting accustomed to the weight. Bay could sense that some wanted to turn away, and she just kept moving forward steadily behind Michael. The others turned back to her and followed.

Michael was surprised he was sweating in such cold. He was bundled tight by Sarah, but he knew it was more than that.

As they circled the island, he could hear cracks in the ice and the horses breaking through the shallow spots close to the land.

He cooed to them all, "It's fine, it's fine, keep going now."

They made their way into the channel between the two islands, and he was shocked at the quiet. There wasn't much of a breeze, just the sound of the chains, the jingle of the trace harness, the breathing of the horses as they moved across the great whiteness. The lighthouse itself stood as it normally stood and slid with relative ease across the snow and ice.

Bert, thankfully, took up the rear behind the lighthouse. *What's he going to do? Catch it if it falls? Goddamn cheese-eater.*

They were crossing the channel diagonally towards the bluffs on Grand Island. He could see it now. Clear Point jutted out from the island to the north, about 450 yards away. The new home for the lighthouse, thirty feet above the water.

"Here comes the real test," he said gently to Bay.

He brought the team to a halt at the base of the sweep that led to the point of the landmass. Bert popped his head out from behind the wooden structure and held it there, peering towards him. Michael put a hand up to let him know to wait.

Unhooking the chain from the team, he placed it solely on Bay's collar. He looked back to Bert and shouted to him. "Keep an eye on the horses, will you!"

Bert looked perplexed but nodded.

He began to climb the sweep with his horse, cooing to her. "We've just got to get that chain up there. No problem."

The incline was fairly steep, but he and the mare climbed it with relative ease. At the top stood a large iron capstan with two small arms. The device had come from one of the freighters on the Great Lakes, *Northern Spirit*, out of service and sold for parts. His father had bought it to use as a sort of winch on the farm. He had taken the great hulk of iron and placed it on a wooden structure he fashioned with wheels, which he secured with short chains to a massive oak and a mature maple. Michael unhooked the chain he had around Bay, wrapped it twice around the capstan, and then back to the collar on Bay.

"Here we go, honey, you and I."

He looked behind to see the top of the lighthouse staring at him. Doubt seized him and self-recriminations. *I should have done this with a team. Why did I have to go through all of this trouble just to prove something to Hazelton?* He paused, sighed, and spoke aloud. "Well, we're here now. I've made this bargain. And I have a right to make bargains after being pushed and bullied into this whole goddamn affair."

With that, Michael placed both hands on the chain and began to pull with Bay. The horse sensed his motion and joined him. With their forward motion, the capstan's ratchet clicked through a couple of notches, holding them. The chain tightened, the horse strained, pawed a little at the snow and earth, but began to move the lighthouse towards the slope.

As the structure reached the sweep of it, the horse struggled. Michael grimaced. "It's a mighty load, I know." He heaved again with the horse on the chain. The capstan clicked and clicked again. And then stopped.

"Easy, now. Take a break."

"Everything okay up there?" he could hear Bert hollering.

"Always!" he replied.

Michael walked to the device and picked up a large metal rod that lay beside it. Nearly six and a half feet long and five inches thick. *I thought I might need to use you and I guess I was right.*

He dug one end of the rod into the ground and rested it against one of the metal arms of the capstan. As he leaned into it, he hollered, "Let's go, girl."

The horse strained and the device clicked. Michael moved forward and put all his weight on the heavy lever. Groaning, he pushed with his full force.

"Click."

*It's going to need more from me.* And with that, Michael heaved himself against the lever.

"Click."

*There it is, then. I'm going to have to toss myself into it.*

He stepped back and threw his body at the metal rod, grabbing it in the midst of his flight. He and the horse continued like this, his body straining, banging and bruising with his charges against the metal, and the horse breathing heavily into the cold air, sending a fog.

"Click, click, click."

*There you go. Three clicks for each attempt is good measure.*

Both Michael and Bay were spitting into the cold air and dripping slobber from their mouths. Their bodies steamed from sweat. Michael groaned low. Over and over again, he threw himself at the lever. The groans became grunts as bruises formed and ribs were bruised and then cracked.

His mind began flashing scenes from his life. *They never quit speaking to us like children, did they? Like we were dim. Different. Somehow, no matter what, less.*

"Goddamn this. Goddamn this all. My Lord, the pain of it. What else is there to do? Such a fool. What sort of gods! Destroy me, then, if you will. You miserable power. Take the body of me, then. I don't care now."

*If we fought, we got. Fight and fight and fight is all we could do for a scrap of land, but no respect. I don't care what they think anymore. I know who I am.*

He looked like a small puppet handled by a cruel owner. Thrashing against the rod of metal as though he were fighting it.

*Thank heavens for the teacher at the school. A priest, but he still taught us the language and the old tales. Bless him. It gave us a bit of pride, didn't it?*

Tears streamed from him. His head bounced from the pole with one of his attempts, leaving a gash above his left eye and blood running down his face and onto the snow. He blacked out for a few seconds. He continued to strain against the lever, pushing so hard he dislocated his right shoulder.

*I'm in pieces now. Pieces. So be it. The pain of it. Don't go yet. Now, keep at it. Finish or perish. . . I liked best how the teacher said our names in the Irish language. He'd go around the room and translate each one. And we felt chuffed, didn't we? Oh, there we are. I practised saying it: Mícheál.*

The lighthouse now stood on the hill on the island that was its new home. Just as was demanded of Michael. He sensed the horse found it easier once the building passed the crest of the slope, and he slackened, nearly fell, and held himself up by leaning against the metal bar.

The building was followed by Bert Hazelton, who seemed both impressed and annoyed. "It shouldn't, I mean it shouldn't be done. I don't know how you would do such a thing. It's still foolish," he announced.

He caught sight of Michael. His body was heaving. Patches of snow turning red with his blood.

"Jesus in heaven! What happened to you, Mick?"

Michael didn't answer. His body was in agony, but he refused to let Bert know. He simply nodded to him. He used all of his strength not to fall to the ground and held desperately to the metal rod.

Turning from Bert, he opened his coat and shirt with his left hand. He couldn't move the other arm. He could see dark bruises forming on his skin all over his torso. Breathing was difficult. Sarah would tend to him. He was sure that at least two of his ribs and his collarbone were fractured.

He stared at the structure and the dull grey sky while he tried to catch his breath, his body emitting steam into the winter air.

"May the spirits let me be now," he said to no one between breaths.

"What was that, Mick?" Bert asked.

He had forgotten about Bert. Trying to steady his breath and wincing, Michael looked at Bert Hazelton and tried to speak, but blood oozed from his mouth when he opened it. He wiped it away with a bloodier hand that only smeared more of it across his face.

Summoning the pronunciation he had heard as a child, he swallowed hard to gain the strength to utter one line.

"The name's Mícheál."

# 3. A Farm

## March 23, 1847–Leadmore West Townland, near Kilrush, County Clare

Dennis O'Sullivan rose slowly from his bed and made his way to the doorway of his small home. He moved gingerly to ensure he didn't wake his sleeping wife. He planned to be the first to check with his grandson, James, about his journey to the landlord's estate the previous day.

*I know it's too early in the season. We just finished planting the crop. But the blight. Will it return again? I can't turn from thinking about it. It's an affliction, I know. I know. I don't have the strength to get past the worry, though.*

It had been a fitful sleep of worry, dreams of violence, and drowning. He was glad to rise and be away from it all and enjoy the calm and peace of dawn. He stretched his back and looked out from the door of their small thatch-roofed home. A tall man, once broad-shouldered, he now stood a bit stooped. His pale skin was paler after a long winter with little in the way of food. And that scarcity had also robbed him of some of his light brown hair. He had been trying to eat less as time marched forward and their meagre stock of food dwindled. It was a quick estimation for Dennis. *I'm the eldest of our lot, and so I should take the least. Even the oats are low now. God knows how long this deprivation will last.*

He liked standing in the warmth and dryness of their home, looking across the verdant fields, past the cottages of the McInerneys, the Collinses, his cousins the Normiles, and down to the sea and islands.

Dennis looked behind him into his home. *We're more fortunate than most. With solid stone structures and fine thatched roofs on both, aren't we? But there's barely a thing in here now. Ellen has sold anything she could for a few shillings for food. Just a few sticks of furniture left. Not even enough chairs for the four of us at the same moment. And friends with just scraps of wood and mud around them. And some worse! Living in ditches, really. I ought not to make such complaints. But we're low on food, aren't we? And we can't keep going on like this. Some of them, though. Families of ten in one room, I hear. Thanks be that Liam followed my advice and had just the one child. It's saving us, isn't it? Maybe James will follow suit now.*

*We'd surely be done for if we hadn't had the relief jobs on the roads. Ten pence a day for Liam kept us fed, didn't it? But only one man in the family was permitted to take part and, with our begging,*

*Beatrice allowed a few days. Too many needing it. I understand. You have to parse it out fair like.*

*There isn't a soul to be seen yet today. Not even a cow or pig for some time now. Slaughtered or sold for food. It's desperate. Just a few more small homes without their fires lit yet. This quiet scene brings a bit of peace, though, doesn't it? And so far, no lost soul wandering the hills or down by the seashore. There seems to be more and more of them each day. We haven't much to give anyone, let alone ourselves, even if it's considered a slight to the spirits to deny a traveller. . .*

*My sixty-six-year-old body feels at its best this time of day. Tranquility and contentment are rare feelings in our home now, aren't they? For everyone I know. . .*

The town of Kilrush was behind the building, to the northeast about two miles away. His sense of ease was coming to an end as he thought about the day ahead of him.

*I'll need a rest soon enough. And the sights of Kilrush are the stuff of nightmares. Lost, broken bodies. Some children. How much can we do? Pitiful.*

It was then that he felt the hands of Ellen on his back. Like Dennis, she had been a fit woman. But now his wife's broad hips were the only aspect of her that seemed to convey strength and health. She had the same ghostly skin and hungered look.

"Up already, then?" she asked.

"Appears . . ."

"How are you?"

"Low. And how is your health, then?"

"Ah, the same, isn't it?"

"Rest, then."

"No. I'm up now. You can."

"I have to be helping Doyle mend his roof."

"You know he can't pay you. Not in food or shillings."

"I do."

"But you'll do it anyway."

"I will. He's our neighbour. For years now."

"He's sick too, isn't he?"

"Just unfed. No fever."

Ellen shook her head but said no more. *I suppose he needs this,* she thought. *To work and to give back what he can.*

She gestured with her head beyond the door. "Shall we?"

The two walked slowly to the garden patch. The soil had been tilled, potatoes planted, and their grandson had visited their landlord, Crofton Vandeleur, the day before to see about other seeds for their garden. They were told that a government program was to be put in place so that families could plant other vegetables this year in case the potatoes were stricken again. Both Dennis and Ellen wanted answers from James this morning.

"Plenty follows scarcity," Dennis offered, as they passed the dark earth of the garden.

Ellen pushed air through her lips and shook her head. "Fever follows scarcity," she said. "And you know that to be the truth. Not conjecture."

They both looked down the dell to their destination: the small home in which their son, his wife, and their grandson and his family lived. It bothered Ellen to see them all sharing such a small building.

*If there's a sign we've fallen, it's that,* she thought. *And there's nothing for them to do. There's no work. Well, you can always find work. Lately just the relief work. But nothing fruitful. No, there's no fruit for us at all.*

Dennis was thinking about opportunities. *Two years of potato failures. Where do I go now? There's talk of a lighthouse on Scattery Island, farther out in the bay, and maybe me being the keeper. I guess with my experience at sea, they think I'd be fine enough at it. But it will be years before they get that done. Years I know I don't have. But maybe Liam could do it. I have history and not much in the way of tomorrows. . . Is that what got me here? The series of choices I've made along the way. Have I damned them? My child and his own.*

His mind turned to his tale, as it had over and over again this last year or so.

Dennis was born in 1781, just after the end of the Penal Laws in Ireland. It meant, among other liberties, that Irish men could join the British military and make some money. Dennis loved the sea and took to it with the Royal Navy at thirteen, with his father's approval and tears from his mother. He was just sixteen and three years into his service when he knew he had to find a new vocation. He was on board HMS *Sandwich* in the Thames when a mutiny broke out. He was sympathetic to the cause—better treatment of the sailors and better pay—but thought the demand to dissolve the British parliament seemed foolish. It was quashed, and after helping a few men remove the body of their executed leader, Richard Parker, from the ship so his wife, Anne, could find a proper burial, he felt weary.

*There were always jobs for the Irish in the military forces,* he thought now. *They liked to say that Ireland was the inexhaustible nursery of the finest soldiers. Like it was supposed to make us feel good about ourselves. But there was little in the way of advancement. That became clear following the events on the* Sandwich. *There was a fog of suspicion around me, wasn't there?*

He had become friends with a young man from Dublin, Thomas O'Shaughnessy, on the *Sandwich*. Thomas's father was a blacksmith in Bray, just south of Dublin. The two served six more months, then went back to Ireland with the plan to become blacksmiths under the tutelage of Thomas's father, Malachi.

They arrived to find Malachi was heavily involved in an organization known as the Society of United Irishmen. The society's expressed goal was to create an Irish parliament where all the people would have equal rights. Both Thomas and Dennis were inspired by the organization. As young men with military training, they were attractive recruits and joined in the plans for an armed rebellion. So, little work was done in the forge, and soon Dennis's plans to become a blacksmith were behind him. When news that the first phase of the rebellion in Dublin had been put down, Dennis and Thomas joined thousands of other men to fight at Vinegar Hill.

*The soldiers were so young. Not just us but the Brits too. I had to try and hate them. I had to put that feeling into my heart so I could load and fire the musket, didn't I? And most of the men near me were only handed a pike. A stick and spike to hold off the trained and armed British soldiers. Some others, just farmhands and fishermen, swinging scythes at cannons. My heart fell, didn't it? I knew we were doomed. The din of it. It's still with me. Rattled by the sound of shots and cannonballs still today. A loud noise can take me back there. But it's the wailing of men and the sight of them that haunts me. Robbed me of peace for so long. Maybe I shot one. I stabbed at two with the bayonet. But I was not fierce. No, I was not. Gerard McCarthy, who got through with me, liked to regale me and others with the bravery he saw in me, but it was just fear. I couldn't summon much hate, but the terror of it all washed me away like a great wave on the sea. No one knows that, do they? I was just fighting to stay alive. . .*

*As I stepped through Needham's Gap and out of the horror, I just kept running for peace. Poor McCarthy could barely keep up. I wanted to be as far as possible from the battle and the plans of men. West. And west I went to the home I knew. Where the Shannon meets the western sea. I held it hard in my head, running, walking, or travelling by cart back there. The rolling hills I knew in peace as a boy. Soft days and nights with the stars growing quietly above us and where I tasted joy as a child. It wasn't until that day that I knew peace means joy for us grown now.*

Dennis's head was swimming, and his legs grew weak.

*Ah, there it is*, he thought. *I'm not well, am I?*

He felt hands on his back once again.

"You're all right now," Ellen said, as she held him.

"I am. And thanks to you."

"What were ya thinking about? Your head was off somewhere else."

"The summer I returned here . . . and you were as bright as a bundle of sea thrift blooming." Dennis smiled at her. "You still are that to me."

"Stop it now," she replied, smiling.

When he returned, there was little in the way of work, so he became a labourer on farms until he met Ellen and became a tenant farmer himself. He had ten acres of land now.

Ellen was happy Dennis was smiling. *I fear that with the rains, the blight will be back*, she thought. *That's what they say does it. And if I see the spots this year, I don't know if I can stop myself from wailing about it. And the children don't need to see that, do they? And it's them I'll be crying for, not myself. I'm not sure how much I have left in me. Nor Dennis for that matter. He's likely to blow away in a gale from the sea, isn't he?*

It had been a rainy night. The skies had cleared at dawn, but the ground was still wet. They reached the small home with clay walls and a thatched roof just a few hundred yards from the sea. They relied on the dulse as a source of nutrients for the potatoes. The previous year, they had seen many eating the dulse itself out of desperation.

Smoke was rising from the chimney, which meant at least Beatrice was awake. They both paused before they entered, afraid of what they would learn from their son.

"Good morning, is it?" Dennis asked as he opened the door, trying to sound cheerful.

"Oh, I wish it was," said Beatrice. She was sitting by the fire to stay warm.

Dennis and Ellen make their way into the small, dimly lit room. The cottage was the same style as Dennis and Ellen's, with a room with a fireplace for warmth and cooking and one bedroom. Liam and Beatrice had used some boards to create privacy for the bed used by their son, James, and his wife, Genevieve, in the main room.

"Is that the case, then?" Ellen asked.

"'Tis," said James emerging from the makeshift room. Liam appeared from the bedroom.

"So, Vandeleur had no seeds for you, then?" Dennis asked.

"He did. But at a price. From the office at the market," James replied.

"Really?"

"I'm afraid that is the truth. He started talking nonsense about free markets and so on. As if I had any care for that. And saying the government can't solve the problem."

"No, they can only create the problems," replied Beatrice.

"And that they do. You're right about that, Bea," said Ellen.

"But I have other ideas," said Liam.

"Oh, you do?" Beatrice asked.

Liam nodded.

"And would you be sharing your great schemes with us, then?"

"No. Not yet, I will not."

Beatrice shook her head.

"He won't even tell me," James said.

"If Vandeleur can take an advantage and a few shillings, you can be sure he will make a bargain," Ellen said.

"It will have to be a grand scheme to make a man pass through town again to his estate. The horrors along the way were unspeakable. So many in a desperate way," Beatrice added.

"He also offered passage to us," James said quietly.

"What's that, then?" Ellen said.

"You know. Some of the landlords are offering to pay the passage for families to Canada."

"Oh, they're pleased enough to be rid of us, aren't they?" Ellen replied.

James was surprised that he could see a look of consideration in his grandfather's eyes.

"Well, I suppose this is the start of the end," Ellen said. "And you know it won't be just us."

"All of us are in it now," said Beatrice.

"That we are," Dennis agreed.

*There's no denying it*, he thought. *What a mess. It's a terrible thing. The Brits have no care for us at all. They want to keep us alive so we can provide more money for ribbons and wines. If they offer a little bit of healing with the left hand it's so the right can keep striking you and taking from you for the rest of your days. What a devil of a situation. . . It builds hate in your heart. And that is also part of the death of us—all the hate and hopelessness.*

# 4. Rum-Runner

April 1928—The King George Hotel, Kingston, Ontario

Colin O'Sullivan had never been inside the ballroom of the King George Hotel in Kingston. And he never guessed the parties it held would be so extravagant—and wild.

Since his youngest brother, Pat, had become a bartender there, he had taken his middle brother, Michael Jr., a student at Queen's University, to the bar, but they had never entered the hotel's ballroom.

Colin and Pat were clearly their father's sons. Tall, broad-shouldered, and a bit bigger than their father. Both six foot two. They also had the wild, thick locks of chestnut hair. "Beyond control," Pat joked. "No sense botherin' with them." And when each of them smiled, his eyes were set dancing. Michael Jr., contrary to his name, was very much his mother's son. Quieter than his brothers, fair-haired and dark-eyed, with a slim frame. The boys were born in quick succession, with Colin now twenty-one, Michael Jr. almost twenty, and Pat eighteen.

"It's reserved for some of the fancy parties and weddings and so on. But Joe said I could invite some friends to his party here," Pat explained. Joe Haggerty was the leading rum-runner in Kingston. Everyone knew about it. And this was one of his famous parties.

Colin didn't have the heart to tell Pat that Joe had also invited him to the party. It was last week, when he was coming out of the mill. Joe was waiting for him, and that's when he invited him and made a proposition.

What an affair, Colin thought, as the three brothers entered the packed ballroom. Cases upon cases of champagne. Food he had never seen before: fresh oysters on ice, cured meats, and cakes. And the women. Joe must have shipped in, along with the band, at least a dozen of these girls, from Toronto. The place was wild: dancing, the early stages of sex in some corners, loud conversations, and the jumping music.

"I've gotta use the bathroom, guys," he told his brothers. He climbed the stairs, turned into the men's restroom, and stumbled upon Tom Donovan with one of the Miller girls, undressed in an open stall. Colin gave a wink and shut it.

As he washed up, he caught his reflection in the mirror and began to feel self-conscious. He had put on his best clothes for the night. A suit he had worn since he was seventeen for church and rare formal events. It seemed shabby, and the scuff marks on his Oxford dress shoes seemed so obvious when he thought about his surroundings. But then he thought about his brothers and some of the familiar faces that were just as awestruck as he was and knew they came from a similar background. He loosened up as he walked back downstairs and joined his brothers at the bar.

"This is some party," Michael Jr. said when Colin reached them.

"Isn't it?" said Colin.

"Haggerty knows how to do it up," Pat said. "He has one of these every three months or so."

Colin heard a sound that seemed to rise above the noise of the band and the crowd of people. Unbridled and carefree laughter that was like a song. It startled him, and he sought to find its source. He caught it again, another peal of joy. Then he saw her animated face, eyes that seemed to dare you to stare into them. They would surely ensorcell you and you'd be lost to her, he thought. And he was. Immediately.

Eva Murphy was the eldest daughter of James and Siobhan Murphy. James and his wife were tailors in the city. Eva ran the shop.

Colin was unaware that he was moving towards her. He reached her and her ensemble of friends, who stopped speaking at this strange arrival.

Eva met his gaze. She looked him up and down while he remained silent. "I'm sure you have intentions, don't you?"

Colin smiled a broad smile and laughed. He nodded his head.

"How forward," she replied, and offered a smile in return.

Colin was working on a response when Joe Haggerty grabbed his shoulder. He turned, shocked.

He knew Joe. Everyone did, and the shock faded. Joe could do nothing delicately. There was no physical act he could do without being forceful. Colin was sure Joe meant no harm. It wasn't just that he was a large man, just a little shorter than Colin but thicker, with thirty-four years of living behind him. He had gone from farming to the war to farming again and then smuggling. *It was the war*, Colin thought. *Dad said it took him a few years to settle in again. He would often take off for long hunting and fishing trips in those years after the war to "get right," as he put it. Joe brings an intensity to each situation that tells you it is something he carries at all times. He's closer to my father's age than mine. He's lived. And those scars on his face let you know it's true. The gas in the trenches, they say, did that to him.*

Joe gestured towards the door and tried to say "Let's talk" over the noise of the party.

"Go with your friend," Eva offered. "Maybe he can help you find the right thing to say."

Colin nodded and laughed. "I don't know if there are words that could sum up the pleasure in finding you here."

"That's a good start," she replied, clearly touched, and amused.

Joe pointed to the side door to the street. Colin followed him, and when they were on the sidewalk, Joe said, "Come around back, to the alley."

If Colin didn't know Joe, he would have been nervous. The small, dark alley was known as a preferred location for brawls.

"It's so goddamned loud," said Joe. "Between you and me, I throw these parties to keep everyone happy. It's the price of doing business, I suppose." He moved in close. "You know how I got the money for this party? I know you do. And there's a hell of a lot more coming. Have you thought about what I mentioned last week?"

Colin nodded and smiled.

"I don't really break the law, if that's what worries you. We pick up the booze in Toronto. Legal. We just drive down here. Legal. Throw it in a boat. Or two. Legal." He smiled at that. "We could have two boats. All legal. And we cross over to the U.S. side. Then maybe for thirty minutes or so we're breaking U.S. law, and that's it."

Colin laughed. "Those thirty minutes must feel like thirty hours, though."

"Not really. We have our people over there who take care of everything. Come on, Colin. You know the lake and the river here better than almost anyone. Hell, better than me. And I trust you. We're only limited by the number of boats. I'm taking one boat, and I want to find a guy to take the second. You. We split it evenly, you and me. Do this for a year or two, you'll have your own house and money in the bank to do whatever you want."

Colin wondered if Joe could tell he was bored with this life. Working at the mill was dull. He had no intention of being a lighthouse keeper like his father. Maybe a fisherman. He wanted turbulence. Rough waters.

"It sounds like a hell of a good time," Colin laughed.

Joe chuckled. "I guess it is. Beats working in a mill or something."

"Okay, Joe, let me think about it, but I won't say it's not enticing."

"Fair enough. I know you need to sit with it, but it would be good if you could get back to me in the next day or two."

Colin knew he was going to say yes, but he didn't want to rush it. The decision was large and deserved that. *I'd look too eager or desperate if I just said yes. And it's bad enough that I feel both of those things.*

"Let's get back to the party," Joe said. "Eva Murphy is waiting for you. Beautiful girl. And she's a Catholic like you."

"That's her name? Eva?"

"It is."

"I like it."

"If her name was Beef Stew you would still like her."

Eva had watched the door Colin left by, and she was pleased to see him return. She liked feeling she could let him see her watching. *I don't have to play games. He doesn't play games with women. I can tell it. He just wants me. What a relief.*

As Colin made his way towards Eva, the female singer started with "I Can't Give You Anything but Love, Baby."

"A dance?" he asked, as he reached her.

"I don't dance with nameless men."

"Colin O'Sullivan."

"Is it?"

"So they tell me."

"Well, Mr. O'Sullivan, my name is Eva Murphy."

"It's a pleasure. . . So?"

"I suppose, now that we're such good friends, it would be rude to deny a friend a short dance."

"And I appreciate that."

Colin took her hand, just as his mother had taught him, placed a hand around her waist, and began to dance. *Thank God for the dances on the island,* he thought.

The band played, and he looked from Eva to the smiling and laughing faces around him and thought his life had finally opened up. Here he was, dancing with a beautiful, golden-haired girl at a fantastic party, and he had an opportunity to make something of his life.

He danced with Eva all night and introduced her to his brothers. They joined her group of friends. Just before midnight, Eva asked Colin to take her home. He let his brothers know his plans and left with her.

Both were elated. And as Colin said goodnight to Eva on the sidewalk in front of her parents' home, she leaned in and kissed him.

"Let's get that out of the way," she said with a smile.

"And now let's do it again," he replied.

He held her hand. She liked it. He didn't push for more. She felt as though she were in his care, and she liked being in that place.

"I'm going to have to go in."

"Can I see you again?"

"You have to."

"Good. How about I take you to the movies tomorrow night? The Allen Theatre has a new one. *The Circus,* I think it's called."

"That sounds like a lovely idea."

"I will pick you up at six, then."

"Yes, you will."

With that, Colin gave her a small kiss on her cheek, squeezed her hand, and began to walk away. He looked over his shoulder and was happy to see her watching him. He shot her a smile and she began to walk towards the front door of her parents' home.

The next day, Colin confirmed with Joe that he would help with the shipment, and if all went well, he would continue.

It did go well and he did continue.

By their third run to the States, Colin had earned a newfound place in Joe's heart. They'd had two runs with no sight of any authorities. They were feeling confident. But of the two men, it was Joe, especially, who remained cautious.

They were making their way between the foot of Grand Island and the little islands at the head of Granite Island just after dark when they spotted trouble. A coast guard picket boat was in between Dickson and Pine islands. Joe was in the lead boat, while Colin followed close behind in the second vessel.

Colin watched Joe veer upstream. He was perplexed and then caught sight of the coast guard craft, east of him.

*Joe can't outrun him*, Colin thought. *His engine can't beat that monster.*

With that, Colin swung his boat towards the authorities, drove the throttle down to achieve maximum speed, and made his way towards the cluster of islands.

It took him a few moments to devise a plan. The best he could muster was "Pursue! Pursue the craft!"

The picket boat, though it could reach impressive top speeds, took longer than Colin's boat to do so. Colin knew he could beat them in a sprint. And as long as he stayed dangerously close to the shore, it was unlikely that they would fire on him, as they risked hitting someone in one of the cottages or houses that dotted Granite Island's waterfront.

As Colin howled into the summer night, he looked past the stern of his wooden vessel and saw the coast guard's boat fall behind him. He continued for eighteen miles or so, weaving between the islands with the boat's running lights off. With the islands so close, and Colin veering near them and the shoals, the picket boat, following a more cautious route, lagged a growing distance behind. He made it to Stoneport River, headed upstream until he found an empty boathouse, steered his craft into it, closed the doors behind him, and slept there until dawn.

When he reached Joe's house the next day, he found him sleepless on the porch.

"My God, man! How did you fare?"

Colin laughed a little. "Just fine, just fine, thanks."

As Colin relayed his exploits, Joe's face moved from concern to a clear expression of respect and awe.

Colin felt a growing pride. "It was a night, Joe, I'll tell you that."

"That it was! Get in here and let Irene make you a breakfast!"

Colin's trips to visit his parents on the island had become less frequent. Usually about once a month. And that was at the request of both of his parents.

The lighthouse and the story of its transportation had quickly become a legend in the area. Some didn't believe it was true. Michael and Sarah would often find cars parked at the side of the road and see people wandering on their property. Michael didn't like speaking about it. When it was brought up, he would go quiet and change the subject.

In the weeks that followed the transportation of the building, he sat in his big chair by the fire in the living room. In the quiet of these moments, his mind would often reflect on what he had done. *Thank God the dreams have subsided. But why was I forced to do this? Why did I need to move the building? Could I not wait any longer to see if somehow the ice would knock it down? But if it did, why would that matter? They could just build another. . .*

*My shoulder still aches. And I can feel it when I breathe. Who wants to have that? A reminder, you're alive now. Hopefully, that will pass.*

It was just over two months after the "great diaspora," as Michael called it, to mock the accomplishment, that a rare occurrence took place. It was late March, and the air and water were warming. Lake Ontario was releasing its sheets of ice, some pieces less than three feet long and some 150 feet in length. All were at least a foot thick. A great and unusual storm rolled in from the west, pulling ice from the lake down to the narrows near the islands. The wind swung to the north in gale force and then stopped.

Michael stepped out of his home that morning, surveyed the coast, and saw massive white piles of ice along the shoreline. The north wind had blown and stacked them there.

"My God, that must be piled twenty or thirty feet high," he startled himself by saying out loud. He strode to the lighthouse and found the ice piled all the way up the sweep to the base of the building.

"It's just as I dreamed it. My lord."

After staring at the scene for more than ten minutes, he walked closer to the lighthouse. He placed the palms of his hands on the white-painted wooden sides. He spoke in hushed tones. "That's right. You're safe here. It must have been a thing for you to watch last night. No need to thank me for saving your life." He smiled. Laughed a little.

He was surprised to feel content for days and weeks to come. And he was glad to let others come to the realization that in its old location the lighthouse would have been demolished in the storm. The joy stayed with him for months.

As the months passed, Michael's life returned to the rhythms he knew: solitary fishing, time spent about the house and farm, and tending to the lighthouse. But as he sat in his skiff that summer, a new thought began to emerge. One that haunted him.

*Yes, I saved the light from falling in the storm. But if it had fallen, another could be built, and in this location. Sure, it would have taken some time to build another, but they would have got it done for the spring. It was too important to shipping in the area. In that span of time, there would have been no lighthouse, but there was no sign its absence would have led to any sort of calamity. So, why did I need to move it?*

The spring also delivered the last of his three sons, Pat, off the island and into Kingston.

*First Colin, Michael Jr., and now Pat. They're all there. Just working for a wage or getting ready to do so. Not one of them cared enough to stay with me or their mother and tend to what we have. It's Colin that surprises me the most. A natural. He could handle a boat like no one else. And read the lake. He loves being out on the water.* He had joined Michael fishing until the end of the previous season.

*If my father were alive, he would love to see Colin handle a boat. He too was always on the move, a captain of a schooner and all by the end. One of the first Irish to captain a boat out here. He had a hard go of it, as they weren't keen on Catholics, he said. And the jibes never ceased. I bet that's why the man wouldn't touch a drop of the drink. And he said the same to me. "They want you to fail. They want you to be the worst version of yourself so they can put the hate they've been holding for years into someplace. Don't give them a fresh breath of satisfaction." It took him extra years to get there. Piloting the boats he could captain. As much I like being out here, I wouldn't want to have to do the same. I didn't have the fire for it like he did. If the boys knew the fights we fought to get here. Maybe I didn't do enough to let them know. Just telling the story of the assassination of D'Arcy McGee isn't enough, I suppose. Colin seems lost. As though he's looking for something out there but he doesn't know what it is. . .*

Michael's thoughts turned to his two other sons. Michael Jr. was at the university, and his mother was proud of him for it. He was studying mining sciences at Queen's University, in Kingston. Michael laughed when Michael Jr. told him his plan.

"Mining? You wanna climb into a cave? Why would you wanna do something like that?"

Michael Jr. blushed, and his father felt bad. He forgot that the boy wasn't much for arguing with him. He was his mother's son. So, Michael went silent. His son took it for disapproval, and the two rarely spoke of it again.

Michael wasn't aware of the work his wife and son had done to get him into the school. It began with his name. Queen's was a Protestant university. Presbyterian, in fact. And he was Irish. That meant Catholic. Neither was found or liked much at the school. Sarah remembered her father telling the stories of the riots in Toronto and the signs in the window: "Irish Need Not Apply." *And we're no well-to-do Irish family,* she'd thought. *There's nothing that states he can't apply to the school, but it's unlikely he'll get into it. There will be some reason that never mentions religion or national origins. It will be a reasoned answer. Maybe enrolment numbers. . .* So she devised a plan.

"You'll need to take on your middle name as your last name. Thomas. Michael Thomas. That should settle them down," his mother said. "And if they ask you, you tell them you attend St. Andrew's Church. Presbyterian. And you're going to have to start going to it on Sundays. It's the only way, Michael."

Michael Jr. was surprised. He felt wounded, but not by his mother. The aggressor was unseen. Later, he sat with it and tried to figure it out but had no answers. Instead, he turned back to the logistics of the situation. *I've heard of Catholics attending university in Ottawa or Toronto, but the thought of going that far from home is too much. It just is. I know I'm different from my brothers. My life will be different from theirs. I won't be able to offer grandchildren. I will likely be alone. But if I stay here for school, at least I will have my family. . .*

But the greater realization seeped in like poison, and Michael Jr. was surprised to feel tears coming down his face as it culminated into a terrible thought. *It's as though a stain is growing inside me that I could hide. I can keep it to myself. It isn't for something I've done but for who I am. It's what I've dreaded: that I'm less than others around me. That I'm irredeemable.*

Pat, the youngest of the three boys, was tending the bar at the King George Hotel. He was young, his father thought, as he sat fishing in his skiff. Why not have some fun? That seemed to be all they wanted to do anyway.

And that brought Michael's thoughts back to Colin. *Throwing parties at the King George Hotel with Joe Haggarty.*

He had begun to hear a rumour about Colin from islanders. It was a tight-knit community, and there was an unspoken rule that if you left the island you still looked out for each other. So, Michael wasn't surprised when Frank Donovan mentioned on the ferry one day that he heard Colin and Joe Haggarty were holding lavish parties in the ballroom of the hotel.

*Frank thinks he's being subtle. And he's pleased to be telling me. Everyone knows Joe Haggarty is running whisky stateside. So, Colin is taking part in this. My lord. I'll talk to him, but it will be of no use.*

Michael drew up his net. Just a few small fish in it, young walleye and bass, and a few perch.

He looked at his catch and sighed. "Nothing's quite right, is it?" he told the fish. "I can't even pull some decent fish. And Colin, he's out here at night running whisky. Have you seen him?" With that, he threw the net back in the lake with the fish. "Keep an eye out for him, would you, please? And report back."

*Sitting here, talking to fish. I'm going in. I'll talk to Sarah. I've got to do something.*

Michael unloaded the nets, leaving them on his dock to dry. He made his way to his barn to feed Bay. On his way in, he paused to look at the chain. He had put four great iron nails into the wall of the barn to hold the links. He liked passing it each day. It gave him a lift. But lately, it perplexed him. So he moved on.

"Well, he's a grown man, and you're not gonna change his mind," was all Sarah said at dinner.

"I want him to know that people are talking. Sure, no one is likely to rat him out to the police, but in time it's gonna slip, and he's gonna be in trouble."

Sarah knew there was no sense arguing with Michael. He was upset and had made up his mind. All there was left to do was get out of his way or trip him as he stomped by you. And she didn't want to do the latter. If he could stop Colin, that would be for the best.

"Well, I'll invite him for dinner. I'll talk to him," Michael decided.

Colin accepted the invitation, and the following Sunday he arrived late in the afternoon. Michael watched him approach the dock through the living room window.

*He has a new boat. Dark wood. Mahogany? My lord, listen to that engine. It must be massive. He's making sure he can outrun anything out there. Later than when I asked him to arrive. But I won't say anything. Pick your battles, Michael.*

Sarah was just finishing setting the table when Colin stepped into the house. He seemed hesitant but smiled broadly when he saw his mother.

"Look at you there, Mom!"

Sarah embraced her son.

"You look thin," she said, stepping back to look at him.

"Maybe. I still forget to eat."

"But not to have a drink," Michael announced as he entered the room.

Colin's smile fell.

"C'mon, Colin, I was just joking around."

"Okay."

"It's good to see ya, son."

Colin was taken aback by the kind words. Unaccustomed to them. He felt uneasy.

"Your mother has broiled a great chicken for us. Take a look."

Waiting in the kitchen was a platter of chicken and vegetables.

"Looks good," Colin replied.

The three sat down for dinner in the dining room. Most meals were taken at a small kitchen table or, for Michael, on the run. The formality let Colin know something was afoot.

"And how are you two?"

"We're fine," Sarah announced. She looked down at her plate. "Michael, will you cut the bird?"

"Let's let our guest do it."

He handed the carving knife and fork to his son.

"Oh, okay, then."

*Another first*, Colin thought. *The old man never lets anyone cut a bird for him.*

"So, what are you doing for work these days, Colin?" his father asked.

Colin looked up from his task. "Well, mostly cutting chickens."

Sarah laughed. Michael wasn't so entertained. He wanted answers. This was evasion. *But I better laugh*, he thought.

"Right. Good on ya. But seriously . . ."

"I do have some cash from last year's fishing with you, and I've been trying a few things to see what would stick."

"You are, are you?"

Colin placed a drumstick on his mother's plate. "Dark meat, right?"

"Yes, thank you. Same for your father. Well, I suppose it's good to try your hand at a few things while you're young."

"Right."

Colin placed the other drumstick on his father's plate. Sarah scooped vegetables for Michael, then herself.

"I understand you've been doing some work with Joe Haggarty," Michael added.

Colin paused in the middle of cutting a swath of breast meat. There seemed to be no good reply to this assertion.

Michael waited. "From your silence, I guess that's true."

Sarah sighed.

"The export of alcohol is not against the law."

"But when you're rolling up on stateside shores, what do you tell yourself then?"

Colin dropped the utensils, picked up the serving spoon, and quickly scooped some vegetables.

"The Americans aren't going to put up with it," Michael said. "I've been reading that all the smuggling on the Detroit River came to a close because the smugglers were shooting each other and the authorities stepped in and did the same."

"There's no gunfire out here."

"Not yet, Colin."

"I'm just doing a few runs. It's not like this is what I'll do for the rest of my days."

"If your days are cut short, it might be," said Sarah.

Colin sighed. *Just get through the meal and you can go*, he thought.

"I can do it for a few years and make more than I ever will hauling nets or tending a light."

"There's always a way to make more goddamn money! It's just a question of what you're willing to do!" Michael was bellowing now. His fist crashed onto the table. The plates, glasses, and cutlery jumped, along with his wife, but not his eldest son.

*They got me. They pushed me, and here I am*, Colin thought. He stood. "I've got to get back. I've gotta get back to work."

"*Work* you call it, do ya!" Michael hollered from the table as Colin left the room. "*Work!* That's what an honest man does. Can you say that, Colin? Can you say it's an honest thing?"

Colin strode from the house, paused, and turned to the barn. The sun shone through the doors and glinted off the chain hanging, ceremoniously, like the picture of the pope in the kitchen. He glanced over his shoulder, saw no one was following him, and walked up to it. He lifted its great weight from the nails and then headed down to this boat, dragging the metal links behind him.

Michael and Sarah sat at the table. One fuming. The other weeping.

Days passed, and then weeks, and finally months. Colin continued to keep his distance from his parents while he and Joe continued their deliveries. One per week. Colin made one adjustment to Joe's approach. Instead of going ashore on the U.S. side, he dropped the crates of whisky or beer into the water, where they could float, and ran the great chain of his father's through the leather handles on the crates so they remained together. This way, he and Joe never had to touch U.S. soil. Stepping onto the American shore seemed the most risky part of the enterprise for Colin. There was no quick getaway if the police or coast guard found them. And, if he was honest, there was an ethical aspect for him. *I'm just dropping this in a bay. What happens next is not my business,* he thought. *I am not entering a foreign country and breaking its laws.*

Joe thought it seemed smart but found it odd that after each trip Colin needed to retrieve the chain.

"My God, man, we make enough money. You don't need that goddamn chain. We can get a new one each time! And why not use rope?"

"First off, the chain has a weight to it that keeps the load floating low and less likely to drift away. And, well, getting it back is my problem. My risk. And I won't utter another word on it. But I will never impose on you to get it. It will be my duty."

"Okay, Colin," Joe replied, shaking his head and laughing. *The guy is never that serious,* he thought, *but he is now, about a chain.*

Colin walked away from Joe and turned to his own thoughts. *Not losing the chain is the least I can do for the old man. And if I'm honest, that's about all I ever do for him or anyone: the least.* A great hollowness welled up in him. And he could think of no resolution to it.

His plan worked. After each run, he would pick up the chain on the shoreline closest to where they dropped the load. He arranged it with their buyers in the States.

It was late June 1928. Michael checked on the light as part of the daily maintenance. He had begun to dislike the task. The more the story of his delivery of the building grew, and the longer he sat with the unanswered question of why he moved it, the more his joy at tending the light decreased.

*Sure, I saved the building from being knocked down by ice. But who cares? That hardly seems vital enough to be bothered by spirits.*

From the lighthouse, he took a look at the shining lake. The sun was setting and turning the sky and waters ablaze. He opened the small window at the top of the building and felt the kind wind from the southwest.

*But it's still a mighty view from here.*

As he looked out to the north and Kingston on the far shore, he noticed more activity than normal on the lake. Speedboats, with floodlights turned on to compensate for the coming dark.

*More of those than fishing boats now,* he thought. *Maybe he's out there racing. He would like that.*

Michael turned from the scene and started down the stairs from the top of the lighthouse.

On the other side of the island—the south shore—some ten miles away, Colin stood in Beth Thompson's kitchen apologizing.

"I'm sorry, I'm getting the kitchen floor all wet."

*Why does it have to be Mrs. Thompson's house? My teacher.* It occurred to him that he could wait outside for the phone to ring, but he wanted to be near.

Beth raised her eyebrows. *I can't believe he wouldn't call his father directly for help*, she thought. *I mean, I get it. Michael O'Sullivan will be livid with him. Just livid. And Colin, he wanted Joe's wife to call Michael. Michael will still know that he's here. Funny the things people choose to care about.*

"I'll be on the porch."

"Just stay close to the house, then," she told him.

*He will never forgive me for this one*, Colin thought. *He doesn't know how. Forgiveness is a foreign language.*

*The night is calm and warm. One of those summer nights I loved when I was young. It used to feel as though time stood still. The whole world was in bloom. Only a few years ago, this would have made me smile and swell with joy at the possibility in life. But tonight doesn't feel like that.*

Standing here, wet, he felt old. There was no expectation of great days ahead.

*I can't think about it. With one wrong move tonight, this whole world I know could be done. Dead. We don't even have a twenty-two on board, and those guys have mounted machine guns.*

The U.S. government was taking the smuggling of Canadian liquor and beer into the country more seriously now. It had become a hot political issue. In American fashion, they responded with force.

It was just after 10 p.m. when the phone in Michael and Sarah's kitchen rang. Michael was slicing an apple for a snack. A ritual of his before bed. He picked up the phone.

"Is that Michael? Mr. O'Sullivan, I mean."

"It is."

"Fine. Hello. This is Irene. Irene Haggarty."

*Irene Haggarty. I believe she's Joe's wife*, he thought. "Oh, what can I do for you?" Michael asked, feeling guarded.

"Well, I know that you may not agree with what Joe has been up to, but he and Colin"—*oh no, I wasn't supposed to mention Colin*—"are stuck in a boat at the east end of the island with a load of . . . well, you know."

She waited, but there was no response. So she continued. "They were almost to Cape Vincent, on the U.S. side, when they saw a couple of the coast guard's picket boats. They turned back for home and came across the same in Canadian waters, near Kingston. They're blocking the harbour for them to get home. The boys assume they'll send boats out here soon enough. Circling the island. They can't make a run for it, because the other boats are faster. They can't go to drop the load, because they're not sure that there aren't men onshore as well. And they're afraid to try and unload the boat here. They may have no time, Mr. O'Sullivan. The coast guard has got those machine guns on the bows of their boats."

With that, she burst into tears. "I know, Mr. O'Sullivan, that they brought a lot onto themselves, but should they be shot for it? For a few cases of whisky?"

Michael sighed. "I don't know what they deserve. Do you? You seem to know a lot."

"Sorry, sir?"

"Well, how do you know about their misadventure this evening?"

"Yes, sir. Colin swam ashore and got to the Thompsons and called me."

"Did he?" He wanted to ask why his son hadn't called him, but he knew the answer.

"Yes, he did. If you can turn off the light, or break the light, and call the authorities and say that no boats can pass the island, then the coast guard may stop their search and the boys can make it home."

*Goddamn it, Colin. You probably love doing this to the old man.*

"Mr. O'Sullivan?"

"What if they just surrendered?" Michael asked. "You could have him call the authorities and surrender, and Colin can go to jail with your beloved Joe. No one dies."

"Michael, you don't mean it. And you know they won't do that."

"Then maybe it's out of my hands. Maybe they made their own choices, one after another. Choices that led them here."

She waited on the phone. She knew with men you often just had to wait. *You just have to let them get there on their own. If you force him, they're more likely to go the opposite way or another foolish direction.* She could hear him breathing heavily and grunting.

"It will be done. The light will be out and I will make the call."

"We need to do it quick, Mike, I mean Mr. O'Sullivan."

"Do we?" answered Michael.

He slammed down the phone, breaking the cradle for the receiver.

Sarah had woken and come downstairs.

"What's all the noise?"

"Sorry."

Michael left the kitchen and strode outside.

*Well, the thinking is done now. It's just the doing left,* he thought.

As he crossed his property toward the lighthouse, he picked up a rock. Fairly round, and about eight inches in diameter. He climbed the staircase in the lighthouse to the top. With his elbow, he smashed the glass of the window. He paused when he felt a sharp pain in his arm, just above his elbow.

*Goddamn foolishness. I didn't even think about what I was doing.* A two-inch piece of glass protruded from his arm.

He then looked at the constant red light for a moment before he struck it with the rock and burst the glass. He tossed the rock through the broken window.

Michael shook his head and then went back down the stairs.

He entered the kitchen, picked up the phone, and finally noticed the broken cradle. He was surprised the phone still worked.

"I got a call from one of my neighbours. Asking about the light. It was out. He had been coming home and he didn't even know where he was. It's a moonless night. Dark enough that you would need the light. So many shoals. . . Yes, we'll have to get it fixed. I'm sure it can be done within a few days. For now, we need to alert the authorities to issue a notice not to travel in the channel close to Grand Island. . . Yes. Fine, then. Thank you."

The phone rang at Beth's house.

"Okay, then. I'll let him know," she said.

She stepped onto her porch.

"Your father said that the light is out and in time you'll be free to pass on the north side of the island. Your father has got it done." With the last line, she nodded her head. "And he isn't happy about it," she added.

Colin sighed. "I would imagine he's not. Thank you, Mrs. Thompson."

"Now that I'm a co-conspirator with you, I think you can call me by my given name, Beth. Go on, now. Just get yourselves home."

Colin nodded. Saddened. *Everyone is paying a price for this. Including my former teacher. I'm free tonight, but there is a whole world of trouble coming for me.*

And with that, Colin turned his back and made his way across Beth Thompson's lawn to the lake. He swam to the boat. Joe's boat had been roped to his own, and they were anchored in the bay. He relayed the news to his partner.

They waited a couple of hours for all of the government boats to reach their docks. At about midnight, he and Joe started their boats, untied them, pulled the anchors, and headed for home.

As he crossed the channel between Grand Island and Kingston, he had no idea that his father was watching from the lighthouse. He had stayed there all night, only leaving for tea and to use the bathroom.

*And that will be him, no doubt, in one of those quick little crafts with no floodlights on,* he thought. *Godspeed, my son.*

And with that, Michael was surprised not by the feeling of relief but by sadness.

*Have I lost you, Colin?*

He picked up his teacup, took a final look to the east and the rising sun, and climbed down the steps of the lighthouse.

Colin's and Joe's boats were safely back in the inner harbour in Kingston. The crates of whisky were unloaded and left in the warehouse just up from the docks. "The delivery will have to wait for another day," Joe announced.

Colin lay in bed a short time later and drifted into sleep, thinking about his father.

*The old man got it done. I'd like to thank him. But how can I? My thanks will just be met with anger and disapproval. But I need to call him. Let him know I'm all right. If Mom knows, she'll be in a state. I can put up with his fury, I guess. It's the least I can do.*

*This is who I am now, I guess. There's no way back. I'm not going to be getting into the skiff with the old man again. He won't have it. I'm a runner now.*

As Colin slipped into sleep, Michael gathered his 12-gauge shotgun from the closet along with three rounds from the shelf above it.

He went down to the shore and found a flock of geese on the lake.

*You can always count on the birds.*

He shot once, looked up from his gun at the goose floating on the water and the rest flying away. He waded into the lake and took the dead animal by its legs. Back on shore, he dropped it on the ground, pulled out what shot he could find, and wiped away the blood on its feathers. He stepped back, looked at the goose, and nodded his head, then picked it up again and made his way down the shore to the lighthouse. He dropped the bird at the foot of it and turned to make his way back home.

*Well, the inspector will like a little evidence of the unfortunate incident.*

He stopped, went back, and placed his hand on the breast of the fowl.

"Needless. I'm sorry, and I thank you."

Sarah was in the kitchen, bright, and waiting for him.

"Colin called. He wanted to let you know he borrowed the chain. And he also wanted me to tell you that he's doing just fine. He offered apologies about the other night. That's nice, isn't it?"

Michael didn't want to share the truth with her now. She was so happy. *Why should I not let her have that? There's always time for bad news. She wants her family whole. So do I.*

Michael smiled and nodded. "Well, that is nice to hear."

Few questions were asked of Michael about the lighthouse. It was inspected, and Michael was told it would be repaired within two days. "It's easy enough for some geese to fly into the light," the official told him. The lamp itself was replaced and running again within the two days, as promised.

Colin and Joe met the following day. Living only a few blocks from each other, just up from the inner harbour, the men were often at each other's homes.

"That was a close one," Joe announced as he entered the room.

"That it was," Colin replied.

Both men smirked.

"Well, we still have to get rid of that load," Joe said.

"Indeed. And with that light gone, we have a few days with no traffic out there. What do you think?

"Good call," Colin said with a nod. "It will be a dark night, but that's to our advantage."

"Right."

Colin felt a strange pang of regret and pushed past it. He knew its source, and there was nothing to do but ignore it.

*It's funny*, he thought. *Joe is chomping at the bit for the money. How much is enough? He owns a house, a boat, he'll likely get a car soon enough. The guy dresses like a solicitor on vacation. He's got cash stashed at his dad's farm.* And then he thought about when Joe came back from the war. *He looked so skinny. And those scars along the jawline on the left side of his face—from the mustard gas, he said—spoke about things I'll never know. Maybe, after all of that, he needs money, success. . . Well, it's still fun for me.*

His mind turned to his work at the mill at the old harbour. Mindless, tedious. And when he thought about his options—sitting in a skiff with his dad and being harangued for his smuggling or working inside at the mill or somewhere like it—he sensed the narrowness of his life.

After their near capture, it was Joe who wanted to expand the business. Colin liked the parties, especially taking Eva to them, but he didn't care much about money. It had never played a major role in their house when he was a child. In two trips, he would make a year's wages. He was aware of it. But it was the rush of it all and the freedom he loved most.

So, after buying a house for himself and Eva to move into after their marriage in the fall, the money was "lent and spent," as he liked to say. And the lending never really was lending—he never expected it back.

Eva was aware from the start that Colin was running rum. Like most people in Kingston. But it was accepted. Even her parents didn't have an issue with it. Her father was impressed at Colin's enterprising ways.

Many young men in Kingston wanted to join in the business. Colin was hesitant, but Joe was adamant that it was vital for their success.

"Just think of the money, Colin. We hire them, give them a cut, and take the rest of it ourselves. No risk, all reward."

Joe rarely pressed him, so Colin felt he should consider it. *When we're in tight spots, it's me who comes up with a plan to get us out of trouble. Not Joe. Joe likes the money. He collects it. He doesn't take much joy in the trips. I remember that first run together. He was quiet as we loaded the crates into the boat. And when we started the engines, I looked at him and saw the colour of his skin change a bit. He was grey as stone. I assumed he was a little under the weather.*

He looked to Joe and to the boat he would captain. It was thirty-two feet long, made of deep-hued mahogany with a glistening finish. The engine was 110 horsepower. The largest he had driven in his young life.

"There's nothing out here that can get us, Joe. I promise you. Between me and this boat, you're confirmed for success."

"I know, I know. Remember, I've been doing this a while now."

"But have you been doing it with such a dauntless and handsome partner?"

Joe shot him a look. He was perplexed and then amused.

He was finishing a beer. He took a swig and then reached out from his boat to Colin's and broke it on the gunnel.

"You're christened now, my boy!"

Colin laughed. "What's her name?"

"On this trip, we'll call her *Firefly*. Light and fast, doing no harm."

"Nice? This trip?"

"We change the names to throw off the coast guard. Now, get the goddamn boat there and back in one piece."

"Okay, Joe."

Colin's mind turned back to the issue at hand. *Joe's scared. He wants more money and less risk. So hiring the younger guys makes sense. But I doubt any of these younger lads could get themselves out of trouble when they find it. And find it they will.*

He didn't want to do it. But he liked the young men they were considering and thought, *Well, I guess this is what partnership looks like,* he thought. *Like a marriage. I guess you just try to make sure you're doing at least half of what you want to do, and getting half of what you want to get, and the other person does the same.*

It was Vic Hunt and Sam McIntosh they hired. Sam had been a fisherman, just like Colin. With his dad as well. Vic was from a farming family just north of the city. Colin outfitted him with the boat. He even gave it a name: *Hummingbird.* "She's fast and can move with greater agility than anything out here." It was a speedboat with a 100-horsepower Kermath engine, a motor larger than any belonging to the coast guard.

Vic and Sam did a couple of runs with no real problems. Sam knew the waters. Vic was a good guy who worked hard. The boys had met in high school. They were barely out of it.

Over the last few months, the increased presence of the United States Coast Guard pushed the men to drop the whisky further afield. Out in the middle of the lake, at the Danish Islands. It was far from anyone. And any boat coming for you could be seen for miles.

It was an early November evening, and Colin was at home. He wasn't thinking about Vic and Sam out on the lake, making their way to the Danish Islands. Sitting in the living room of his little brick home on King Street, he was talking with Eva, by a fire, when the conversation found a pause. He heard a slight tapping on the windows, and then it quickly grew louder. He saw rain coming down.

*What's with the sound? Freezing rain, on the windows. It's getting louder. No one called for freezing rain today. I checked the forecast in the newspaper, because the boys— Oh, shit! Those guys are out there tonight.*

The boats were open, with no cover except for the cases of whisky. The sudden drop in temperature and the rain would make the long run to the Danish Islands treacherous. They would be out there for hours, taking on the rain in their boats, along with the water of the waves, now that the wind had picked up.

He jumped from his seat, quickly dug his feet into his boots, and was putting on his coat as he made his way out the front door.

*What a mess of an evening.*

"I'm heading out," he called, not looking behind him.

He strode the six blocks to Joe's house. The freezing rain continued to fall, and the wind was coming in gusts.

"Jesus Christ. What a night. What a mess!" He hollered this aloud to no one at all.

He knocked and entered Joe's home in one movement.

"Joe, do you see this weather?"

"No."

"It's a mess out there. Freezing rain. And the wind."

Joe's face changed.

"God knows what it's doing in the middle of the lake," Colin said. "It could be a fuckin' blizzard out there. It's freezing."

He could see the dread growing in his friend.

"And the winds are getting stronger, Joe."

Joe just stared at him. "Not much we can do," he said.

Colin didn't like the answer. He wanted action. He wanted to do something.

"Joe, they wouldn't be ready for this kind of weather."

"We'll never find them, Colin." Let's wait for the morning. If they're not back by then, we'll know something's gone wrong and we can actually see out there and find them."

"Fine. I'll go down to the harbour in a few hours and see if they're back."

"Good call. I'm worried too, Colin. Don't think I'm not. But they're men now. I was with younger ones in France. If all's gone well, they only hit a few minutes of the storm on the way back."

"Right. Well, I'll check the harbours. If there's no sign, we'll go in the morning. First light."

"Yup. Yes we will. I'm agreeing with ya."

It was just before 11 p.m. that Colin arrived at the city's main harbour. He walked the docks and saw no sign of Vic or Sam or their boat. Or anyone. The same was true at Portsmouth Harbour. The wind was blowing harder. The freezing rain had turned to sleet.

Colin didn't sleep. He sat in the chair in the living room with a bottle of Corby's whisky beside him, sipping it through the night. When dawn's glow appeared, he made his way out to his car. The rain and sleet had ceased, but he nearly fell as he stepped off his porch. There was at least an inch of ice on the ground. And the trees, the house, the entire street. The temperature had dropped further.

He scraped the ice off the car windshield and slowly drove the frosted roads down to the harbour.

Once more, he scanned the docks.

He stopped at Joe's, and the two men went to the other harbours in the city. There was no sign of the boat. When they reached the end of the dock at Portsmouth Harbour, Joe turned to him.

"Goddamn it!"

Colin made his way back to the car. Joe followed him.

Colin didn't want to talk about their next steps, and he didn't want to hear anyone's opinion about what he would have to do. Joe also remained silent, seething.

It took nearly two hours for them to get to the Danish Islands. The day was cold, and a great fog met them in the harbour and stuck with them all the way to their destination.

*As much as this fog is a hassle, I love it, every year. Such a wonder to me,* thought Colin. *Still.*

The air grew colder. In the middle of the lake, where the Danish Islands stood, it was a different place. It had its own weather, separate from that on the mainland. Colin remembered being out here with his father. It felt otherworldly. So far from anything. The winds, the air, the light. It was exotic.

*I feared it and loved it,* he recalled.

As the islands came into view in the distance, the wind picked up again. Waves rolled in. Still no sign of Vic and Sam. They pushed around from the north shore down the east side, and there, in the mouth of the bay on the northwest of the island, with even greater waves rolling in, Colin and Joe finally found them. They were still two hundred feet from the shore. They had likely tried to make it and been swamped by the waves.

Their stern was sinking into the lake. The men were moving about the boat. As he and Joe grew closer, Colin saw they were bailing water out of the vessel. So consumed were they by their task, they didn't notice Colin and Joe's approach.

Breakers were coming in more than six feet high, over the sides of the boat. At times, knocking the men around and nearly into the lake.

"Oh, shit! What a mess!" Joe exclaimed.

"Take the boat, Joe. Take it now," Colin said. He left the helm and made his way to the stern compartment.

"Right, then. Right. Got it."

Colin looked for a rope. The only one they had was tied to the anchor. He quickly loosened the knot that held the anchor. He threw the line hard into the wind towards the other men. The wind pushed it back.

"Goddamn it!" Colin hollered.

He paused and then turned back to the bow where the chain was stored. He began pulling on the links of his chain and hollered to Joe, "Keep her pointed towards the waves. Don't let them hit us beam on. The big bastards will sink us, for sure!"

He could hear Joe trying to hail the men. "Vic! Sam!"

As Colin pulled the last of the chain out, a whitecap crashed into them, nearly sending him over the side. He bounced off the port gunnel, gathered himself, and got back to his task. He wrapped the end of the chain around the rearmost cleat on the starboard side.

"Joe, bring 'er in closer! As close as you can, but try to keep that bow pointed into the waves."

"Right! What are ya planning?"

The boat moved in closer to the men. Joe found it hard to concentrate. He was being tossed in his seat, the motor was running low and loud, the wind howled, and the chain rattled ominously.

"Listen, now!" Colin called, waving his arms to get the attention of Vic and Sam.

"Boys, I'm gonna toss this onto your bow. Ya gotta—"

Another wave crashed and sent Colin tumbling to the stern.

"Jesus, man!" Joe hollered.

He hopped up again. The chain had been knocked from the cleat. Its links were too big to wrap around it. Colin searched for a new way to secure it.

"Colin!" Joe hollered. "We gotta get this done! We can't stay out here!"

The boats were under twenty feet from one another.

Colin wrapped the chain around his waist twice.

"Easy, now, Joe. We don't want to get much closer and send them both down!"

"Jesus, Colin! What are you doing, man!"

Colin shrugged and turned to the other boat.

"Ya gotta grab it and hold tight, then jump into the lake! I'll pull you close and you can climb up in here!"

Vic and Sam hollered that they understood.

"Get up to the bow, boys!"

They were about twenty feet from the boat. "Hold her there, Joe. Hold her now . . ."

*Close enough. You can see the fear in their eyes. The poor bastards. There's never been a toss that mattered more in your life, Colin. Get it now. Get it right.*

He had wrapped the end of the chain on itself so it formed a ball he hoped could help take it the distance. He quickly moved to the stern, then sprinted forward and threw himself and the chain as far as he could. He landed on the bow of his boat and the far end of the chain came down on Vic and Sam's. Both with a heavy thump.

Vi and Sam lurched for the unwinding ball of metal links as a wave came in and sent it into the lake.

"Goddamn it!" said Colin. He yanked the chain back towards him to make another attempt. He used the same method: balling up the links, running forward from the stern, and heaving it to the other boat.

As it landed, Sam desperately leaped for it and went over the bow. The chain remained hung up on the boat above him.

"Grab the line!" Colin hollered. But Sam was flailing his arms and legs in the lake. Immune to Colin's instructions. Captured by the drink.

Vic was lying down on the bow, trying to reach Sam, when another wave struck the boat beam on, knocking him and the line into the water. The chain disappeared beneath the waves.

"Swim!" Colin hollered.

"Swim!" Joe echoed.

But the men were thrashing madly. *Just scared,* Colin thought. *I'll send the line over again. Toss it onto their heads if I have to!* He was leaning over the side, pulling in the last of the chain, when he realized the men were no longer making any movement. He searched the water. Neither could be seen. He stood up and searched near and far. Nothing but big, unforgiving grey rollers. A terrible realization struck him. Like too many who lived on or near the water, neither of the young men knew how to swim. They were gone.

Colin fell backwards into the boat. Stunned.

Joe began hollering.

"Colin! What are ya doin'?"

"They're gone, Joe."

Colin climbed off the bow and stood beside him, staring into the lake.

Another big wave struck them on the port side, a great portion of it pouring into the vessel and sending the men reeling.

They realized they were in trouble.

"Jesus!"

"Spin 'er around, Joe. Or better yet, let me."

With that, Colin took the wheel and turned the boat towards the island.

*I have to get my wits about me. Let's take her to shore. That's why the boys hadn't jumped out of the boat. They were only two hundred feet or so away, but they couldn't swim. And it's cold. Jesus. If they could have just grabbed hold of the chain.*

Colin paused and looked back to where the boat had wallowed in the water. Now only the bow was above the waves, rising up and falling like an impermanent grave marker.

Colin kept his bow into the waves as he made for the sandy shore.

"I'm gonna beach her, Joe."

"Right!"

"There's nothing else we can do."

He looked at Joe, who was wet from head to toe, just like himself. Water kept coming at them.

*He's green. The waves have got to him.*

"I'll get ya to shore, Joe. The islands are really just a big sandbar. There'll be no troubles for the hull."

He made a direct line for the shore.

The boat touched the bottom and began to slow. *What a relief to hear that sound of sand running along the underside.* They were far enough into the bay to be out of the worst of the storm that whistled around them.

Colin hopped into the shallow water and headed to the shore with the rope in hand. He turned back to look at Joe.

"Tie her to all the cleats on the bow, Joe."

Joe didn't move.

Colin stopped in the water. "Come on, now," he said.

*They're in here,* Colin thought. *Somewhere. My God, boys.*

He looked back to see Joe had finished his work and was wading towards him through the water.

Colin tied the rope around the largest cedar he could find on the shore.

He turned back into the water, passing Joe on his way to the land.

"What are ya at now?" Joe said.

Colin didn't answer.

"Colin?!"

Colin was wading past their boat.

"I gotta find them, Joe! I ain't leaving them out here."

He was swimming now.

"Colin! Jesus H. Christ! You'll never find them, man! There are currents from all directions here."

Colin had reached where their boat had been and was diving beneath the waves.

Joe stood in the water, watching.

*I've seen this before. New recruits after a battle would go mad. That's what this looks like. I remember Taylor out of Hamilton. Collecting body parts. And then putting them back together. Thinking he could build a new man? Jesus. It just makes it all worse.*

"Get yer ass back here! Who knows where their bodies are. And they're in twenty feet of water. You'll never dive deep enough!"

He could see Colin was slowing.

*The cold is getting to him. Soon enough, he won't be able to raise his arms, and that will be the end of him.*

Colin was thrashing in the water, screaming.

Joe moved closer but was still some thirty feet away.

*If I swim out there, he'll drown me.*

Joe went back and unfastened the rope from the tree and the boat.

*It will be fine for a few moments.*

He swam towards Colin, who oscillated between bobbing and thrashing in the water as his energy waned.

He swam up to his friend, who didn't see him, wrapped the rope around him, and began to swim away holding the line.

"C'mon, ya bastard! C'mon, now!"

*He'll only hear me if I scream and take control. That's all you can do.*

Colin was unaware of what was happening to him.

*My God, he's a big lad,* Joe thought.

Joe quit trying to pull him and swam sixteen more feet, until his feet touched the sandy bottom. And then he pulled hard.

Colin screamed at him. "Goddamn it, Joe! Goddamn you!"

When Colin was close enough, Joe grabbed his head between his hands.

"Stop it! Stop it, now! They're gone. And if you don't stop it, it'll be the end of us!"

Colin hung his head. He wept.

"I know. I know," Joe said. He placed his hands on the younger man's shoulders. He stayed like that for a moment, then unwound the rope from Colin and secured the boat once more.

Joe helped Colin to the shore and the pair sat down. The storm was still blowing cold rain. Colin brought his knees to his chest and rested his head on them.

*He looks like a kid,* Joe thought.

"They taught us to swim in the army. If they hadn't, my God . . ."

Colin stared at him.

"It was my Mom," Colin said. "Living on the island, she was adamant that we learned to swim."

"It's cold, for sure," Joe added, and joined him in the same position.

The men sat there for nearly three hours, waiting for the storm to pass, their clothes freezing on them and becoming stiff.

Every few minutes, Joe would stand and do some of the exercises he remembered from his time in the war. Jumping jacks, push-ups, and lunges.

"C'mon, Colin, if you sit too long like that you're bound to freeze up."

"Fine, Joe. Fine"

When the storm had subsided, Joe said, "I suppose it's time, Colin. We'll make our way back now." The day was dull, grey, and the water the same.

Colin remained silent. "Who do we even tell?" he said, when he finally spoke. "The police? The boys were out here running rum."

"Yes, we tell the police. As far as they're concerned, we weren't breaking any laws."

"Right."

"It's telling their families that I dread."

As they unwound the rope from the tree, waded into the lake, and pushed the boat off the sand, Colin's mind was moving from the question of how to survive the day to how to live with it. *Vic and Sam are dead.* A new phrase he would have to utter. He had never hated language so much. *I don't want to say it. It makes it too real.*

They had been wet for hours now in the November air, nearly freezing. Both men were pale, and their lips blue. When they spoke, they could hear the chill overtake their sentences with its chattering sound.

"It's a mess of currents in here. Let's just circle the area before we go, maybe we can see ... something." Colin couldn't bring himself to utter the word *bodies*. After circling the area for nearly two hours, Colin said what had to be said. "Joe, we gotta go back. We're gonna run out of fuel."

It was a silent journey back to Kingston. Both men stumbled off the boat in the harbour, exhausted and frozen.

"I'll make the call," Colin offered. Joe looked rough. Pale skin and dark circles around his eyes.

"Good, then," was all he said. He turned and walked up the street towards his house.

Colin felt compelled to watch him go. He didn't want Joe out of his sight. He found the payphone in the building near the docks, and picked up the receiver.

He was loath to see anyone else, even Eva. When he stepped into his house, the warmth wrapped around him and his body responded with great shivers and waves of pain.

"My God, Colin, you look terrible!" Eva exclaimed when she came out of the kitchen and saw him in the hall.

She knew by looking at him that things had gone wrong.

"Are they hurt?"

"I wish they were."

"Oh, my God, Colin. Jesus, Mary, and Joseph."

Colin only nodded.

News of the incident spread through the city and beyond. The police began a search for the bodies, with no luck.

Joe and Colin both became ill in the days that followed. Both were visited by doctors, who said they had hypothermia. It was followed by pneumonia. Just after Christmas, the day before New Year's Eve, Joe succumbed to it. When Colin heard the news, his condition worsened.

Colin hung on, but he was low. The muscles of his body faded, and the bones in his face stood out. Eva had never seen him like this. *And he's so quiet but yet easily agitated*, she thought.

By the third week in January, he was up and moving around the house. He rarely went outside and avoided visitors. He took to reading the newspaper and sitting by the fire in the living room.

It was in April, with the breaking up of the lake ice, that the bodies of Vic and Sam washed ashore in Collins Bay. When the news reached Colin, his health took a turn for the worse. He took to his bed again and began to develop a cough that troubled Eva.

She had called Dr. Webster to check on Colin over the winter. He came back as Colin's condition deteriorated.

"What can I tell you, Eva? He's young, he's strong, and he can get over this. But he's got to want to get over it. He needs to get up and get out of bed, eat food. He must have lost twenty pounds these last few months."

Eva was at a loss as to what to do. *He's slowly letting himself drown in the fluids, the pus and phlegm filling his lungs. He refuses to speak. He just shoos us away. Me and baby Brendan. I know fathers often steer away from newborns but this seems strange . . .*

On Grand Island, Michael had heard the news. The McIntosh and Hunt boys had been presumed dead, and now the presumption was proven correct. . . The story going around was that the pair had turned back that night when the storm blew in. They were at Old Town Tavern in Portsmouth Harbour, after hiding their boat with its full load in Pete Turner's boathouse. When the storm came to an end in the wee hours, they had decided to make the run. When they reached the island at dawn, another storm must have moved in again.

He couldn't let Sarah see that he was more than just angry.

*That son of mine. Leading young men to ruin. There's no way around that fact. The wastrel. That's what he is, there's no way around it. Might best just call it what it is. Of course, no one is saying that about Colin. In fact, they're saying they destroyed themselves trying to save the two. But Jesus. Yes, they tried to save them after they set them up to fail. Well, I guess the storm was an oddity. No one's fault for the weather. But goddamn it, Colin!*

It was early April, one week after the early Easter, a dinner with just two of his three boys, when he received the call.

"Hello?"

"Hello, Mr. O'Sullivan."

*That's Eva's voice. I know it is.*

"Sarah! Phone!"

*I don't trust myself,* he thought.

"Sarah! Telephone call!"

"I'm not deaf, you know. I can hear the thing. I can hear you bellowing even louder."

"It's Eva."

Sarah paused.

Eva was trying to compose herself. She had been surprised to find that getting dressed in one of the dresses she wore to church and putting on a bit of makeup gave her a sort of strength for the telephone call.

*The O'Sullivans are a tough bunch. I'm best not mincing words.*

"Sarah? Sorry, Mrs. O'Sullivan."

"Sarah is fine, dear. How is he doing?"

"He's not doing well."

Sarah's breath escaped her and she couldn't get it back. *I should have called before now. Michael and his anger pushed me not to do what I knew I must, what was natural. Damn him.*

"Sarah, are you there?"

"Yes, I'm here. Of course. What's going on with Colin?"

"He could get better, the doctor says. But he won't get out of bed. And that's allowing the sickness to grow. He's taking it all so hard. It was a real blow. He won't get up from it. . ." Eva fell into sobs.

"There, there, now, Eva. You think I should speak to him?

"Well, he won't get on the phone."

"Should I come there?"

*I don't know what else to say,* thought Sarah. *What should I do?*

"I don't know," said Eva.

"We're coming there. Let me arrange it, Eva."

"Okay, thank you, Sarah. Thank you so much. When do you expect to be here?"

"Tomorrow. Without a doubt. Try to feed him some soup tonight. Clear broth. We will be there tomorrow."

"Thank you, Sarah. I will."

"I'll see you then, Eva."

Sarah sat in the chair by the phone in the kitchen, stewing. *A curse on you, Michael. I should've never listened to you. You know nothing about people. About what they need. I can't get him out of that bed. He's Michael's boy. Whether either of them knows that or not. Each is the only one the other will ever listen to. They would like each other a whole lot more if they weren't so alike.*

Sarah began to cook.

*We'll get this sorted over dinner, Michael O'Sullivan. We will. If it kills you. I may kill you.*

When he scanned the platters and bowls on the table, Michael was impressed. It was his favourite meal. Lake trout and green beans with lemon dill sauce and some fresh potatoes. *She must have gone shopping to get this.*

"What's the occasion, Sarah?" he asked.

"It's the last supper," she replied, so quietly he wasn't sure he'd heard.

"Sorry. Last supper? For whom, then?"

"Sorry?"

"It's the last supper for whom?"

"Your son. The eldest."

Sarah took her spot at the table.

"What? Colin?"

Placing her napkin neatly in her lap, and then unfolding it, she let Michael wait a few moments for her answer.

"Eva, who you rudely ignored, was calling to let me know that Colin is likely to die. Any time now. Pneumonia."

Michael was still standing.

Sarah placed a whole trout on her plate.

"Will you sit down, Michael? Towering over me like that and the dinner is cooling."

Michael slumped onto his chair. He absently picked up a serving fork from the dish of green beans and threw it down angrily on his plate.

Eva continued. "He got pneumonia trying to find those boys, and he won't get up and out of bed now. The fluid is just sitting in there in his lungs and it will drown them in time. Soon now. It's filling his lungs."

Michael's head was swimming.

"That's just foolish," was all he could muster.

"Well, there's nothing Eva can do. Imagine a young family like that. And I expect another child is on the way."

"That boy. You can't tell him to do anything," Michael replied.

"All he needs to do is get up and move around. That's not much to ask."

Michael was lost in his thoughts but snapped back to speak to Sarah.

"I know what you're doing, Sarah. You're pushing me in your own way. And it's not a delicate thing. And you should be delicate."

Sarah paused. *Hold your calm demeanour. Give him the facts.*

"Michael, he's ill because he was trying to help other people. When those boys were lost, he could've stayed home, but he didn't. He went searching for them, and it nearly killed him. It did kill poor Joseph Haggerty. And now he's alone in this mess."

Michael saw the life of his son in his mind, from cooing baby to the youngster rolling on the grass, bringing him tea, to his recent adventures with smuggling. He felt as though he had been struck by a bolt of lightning. One notion blazed into his mind and shook his body.

*I had to move the lighthouse and place it on the hill so it wouldn't be knocked down by that ice. Soon after, I had to turn it off to save my boy. That's why I had to do it all. I've been a fool. Stubborn.* He sat with the thought. In shock.

Finally, he spoke. "We'll go."

"Sorry?"

"Tomorrow. First boat."

"Fine."

"Fine."

He lay in bed that night thinking about it. Awash in realizations and recriminations. *I'm not going to let him down now. My sole purpose with that infernal light was to keep him alive. Sure, if the light had been knocked down by the ice, they would have built another there, but it would never have been built in time for me to turn it out again. It was my responsibility to help him, to save him, I guess. It never ends, really. And that's fine. The only morality is love. For all my consternation and fits, the only code to follow that means anything is to love those that cross your path with as much love as you can muster. That's it. That's all. And Colin and the rest of my family deserve more from me.*

The next morning, Michael stood at the foot of Colin's bed. He had closed the door behind him.

*He is pale and all pointy features. He still looks the boy when he's asleep. All the world drifts away as they enter into sleep. It's a magical thing, really. I could watch him for a while.*

Colin stirred. He was surprised to see his father. Groggy, he pulled himself up to sit against the headboard.

Michael cleared his throat. "I think you're about done now, aren't you?"

Colin's jaw tightened.

"With what?"

"With all of this, then."

"I suppose I am."

"Well, good. I need your help. At least for this summer."

"With what?" *He has never said those words to me before.* I need. *And* help.

"It's too much for me with the farm, the lighthouse, and fishing."

Michael shifted his weight from foot to foot and looked down at the wide-plank floor.

"Please, son." And then he stared into his son's face.

Colin saw tears forming in his father's eyes. He felt tears forming in his. Burning. He coughed and rubbed his face.

"My God, son, you sound terrible."
"I know, I know. This summer sounds good, though."
"You can start by returning my chain," Michael said with a smile.
Colin sat up and slowly got up out of the bed.
"It's in the boat. Let's get it."
"How about a bit of soup first?"
"Okay."

# 5. Rebel

March 25, 1847— Leadmore West Townland, near Kilrush,<br>County Clare

Liam only gave it a day of thought.

The notion came to him like a vision, and he sat with it by the fire. It held. He decided he needed to walk the notion down to the estuary. After some thirty minutes of watching gulls on the winds and staring into the calm waters, he felt more certain.

It would involve travelling to Kilrush. A prospect that brought apprehension.

He was often told he looked like his mother, open-faced, broad-limbed, and athletic, and he would often see members of her family in the town where she had been raised.

*The Shannon and the sea always bring me answers, don't they? I would have been at home as a fisherman. I know it. I would have. But there is no life for a fisherman in Kilrush. We've never had the means to build the boats needed to take us to the big waters of the western sea. No, but she gave me answers today, didn't she?* He nodded towards the estuary and turned to walk home.

He kept the plan to himself for the rest of the day and at the meagre dinner of turnip soup and milk with Beatrice, James, and Genevieve. They all said how quiet he was, but he waved them off and went to bed early that night.

The next morning, he was sure. *Yes, I will raise money enough to buy seeds to grow food for us all. No great crop of corn or rye, no. There's no doubt Vandeleur will just seize that, won't he? I've heard of such things. Starving tenants, not able to pay their rent, raise a crop and the landlord takes all of it. No, I won't let that happen. We will grow garden vegetables: peas and turnips and so on. We will. And I'll have a few pounds left over to go to the rent, so.*

Liam had a few sips of milk. He had to remind himself that a full-throated swig was out of the question. It needed to be rationed. And wasn't Beatrice on him about it? Like a spy she was for her own dairy consumption board. He laughed to himself.

He dressed quietly so he wouldn't wake his wife, son, and daughter-in-law. He turned to the pig, who had wandered in and was sniffing around the table legs for food.

He whispered to the animal. "Ah, Gilly, you'll find nothing there. Anywhere, truly. Sorry, girl. And you're lucky Bea doesn't see ya in the house. You would hear about it."

He took the walking stick near the door on his way out and then turned back. "C'mon, now, girl, back outside," he said to the pig. "Today the cow will have a new home." He was surprised at how good he felt. "It's been a long time since I had some music in my step and feeling a bit of hope, isn't it? But I do. I'm sunny, Gilly, and I don't mind at all telling you that. You stay here now, and I'll share all the details of my journey when I return."

With a short rope in hand, Liam led his cow down the trail to Shanakyle Road, which would take him to his first destination, on the outskirts of Kilrush. He considered turning left and taking the road that would allow him to avoid the graveyard, but he knew it would add too many steps, and with his limited diet, he worried about the energy he'd need to get all his tasks completed. He never liked passing the graveyard, and with the stories he had heard of late, he wanted to avoid it more than ever. *All the spirits have to be troubled now, don't they?* He sighed and turned to the right and made his way down Shanakyle Road. The spring day was clear and warm, and he felt chuffed by his plans.

He hadn't gone more than two hundred yards when he noticed a solitary figure coming towards him on the road. It was just before he reached the graveyard that he met the woman. He saw she was clad in scraps of clothing and was about his age. As he grew closer, he could hear faint sounds coming from her. He couldn't discern what she was saying but understood the tone. She was distraught. He began to make out a few words: ". . . hungry grass . . . doomed . . . forgotten . . ." Liam realized he feared the woman.

*Maybe she's a spectre. I've heard of them appearing. Oh, what a sight. It's best to ignore it. Pay no heed, now. Move on, Liam. Keep your head down, right?*

He thought the figure hadn't noticed him and he was in the clear, but she turned to face him, and he felt compelled to do the same or risk offending the creature.

*Look at those wild eyes. It's as though they're a storm and anyone who falls into them is sure to be taken into the din of it. . . But what a defeated woman, with her emaciated face and body.*

She spoke as she passed him. "Don't let them make you forgotten. Don't give them that satisfaction," she hissed.

Her body shook and she moved on. "You, stranger, are heading to town," she said as she walked away. "Be a mark upon this world that tells of the injustice and how you stood against it. When you are to fall no matter the actions you take, then you may take the boldest of courses."

Liam was struck. He felt as though he were falling into her spell. *It's like hearing a curse, it troubles me so. Oh, what a thing to say. What do I do with it? Things were bad out in the world. I was hiding from them. And now they must become worse, I suppose.*

Liam watched her uneasy progress down the road. He pulled himself from the moment and forced himself to carry on. His feet were slow, as he knew the graveyard was just ahead.

The graves within the stone walls had frightened him since he was a child. As he approached, he made the sign of the cross, but he still felt a cold shudder rise within himself. He looked away from it and began to sing the song he knew always brought him the greatest hope and confidence: *"Proudly the note of the trumpet is sounding; / Loudly the war cries arise on the gale."*

An unseen horse neighed loudly and a voice spoke. "Easy, now, ya dim girl."

Liam was startled. He looked towards the sound and found his eyes on the graveyard. Three men were riding in a cart that held a coffin. They were entering the graveyard from the opposite side. Before he could make a decision, Liam found himself making the sign of the cross once more.

The men hadn't noticed him.

Liam watched as the two horses drawing the cart came to a halt and two of the men began to move the coffin off the wagon. The third man, the driver, wrapped the horses' reins around a metal hook near his feet and hopped down to join them. Together, they carried the coffin to a large hole.

Liam moved closer to get a better look. The dark cavity had other things in it. *Oh my Lord.* He had to stop himself from audibly gasping. *There are other bodies in there. Just lying there. Some barely dressed at all, with just a dirty bit of sheet on them. Six bodies but there could be more. It's all I can see, so. I swear we're dying like birds in the frost.*

He heard a sudden *whack* as the man who had hopped down to help the first two undid something on the bottom of the coffin while the other two held it over the grave. A body fell from the coffin and into the hole, rolled over, and came to rest with the others. The men glanced down then stepped back from the grave, and the man who opened the bottom of the coffin closed it again. They moved back to their cart.

*Look at what they made us into. Unfeeling creatures, aren't we? Uncaring about it all. And that coffin is scuffed and worn. They do this over and over, don't they? Just dump the bodies with no blessings or ceremony. Ah, that has to leave the spirits troubled. Oh, what are we doing now?*

As the men moved through the graveyard, Liam recognized one as Joe O'Brien.

*Not a bad man at all. Terrible times. They force us into terrible deeds.*

"Come, now, girl, away from all of this. Away now," Liam said, and pulled on the lead for the small cow.

The three men passed him on the road in their cart and Joe gave a friendly wave to Liam, who could only stare at him in return. *What do I do with all of this? It's too much to have in my head. But what can I do? Just move on, I suppose, for now.*

"What are we to do?" he asked the cow, as he moved on up the road. "I don't want to see much more of this world. No. I just want to complete my business and get back home. It's lawless and devilish times out here, to be sure."

Liam walked for another thirty minutes or so before he reached the farm of Allan Walsh, just on the edge of Kilrush. Allan was also a well-known cattle trader, which was why Liam sought him out.

Liam took a moment before he opened the gate to Allan's yard. *Come on, man, compose yourself. You've got to stay calm.*

He was still struggling to find his composure when Allan came out to meet him.

"Good man," Allan said, as he stepped into the yard.

"Good man yourself," Liam replied.

"So this is your beast, is it?"

"She's a good cow."

"She's a cow," he replied.

"But a good cow."

"A cow is just a cow."

"Oh, that's not true at all. She's calm and has a good yield of milk. She's no bother at all. No bother at all."

"All right, then. It's no matter to me about her disposition."

"Well, it should be."

And with that, Liam surprised himself by taking his cow by the rope and turning away and walking towards the road.

"Where are you going, then?"

"To another buyer who will appreciate a fine animal," Liam shouted over his shoulder.

"But I have the money here for you."

"That's no matter to me."

"Come on, now. Come back."

"Fine. But you agree she's a good cow, then?"

"She seems fine."

"She is."

"All right, then."

"All right."

Allan stood confounded for a moment, looking at Liam, who met his eyes and held his stern and angered expression.

"Right," Allan said. "I'll go, then, and fetch the money for you now."

"Fine."

Allan stepped quickly into his house and returned just as fast. "Here you are, now. Four pounds, ten shillings."

"Four and ten? That's the best you can do? It's an affront."

"An affront? It's a troubled time, Liam, you know it. Come on, now."

"Troubled for us, but the sale of corn, butter—everything the Brits want—continues just fine, doesn't it? So maybe you're just trying to find an advantage. No better than the Brits."

"Liam O'Sullivan. What a thing to say to me. I've known you since we were boys, haven't I? To make such a charge against me only leaves me insulted. . . Yes, I'm the injured party here."

"Oh, you can sustain the injury, Allan. It doesn't look like you've missed a meal of late. Not like most of us. Seven pounds or else I will be on my way."

"Aren't you the troubled one, Liam? I'll give you six pounds just to be done here and to lend a hand. You hear that? *Lend a hand.* You're not yourself, Liam O'Sullivan, you're not. And I understand. So let's get this done and look to better days and remember the fair ones."

"Fine, then," Liam replied.

He took the cash and handed the cow's rope to Allan. He put a hand on the animal's head and nodded to her buyer, feeling worse for it all.

Allan turned away without a word and led the cow to his barn.

As he passed the gate, Liam looked back, but Allan was gone.

*Maybe that was a bit too rough, my language. I don't know. Maybe he's right. Maybe I'm not right today. I don't know. But my work is not done, is it? I still have a bit to do.*

Liam continued into town towards the market square. He knew there would be a sale of seeds at the government offices. *As it's April, there should be a good supply of them. There's been talk of relief with free seeds for peas, oats, corn, turnips, and so on, but it hasn't materialized, has it? The thought of it just angers me. Me, having to sell a cow to get seeds to stave off starvation. After the money we've given the powers that be, year after year. And if we grew a crop, Vandeleur would be likely to take it, wouldn't he? Yes, he would. There's no doubt about it at all. No doubt. So, yes, let's stick to the wee garden crops. And I'll have cash left over, won't I?*

*What a line*, he thought, when he reached the building, *and they're chatting quiet like, aren't they?* There were about twenty in the line. He recognized a few. *That's Lynch, from the other side of town, and Peter O'Donnell.* Peter had married into Liam's mother's family. *Both look frail. And they were never frail men. Even the talk is low. No one even has the strength to raise their voice, do they?* He gave both a slight nod as he arrived.

The loudest voices were coming from within the building.

"Give him time, boys, give him time. He's trying to negotiate it," a man a little younger than Liam said to the others in the line.

"What's he trying to negotiate?" Liam asked the group in general.

"Well, he's becoming irate, really," one said.

"Irate?"

"You know, angry like."

"I know the meaning, but why is he angry, then?"

"They've raised the price of the seeds," the first man replied.

"Raised the price of seed?"

"Aye. They did," the man said.

"Well . . . that's just . . . I don't know what to call that," Liam said.

"It's the wrong decision, there is no doubt in that. No doubt," O'Donnell offered.

"I would say so," replied Liam. "There's no relief and then they raise the price. And the government knows about it?"

"That they do, that they do," said the first man. "Talk of the free market and whatnot."

"The free market?"

"Yes. The belief is that the government can't interfere in the free market."

"Isn't that a cozy decision," said Liam.

"'Tis," said all three men. The group started forming a circle to talk.

"This is just not right," Liam said. "We need to do something about it."

"They say the society, you know, is going to maybe give out seeds," O'Donnell said.

"The society?"

"The Quakers, I understand."

Liam's head was getting hot. *I want action. A swift blow that would mean something.* He looked around at the men. *I don't know what sort of resistance we could muster. But a few of us could do something.*

He took a deep breath and spoke. "Let's just take the lot of them, each take a share of the seeds, and hand out the rest. It's madness otherwise. Paying increased prices for seeds when we're starving like!"

A few men nodded and one gave an "ay." A few looked to their feet.

"Come on, now," Liam continued. "We've got to stand together, now more than ever, or we'll be lost. We will. Let's march in together. I'll lead the way."

A few more men agreed. "Right, then, Liam," Lynch said. A few more followed this, and as Liam stepped forward about six men were following him, and none of the others were dissenting from this action.

They moved past the line and into the building, where there was a small lobby, a counter, and a few people within, in the office.

"You can't all be coming in here at once," a man shouted from behind the counter. "One at a time! I keep telling you. One at a time!"

"No, you'll be dealing with the lot of us now," Liam replied.

"I will not."

"Hand them over, then," Liam said.

"What are you on about?"

"The seeds. Hand over what you've got, and we will distribute them now to the people."

"I will do no such thing."

"You will. Now."

The man's response was silence.

"Now!" Liam demanded.

"Mary! Fetch the constable!" the man shouted into a room adjoining his own.

"Do no such thing, Mary!" Liam called, but he could hear someone's movements and a door opening and closing. He stepped behind the counter to look into the room where this Mary was supposed to be and saw no one. But he did see the seeds. There were great baskets and wooden boxes of them, labelled and glorious, Liam thought. He was stunned at the sight of so much potential.

He didn't have much time to consider it, as two police constables came through the door on the other side of the room. The one through which Mary had departed a few moments before.

"What's your business in here?" the younger of the two asked.

Liam looked back over his shoulder. His confidence quickly drained and was replaced by a sense of doom. The other men had not followed him into the second room. They were not even in the first one.

"Sedition!" the man who had been behind the counter yelled as he entered the scene. "I heard talk of overthrowing our offices. Theft from the government! He was riling up the people."

"Is that right?" the first constable asked.

Liam grimaced. *There's not a thing I can do or say to save myself, is there? I can see it all. The choices that led me here. It feels . . . inevitable.*

The constables moved towards him, and as they did, he stepped towards the door.

"Hold on, there," the second one said, and the first raised his shotgun.

"Can I just give my belongings to my neighbour?"

"As long as they're not stolen goods," said the older of the two officers.

"Really?" said the first one.

"Truly," Liam replied.

Liam went to O'Donnell in the crowd, handed him the money from the sale of the cow, and whispered, "Will you see to it that this makes its way back home?"

"Aye, I will," he replied.

"Come on, now," the first constable said.

Liam nodded. As he passed the other men who had been with him, they were all now looking at their shoes.

*There's no win at all, is there? Just a march toward our end. The only difference between me and these souls is that I know it, and mine just might be a quicker step toward my fate.*

"Pick it up, now," the constable said. But Liam continued at a slow trudge all the way to the constabulary barracks and his cell.

# 6. An Exile

December 19, 1957—Horsey Bay, west of Kingston, Ontario


*Three times around my neck, and down the torso and then around my waist, and look at what we've got left.*

With the chain on his body, Brendan bent his knees and bounced a little. Then he laughed. *Listen to that. The chain has a little song in it, doesn't it?*

Brendan O'Sullivan was broad-shouldered, like his father, Colin, and his grandfather, Michael. And about the same height. But fair and dark-eyed like his mother. His frame could manage the heavy metal links. He was dressed in a suit but had put his plaid wool winter coat over top to protect it and to offer some warmth. He wore his boots for the journey ahead.

*It's a great chain that stretches on for miles,* he thought. *At least, that's how I felt about it when I was a kid. Its use didn't matter. It held force and implied great purpose. We mostly spoke about it or looked at it, hanging on the side of the barn. It was a thing to behold. Like the northern lights, I suppose, or some of the sunsets out here. My God, listen to me. Maybe I'm still drunk. I likely am. I suppose Dad wanted me to take it when I left the island. A connection. Sure, I found my reasons, being a mechanic. But it wasn't about that. I wanted it, didn't I? Yes, I would have it, thank you.*

He stepped from the garage and looked out at the yard of the home he had been renting on Horsey Bay. It was morning. Just before eight. A week before Christmas. The house was quiet. His friend Dougie Scott was still asleep. As were most of his neighbours on the bay. The fire in his front yard was now a pile of smouldering ashes. A bit of fabric from his sofa was on the edge of it, unburned. He kicked it towards the coals in the centre.

Brendan thought of his conversation just a few hours ago with Dougie.

"Well, I need to get rid of it all. I need to no longer have any earthly possessions," he'd announced, when Dougie asked him why they were burning the items in the house. Even as he'd said it, Brendan felt the words were coming from outside himself.

At first, Dougie was amused to be throwing sticks of furniture on a fire in the front yard. They'd had a few drinks. It just seemed like a crazy thing to do. Brendan always had mad ideas, didn't he? But it continued with a lounge chair, shelves, and then the bed.

"Jesus, man, why don't you light the entire place on fire?"

Brendan paused. "Well, it's a rental." He threw his bedsheets on the blaze.

Brendan turned back to the house. "Follow me. I need your help."

They walked through the front door and were standing in the living room. "Grab the end of the couch, there."

Dougie was perplexed. "But Brendan, where are you gonna live? How are ya gonna live?" He took a seat on the couch.

*I owe the guy an explanation,* Brendan thought. *I was going to tell him anyway. He's one of my closest friends.*

"If I don't burn it off, I'll never leave. Get it?"

Dougie slowly nodded his head, clearly still confused.

Brendan could feel his face getting hot. He knew that often preceded trouble for him. Like when he got into that fight with the guy at the garage. He took a few deep breaths then turned back to Dougie. "So I guess what I'm saying is that I need you to get your skinny ass off my couch so I can throw it in the front yard to burn."

"You're leaving, then?" Dougie asked.

"That I am." Brendan lifted his side of the couch, dumping his friend from it.

"Ya bastard!" Dougie responded, trying to find his feet. "Does Margaret know your plan?"

"She will, soon enough."

"Okay, then. Well, do you know where you'll be going?"

"I'll let you know when I know. And we'll be back around in time, I'm sure."

Dougie shook his head. "Okay, Brendan. Okay."

Now his friend was passed out on the living room floor.

*It's a wager. Maybe more of a demand. I don't know from who, but I feel it in me. Pushing me. It's early to be on the ice. But if I can make it across, drop the chain with my family, make it all the way back with no one stopping me, or nothing stopping me, then I'll go see her. No, I'll go and convince her that she has to go with me. There it is.*

*So, here we go. What a thing to do. Besides, if I just left it in the rental here, who knows what would happen to it before Joe or Dad got it? I gotta get it back home. Joe can make use of it, I'm sure, on the farm or fishing. It belongs back home.*

He started down the lawn towards the slope to the frozen lake. Brendan paused.

*I won't be seeing Joe anymore. I've known it, but now I can feel it. Baby brother. I'll get in touch with you. You'll understand when I send you a letter. And maybe when things settle down, I can be back here. Yeah, I'll be back. He's fine now. He has Dad there with him and Mom. Soon enough, he'll marry. They'll be upset and then they'll understand.*

*That's what we do. We stomp and holler at meeting newness and slowly accept it. That's just who we are, I suppose.*

He took a long look across the lake to the island, two miles away.

*I'd imagine we'll get married ourselves. Won't we, Margaret? We'll be wed soon enough. Maybe even in a Catholic church? It's no matter. Presbyterian is fine, if it makes a great difference to her. Might as well get married down at City Hall if we're getting married at a Presbyterian church. Nah, that's not fair. Let them be the bigots. Not you. Not you.*

*By week's end, then, wed or dead. That's what you're saying to yourself. That's the gamble you're making. I suppose it is. No one needs to know that. Not even Margaret. Goddamn it, whenever I think about it, my head starts to get hot. Why? Why does it do that?*

Brendan paused and took a few more deep breaths to settle himself.

*It does have a weight to it, the old chain. But I'll be fine. It's just a couple of miles there. Since I'm not taking the ice road, maybe even a touch shorter. There are no questions for me if I'm not on that road. For sure there will be someone or other crossing it, recognizing me, and wanting to talk. Right. The road isn't even in yet. Not for another week or two, I would imagine. Usually just after Christmas. But it's been cold for at least a week now. A few inches of ice out there. Enough to hold a man if not a vehicle. Maybe. Should I just wait a bit? No, no. I've come this far, haven't I? The furniture's all gone away. But damn, my head feels hot.*

Once more, he stopped and breathed deeply.

As he walked out of Horsey Bay on the ice, Brendan looked over his left shoulder towards Kingston.

*I won't miss the city. Working at the machine shop was fine, I guess. There are shops like that all over the world. I could work anywhere. But I will miss the island. It has its own gravity, doesn't it? It holds you warmly. You can escape, but you need a good reason to do so. It's more than family. There's a unique beauty and rhythm to this existence. But why don't I feel it anymore? Will I find anywhere else that makes me feel this way?*

A melancholy settled in him.

*But Margaret. It's all worth it for her. Margaret or bust. Her thick, strawberry blond, wavy hair. I just want to get immersed in it. And her skin, as white and bright like snow. No, it's more like light. As if light had form. That's Margaret. It is. And my God, she has spirit. Like no one else, really.*

He picked up his pace.

*Maybe we'll have Christmas in Montreal or Boston. Who knows? Maybe New York itself. They've got a ton of Irish there. They may mind it, but there's enough of us that I suppose they can't do much about it. . . I've always felt the draw of that city.*

His mind turned to the events that had driven him out here to the ice. *Remember why you're doing this. There's a reason.*

It had been a warm Saturday night in early October. He had met Margaret in front of the pool hall, as they'd planned. He was going to take her to a party at Nathan Yeoman's place. It was at a party that he had met her, just a few months before. They both liked going out, dancing, being with their friends, and it was a way for her to get out of her parents' home with no questions.

And then her father appeared, still wearing his suit from work. They both knew he was coming when he was about half a block away. They heard him first. Raising his voice above the gang of them laughing and goofing around.

"Margaret!" he shouted. They stopped. "Margaret!" Saying it twice, like they didn't hear him.

Brendan was shocked, but she didn't seem that surprised. She stepped away from Brendan, but her father grabbed her anyway. Roughly. Brendan felt like a neutered animal. Raw, but not wanting to add violence. Useless.

"Margaret, you need to come home. Now!"

*And the look he shot me. Dismissive. As though I was a monster. I knew what he meant. If she was out with the solicitor's son, it wouldn't have been a problem. Yeah, maybe Donald McTavish's son. That would be okay. But not me. A mick from the island. A mechanic.*

That was why she never had him pick her up at her house, why she met him in town and, at the end of the night, hopped out of the car so quickly after he parked up the street. He assumed that was for the goodnight kiss, but it was more than that. . .

And she was willing to let it happen. Before her father even spoke, Brendan knew she was going to go with him. He could see it in her eyes. The defeat. Dougie, Elaine, Will, Kat, everyone stopped and watched them. And then Brendan watched her father stuff her in the back of the Chrysler.

They tried to cheer him up and told him to come to the party. No one knew he was in love with her. So he went along with them, then slipped out and drove his car to her place. The large brick house looked dark, but when his eyes adjusted he could see her light was on. He didn't know what to do next, so he parked across the road, and after a few minutes she must have seen him, because she came out. She was so nervous, trying to shoo him away, that he had to tell her. He just blurted it out. "I love you!" She was surprised. She hopped in the car, climbed over to him, and said it right back to him.

They drove off in his old Buick and lay beside the Pickerel River as the stars appeared. What an amazing evening. Naked in the unseasonably warm night air. The leaves were turning.

*My God, I never wanted to let her go. But then it all seemed to go away.*

It had taken just one call. She'd asked Brendan to give her some time to talk to her folks. And now three months had passed without her. Only short phone calls and that visit at lunch at the shop.

*I think I'm going to lose my mind. She was the one good thing . . .* It was her damn father, but today that might change. Brendan would stand in the doorway and ask her to leave with him. *She must want to go, mustn't she?*

Brendan had made it out of Horsey Bay and was moving towards the north channel, the body of water that in warmer months shipping vessels, fishermen, and weekend sailors would populate. Now it was a great expanse of white. No other person was on the ice.

*There's the sun*, he thought. *Almost warm on the cheek. It will be a good day. The start of better days to come.*

A game took shape in his head. *If I can make it without seeing a bit of open water, I will know Margaret and I were meant to be.* He smiled. *I'm in my twenties now, and here I am playing these childish games. . . Well, it's a long walk.*

*We're meant to be. I know it. I don't care what they say. Yeah, maybe we will live in Montreal. I can pick up a little French. So can Margaret. She's smart. Brighter than me. I bet she could get a job in the city. I don't mind if she gets a job. If it makes her happy.*

The ice made a sound that was like a great clap of thunder. Brendan jumped. The iron links draped around him sang.

*Just pressure cracks. All those fishermen from the city are afraid of the pressure cracks. They come up here to grab our walleye, and you can see them scurrying from the ice and you know it's the pressure cracks that did it.*

He squinted in the sun reflecting off the snow around him.

*It's so calm out here. I'd imagine this is what a desert feels like— great space around you and silence. There's a beauty in it.*

Brendan continued walking.

He had no warning. The ice beneath him opened up and the darkness under it swallowed him. It was followed by a crashing sound and the noises of thrashing in the water.

*My lord! What's happening? Oh, God, I'm in the damn lake. Kick. Kick, for fuck's sake! Keep moving your goddamn legs. You've done this before. Remember. You fell through as a child. Why can't I get up on the ice again! Oh, no, the goddamn chain. That weight!*

Brendan struggled and managed to stay above the water. *Keep your wits*, he said to himself. *Come on, now.* He finally had his arms resting on the ice with his body in the lake. The chain was still wrapped around him and trailing into the dark waters.

*Just pull yourself up, you bastard. You can do it.*

But he couldn't. He tried the swimmer's kicks he'd been taught to do as a child if he ever went through the ice but had no luck getting his body up there.

*The mechanics of it just don't work. It's too much weight. Too much on me.*

His arms were starting to go. He could feel the strength leaving him. He didn't think he could even lift the chain off him now.

He bowed his head and began to unwrap the weight from around his neck, dropping the line deep into the expanse of water. "Come on, now!" he hollered to the empty plain of ice.

His legs were losing strength along with his arms. Brendan closed his eyes. *Make a choice. You're going to have to pull on everything you've got, now. You're going to have to let go of the chain, then scrape, pull, and scream your way out of this mess you've made. Or not. You could just sink into the water and it will all be over pretty quickly. You know she's not leaving with you. Today was your last stand, and you took it here instead of in her kitchen. Either way, you were done for today.*

Brendan bobbed for a moment in the cold water with these thoughts. Then he used his right hand to unwrap the chain around the wrist of his left hand, paused, and then let it fall into the cold, dark water of Lake Ontario.

He groaned, kicked hard, and pulled himself up, screaming. "You goddamn son of a bitch! Fuck you and everything and all the whole goddamn world!" He dug his fingers into the snow and ice so hard, two of his fingernails split and shot blood into the wet, white snow. He snarled and spat until he'd pulled himself up onto it. Then he rolled on his back and stared into the endless blue sky while tears streamed down his face. "I know, I know, nothing's going to work. I got it all wrong. I'm sorry, Margaret. I'm sorry. . ." As his voice trailed off and silence pressed back in, he felt even more defeated.

His mind turned to his father, the advice the man had always given him. "This is our bit of the world. This is what we've scraped and fought and died for. This. It's not nothing, and it's the best we've had in generations, to be sure. You need to know that. It's ours." He never liked hearing it. It made him feel small and imprisoned. And his father had a way of saying it in moments of great joy—at a dinner with everyone laughing, or when they finished with fishing and had a great catch of walleye and were heading home in the boat. Something about hearing it only raised defiance in him, but he didn't want to argue with his father. He loved him, and it meant a lot to him, but the weight of those words troubled Brendan in a way he couldn't express.

As he was thinking this, his mind turned to the chain. *I let it go. The one reason I was out here. The last thing I was to do.*

Brendan let out a deep sigh. "Fool of a man." His body then sent even greater shudders through him.

*Damn, it's always strange how water can hurt you. It feels like daggers into yourself. And like the whole world is laughing at me. Crossing the ice and not thinking about the weight of the thing. Imagining you could change your luck with Margaret by just showing up today. Thinking that a whole new future awaits you instead of what's known and been expected of you. What am I to do? Well, you can't stay here. You're going to freeze if you do.*

He stood, and as he did, he thought of the pact he had made just a few minutes ago. It seemed childish at the time. *But I have seen open water. I've fuckin' bathed in it. And I know, now, there's no Margaret for me.* He looked to his destination. He could spy his family home on the bluffs of Grand Island.

"Goodbye," he said.

He took one last look down the hole in the ice and then made his way back towards his house.

"I know what to do. I know."

# 7. A Spectacle

### January 12, 1958–Kingston, Ontario


"You'll have tea, and that's the end of it. I don't want to hear any more about it," Ellen James announced to her daughter, Margaret, who sat on the end of her bed in a pale yellow dressing gown.

She looked at her daughter, grimaced, and turned to leave Margret's bedroom. As she walked towards the door, she offered a final message: "And, you know, you're lucky William has such an interest in you."

"I will be forever in his debt, Mother," Margaret responded.

Ellen stopped and looked in the full-length mirror in the room. She was tall and slim. *Handsome* was the word that was used to describe her, with her height and strong, angular features and light hair and eyes. She was proud of her new blue satin wrap dress and how she looked in it.

*I'm still attractive. And I'm already prepared for our guests.* She remembered Margaret was likely watching her and quickly dropped her smile.

"And take the lozenge, Margaret. Your voice sounds terrible still," she said over her shoulder as she left the room.

Margaret shook her head and fell back in her bed.

*I can't believe I have to do this. Yes, William is fine. He's just fine. I'll never love him like Brendan. But he's fine. He's been sweet, I can tell. He's really trying. Asking me about myself at church, bringing me flowers. But Brendan . . . poor, sweet Brendan. I feel bad thinking about William. But what can we do? Brendan, where are you?*

She remembered seeing him in the park. *Handsome, tall, strong . . . and gentle. There's so much strength and gentleness combined in him. And he's not dim. His hands, so large and warm. And that kiss, so tender, and then I felt devoured. I never knew I wanted to be devoured.*

She turned her head to look out the window into the garden and was struck with the pain in her neck. It had been nearly a week now, but it still hurt. She watched the snow drift down in the grey sky, nearly imperceptible until it settled on the dark limbs of the trees, the sidewalks, and the still-green grass. *Does Brendan like the snow? Is it falling on him now? I've never known him in the winter.* She sighed and rubbed her neck.

Her mother came in again.

"You're just going to lie there, are you?"

She began to look for clothes for her daughter and then turned back to the items lying at the foot of Margaret's bed.

"Oh, this outfit is so nice. It's the new one you got in the summer, isn't it? You were so happy in it. That's why I laid it out for you this morning."

Margaret nodded and looked at the white pencil skirt and blouse, the white jacket with a green interior with white polka dots and matching green neck scarf. *A neck scarf. I get it now.*

"Yes. I was happy then."

"See! Put it on."

"You're daft. I was happy because of Brendan. Not the magical powers of a skirt and blouse."

"Please put it on."

"Don't push me."

"William and his parents will be here in less than half an hour."

"I'm aware of the details, you may recall."

"Do you plan to meet them in your dressing gown? I'm sure that O'Sullivan boy wouldn't mind that."

"Don't speak about him. Especially like that."

"He didn't even have the decency to come to the door and speak to us."

"Because I knew you wouldn't accept him! We've had this conversation!"

"That may be true, but he's still rude."

"You know you're Irish. I'm Irish. Partly, thanks to you."

"We're Protestants."

"No one cares."

"You brought it up."

"Only to tell you that no one cares."

"Well, let's leave that business with Brendan behind us now."

"You're insufferable, and he wasn't the one who was grabbing me on the main street."

"No, I'm sure you were grabbing each other in the alley."

"No, Mother, we did that in his car."

"The mouth on you!"

"Get out and I'll get dressed."

"Fine!"

Ellen paused at the door and looked back at her daughter.

"And are you okay, Margaret, really?"

"No. Really."

"Goodbye."

Her mother slammed the door behind her.

Margaret slipped out of her dressing gown and began to put on her clothes. She paused before she tied the scarf around her neck. *How long did she spend finding an outfit to hide her shame? My shame, I guess. But she's made it her own.*

*I suppose I have to get married. I've put it off long enough. Maybe if I make them happy and date Dad's friend's son for a bit, I can get them used to the idea of Brendan. But Brendan's going to be upset. He won't understand. He's not patient. And so emotional. But I'll talk to him. I'll make him understand.*

She began to do what she'd done as a child when she felt sad or anxious. She rubbed her left palm with the thumb of her right hand. It was like a massage.

"Margaret!" she heard from downstairs.

"Ellen!"

She could hear her mother's feet on the stairs.

"I'm your mother!" she announced as she entered the room again. "Not *Ellen*."

"Right. Thank you! For so long, I thought you were the warden here."

"Not humorous."

"Definitely humorous."

"Will you please finish putting on your clothes and come downstairs?"

"It would be with the greatest pleasure."

Ellen paused in the doorway.

"Would you like me to do your makeup?

"My makeup?"

"Yes."

"I've been doing my own makeup since I started stealing yours when I was six."

"Yes, you were a terrible little thief."

Margaret smiled at her mother, a defiant smile.

"I mean, you know, down here," Ellen said nervously, pointing to her own neck.

"Oh, you think I should wear makeup on my neck?"

Margaret looked in the mirror and saw that some of the bruising on her neck could still be seen—red, yellow, and deep purple marks.

"So much for this ensemble. The scarf isn't working."

Ellen grimaced and looked down at the floor.

"I was just trying to help you." Tears formed in her eyes. "I don't want you to have to answer any . . . awkward questions."

"Or you don't want me to embarrass you? No one wants to buy bruised meat, right?"

"Margaret!"

"Ellen!"

"Margaret!"

"Ellen!"

"I swear to God, I can't do this with you."

"But here you are, doing it, so I guess you have to apologize to God after you apologize to Brendan and me. And we've been waiting for a while now."

Ellen left the room and slammed the door behind her again. Margaret could hear her crying in the hall.

*I can feel it when I swallow*, thought Margaret. *It would be a quick way to get rid of William—just let him see the bruises around my neck.*

She stood at the mirror and began dabbing makeup on her neck. She examined it when she was done, tilting her head to the left, and began to silently cry. She breathed in deeply, patted her cheeks with a tissue from her bureau, and then left the room.

Just a few blocks away from the Jameses' home, Rupert Glendon had a decision to make. He rubbed his greying moustache with his hands and touched the thinning brown hair on his head. He then reached into the small pocket on his suit vest, withdrew his pocket watch, sighed, and reached his conclusion. They would drive.

Rupert owned a series of car lots in the area. He had invested in them with the money his father had made in the logging industry. He had two sons, William and Kevin, though just William would be coming with them for tea at the Jameses'. The family lived only a few blocks from the James family, but while the snow that had arrived in early January had been cleared and the street and sidewalks were passable, it looked like it could snow again today.

He had been deliberating for the better part of ten minutes before he came to his resolution. Muriel would prefer it if they drove. She and Ellen had arranged this. It was all their doing. But she would approve of his choice.

As they moved through the streets of Kingston in his Studebaker, he felt pleased.

"Look, snow now, Muriel. There's snow coming down."

"That's right, there is."

"I suppose you're glad we didn't walk."

"I am, Rupert. Yes. Great foresight."

"Thank you."

"Will the Weaver boy come round to clear the sidewalk and drive?"

"I suppose he will. If he hasn't by the time we've returned, we can call him about it. I would hate to have someone slip. I heard there are scoundrels out there who look for nice houses with snowy walks to fall on so they can sue them. Can you believe that?"

"Scoundrels, indeed."

"Indeed."

In the rear-view mirror, Rupert noticed William was staring out the window absent-mindedly and playing with this tie.

"William, stop your fidgeting back there."

William mouthed something inaudible.

Muriel spoke up. "Rupert, don't be so hard on the boy. He may be having tea with his future wife. Who knows?  I saw you glancing at Margaret today at church, William."

William smiled a little and then scowled.

"William, you could do worse," his father said. They are a fine family. John basically insures the entire city now. He must have two dozen agents working for him."

Rupert looked in the rear-view mirror again and caught his son's eye. William looked away and made a fist with his right hand.

As they reached the front door of the James family's home, Ellen opened it before they could knock.

"Well, come in here. Quickly! It's so cold."

When the door was closed behind them, Ellen called over her shoulder, "Annie, can you please help the Glendons with their snowy coats?"

"Of course. Good afternoon," Annie said.

No one replied. They handed their coats to her.

"Please follow me to the parlour," Ellen said, "and we can make our introductions."

John stood and Margaret remained seated as Rupert, Muriel, and William entered the room. Everyone said hello except Margaret.

"Margaret, say hello," Ellen urged. "Or should I say, wake up?"

Startled by her mother, Margaret stood up quickly and offered her hand.

"Hello, Mr. and Mrs. Glendon."

She turned to William and gave a little wave. William smiled in return.

The Glendons took the spots Ellen suggested to them. The two sets of parents faced each other on the loveseats while William and Margaret sat in chairs across from each other. The group formed a square.

"What a lovely sermon today by Reverend Jenkins," Ellen offered

"Corinthians is one of my favourite books of the Bible," Muriel said. "Hopeful, and such sound wisdom for life and marriage."

"True," said Ellen.

John spoke up. "Well, how is business, Rupert?"

"No complaints at all. And we never stop expanding."

"Well, good for you. And good for me, I suppose. We insurers grow with you."

"That is true," said Rupert.

"Margaret has been helping at the hospital," Ellen said. "I'm so proud of her. I think it was good she took this year off before considering what happens next in her life."

"Well, good for you, Margaret," Muriel said. "I would find that difficult," she added, her voice trailing off.

"Why's that?" Margaret replied.

"Oh, you know." Muriel said, looking with a smile at Ellen.

"It's trying work, Margaret," Ellen said.

"Yes, helping others requires giving a little of yourself. I have no intention of keeping myself on the shelf like one of your Royal Doulton figurines, Mother."

"Let's just watch your tone with your mother," John added.

Margaret began rubbing the palm of her hand with her thumb.

Ellen gently slapped her hand. Margaret stopped and sighed.

Annie came in with the tea.

"Well, here we go," Ellen said. "Thank you, Annie."

"How do you take your tea, Muriel?"

"A lemon slice, please."

"Of course," said Ellen, while Annie poured the tea.

"I think it's great for a girl to have her own pursuits," William said.

"Of course you do," said Muriel, "you've always been a generous boy."

William smiled.

"I was thinking of becoming a nurse," said Margaret.

"Well, that training will be wonderful when you have a family. Knowing how to attend to cuts and bruises with little boys is indispensable," Muriel replied.

Margaret sighed and shifted in her chair.

"Very good point, Muriel," said John. "I've always said no education is a waste, even for young women. Especially something so practical as nursing."

"True," said William

Both husbands nodded.

"And there's no greater joy than in raising a family," Ellen added.

"Really? I've been your greatest joy?" Margaret asked.

The room fell silent.

Margaret spoke again. "Annie, can you turn up the radio and maybe put on that new station? The one I was telling you about."

Annie looked to Ellen, who rolled her eyes and nodded slightly. She left the room, and a few moments later, Fats Domino could be heard singing "Blueberry Hill." Annie returned to her work with the tea service.

"I love this one," said Margaret.

She jumped up from her chair and ran into the kitchen to turn up the volume further.

The four parents looked at one another.

"What do you think he found up there to give him such a thrill?" Margaret asked.

No one answered.

"The singer. Up on that hill. I think I have an idea."

"Margaret!" her mother said with a slightly raised voice.

"Ellen!" Margaret barked back.

Rupert looked uncomfortable. "Well, I think volunteering is a great thing. I remember, Ellen, when you were helping with the Ladies' Temperance Society. The scourge of alcohol is no small problem."

"Yeah, trying to make people do what they don't want to do would be a big problem to solve," offered Margaret.

"Margaret!" Ellen hissed at her.

"Ellen!" Margaret barked back again.

"The tea is lovely," Muriel offered weakly.

Both men were shifting uncomfortably in their chairs.

"Ooh, I love this one. You just have to dance!" Margaret announced. She jumped up from her chair again and began singing along to a Bo Diddley song.

Her father broke the stunned silence. "Margaret! You're making a spectacle of yourself."

Margaret paused. Memories rushed into her mind. Images she had a difficult time collecting. Part of her had tried to suppress them, but now they flooded back regardless.

She'd woken on the couch in terrible pain, her father standing over her and her mother kneeling by her, crying. The first thing Ellen said, while sobbing, was, "Why do you need to make a spectacle of yourself."

She had taken a chair from the kitchen to the garage and found a rope. There was always a rope in there. She knew her father would be home soon and would park his car in the garage. When he did, he could find her there. If they wanted to treat her like a prisoner, refuse to let her see Brendan or even go out of the house, they needed to know what she was willing to do about it. And now Brendan was gone. No one knew where.

She climbed up on the chair under a beam in the garage. She flung the rope over the beam, looped it a few times to make sure it wouldn't slip. She'd made a loop big enough to poke her head through. She looked at her watch: 5:11 p.m. He should be home in a few minutes. She'd stepped up on the arm of the chair, to check the rope, to make sure it would hold, when she heard the car and the garage door begin to open. It startled her, and she'd lost her footing. She felt the rope around her neck. She vaguely remembered her father yelling, and then it all went black.

And the next thing she'd heard was, "Why do you need to make a spectacle of yourself?"

Margaret was standing still in the room. The song was over. "In the Still of the Night" had started. She realized where she was and looked at her mother. She sighed and swayed to the music.

Still staring at her mother, she loosened the bow in the scarf and pulled it from her neck. She held it before her, then let it fall to the ground. Everyone was silent.

"You're confused, Ellen," she said to her mother. "I'm not making a spectacle, I'm just spectacular."

William laughed.

"A dance, darling?" she asked.

William stood, took her hand, and she began to lead him in a waltz.

# 8. A Fire

## June 14, 1958—Kingston, Ontario

William Glendon looked at his brother, Kevin, and his friends Tommy and Brad from Queen's University and felt a swell of pride.

They had just sat down at their table at the King George Hotel. He felt he needed to say something.

"I can't believe she agreed to get married, boys. But here we are!"

Kevin smiled, looked at the other guys, and said, "You've got your hands full now, brother."

William grimaced and then offered a little laugh.

"She'll settle down after we get married. . . She'd better."

*It's been a whirlwind,* he thought.

After their formal meeting with her parents, he had been adamant about going on a date with her. Despite his parents' protests. Especially those of his father.

*She reminds me of a new car. So bright you want to show her off to the world. It feels strange and amazing at the same time.*

"Hey, Romeo, are you with us?" Tommy asked.

"Yeah, yeah."

"To William," Tommy said, his glass raised. The others raised their glasses.

"Come on, let's play some darts," Kevin said.

"Okay, okay," said William.

On their way to the dartboards, they passed the bar, where Joseph O'Sullivan was seated. He was clearly Brendan's brother. Tall, broad-shouldered, and with a mop of thick hair.

Kevin elbowed his brother and said, "Isn't that the younger brother?"

"Whose younger brother?"

"Brendan O'Sullivan's brother, Joe."

The name alone gave William a start. He had heard the rumours about Margaret and Brendan. They troubled him.

"I don't know. I don't know him."

"Yeah, it is."

Kevin walked towards the bar.

"Kevin, what are you doing?"

He stood beside Joe. "You're Joe, right?"

Joe turned to him. "Yeah. Yeah, I am."

"What are you up to tonight?"

"Sorry, do I know you?"

"I don't know. Maybe."

*What's with this guy?* Joe thought.

"And your name is?" he asked.

"Oh, that doesn't matter."

Joe turned away, but Kevin continued speaking.

"But your brother will know *my* brother's fiancée. Margaret James."

Joe paused as he put it all together. *So, it's true. She's going to marry that guy. I guess it's best that Brendan has gone.*

"You meeting your brother here tonight?" Kevin asked

"I don't think so."

"Why's that?"

"He doesn't live around here anymore."

"Oh, that's right, he took a flyer."

"Yeah. Anyway, I've got to meet some friends."

"Well, I don't think I'm done talking to you yet. I want to make sure your brother gets an invitation to the wedding."

"Brendan is long gone. It's over. Your brother is marrying the girl, and my brother left. Let it go, man."

Joe pushed past Kevin, and in doing so caused him to spill his beer.

"What the hell is wrong with you?"

Joe ignored the question and walked out of the bar.

*I'll never make it to the Crown before they catch up with me. Damn it. Spence and Leo are there. They'd help me with these guys.*

He picked up his pace, made a quick right turn and looked down the alley, sprinted towards a piece of lumber on the cobblestones and picked it up. He heard footsteps behind him and knew it was the men he had left in the bar.

"I think you owe me an apology!" Kevin yelled.

"Well, sorry you're such an asshole. We all are," Joe said in return.

"Come on!" said Kevin, but only Tommy followed him, and Joe replied with a swift swing of the lumber, catching Kevin in the knees and sending him to the ground. He did the same to Tommy with the same effect.

"Are we done?" Joe asked.

William made sure he locked eyes with Joe. "Just tell your brother to stay the fuck away from Margaret."

Joe said nothing and walked out to the street.


Margaret was laughing. She was surprised at the sound. It had been so long since she'd heard it.

Her friends Kat, Irma, and Betty were all at her house. They had come to see her ring. Hours had passed, and the girls were now in the parlour, dancing to "The ABCs of Love," when they heard a knock at the door.

Margaret answered it.

"William?"

"That is correct."

"Why? What are you . . . ? She smiled and gave him a peck on the cheek.

"Isn't that sweet? We need to talk, Margaret."

"Oh, okay. The girls are here."

"Tell them you're leaving for a bit."

"I am?"

"Yeah."

Margaret called over her shoulder, "I'll be back in a bit."

"Do you wanna go for a walk or something?" she asked.

"No, let's go for a drive."

"Oh, okay. Are you drunk?"

He got into the car before he said anything, then answered, "Not really. But I should be."

Margaret was still standing by the car. She was waiting for him to open the door, but he didn't. He just started the car.

There was a mickey of Corby's whisky on the seat. Half of it was gone. William was silent as they drove down her street towards the lake and turned in the direction of downtown.

"So, where are we going?"

"Oh, I thought I would take you somewhere that I know you love."

"Oh, okay. A mystery."

"How was your night?" she asked, as they drove through the city.

"It could have been better."

"Why's that?"

"One of the O'Sullivans was waiting outside the bar and attacked us with a pipe. Why do you think he would do that?"

Margaret was shocked. "One of the O'Sullivans?"

"Yeah, it was."

"Which one?" Margaret asked hurriedly. *Was Brendan back?*

"No, it wasn't your precious Brendan. It was his brother, Joe."

They drove into the parking lot of the Grand Island ferry dock and William stopped the car at the back of the waiting line. When the cars ahead of them began to move forward, William started the engine and followed them.

"Why are we going to Grand Island, William?"

"Why wouldn't we?"

*I don't like this*, she thought. *But William is a kind person. He has been . . .*

After William parked the car on the ferry, Margaret got out and began walking to the stairs that led to the open-air deck. It was a nice night. The stars were bright, and the air was cool but not cold. The horn announcing the boat's departure startled her. She stood, looking at the lights of the city and stars above. "Brendan, where are you?" she whispered to the night air. She looked down and saw William was still in the car. Drinking. She knew what was coming.

*Be an ass, William.*

The boat reached the dock in Elizabethville, the only village on the island. Margaret waited as long as possible before she climbed back down the stairs to the car. As she did so, she rubbed the palm of her left hand with her right thumb.

William looked at her but said nothing.

*He's looking at me differently now. The booze unleashed something in him.*

Margaret spoke first. "The cars are moving. You should start the engine."

"It's not your job to tell me what to do."

They drove off the ferry and onto the short street that met the main road on the island's north shore. As they approached the intersection, Margaret spoke up.

"It's a right turn."

William said nothing.

*It's a charming place*, Margaret thought. *It's just across the lake, but it feels like a different world. Both older and sort of timeless. You can sense a slower pace to life. People know each other here. It has a sort of intimacy I'll never experience, I bet. Not in the city.*

They drove west on a quiet two-lane road with no cars. Cottages and small farmhouses sporadically appeared on the shoreline.

"It's about two miles from here," she said.

William grimaced. "I suppose you're happy to go there," he said.

"I suppose."

Margaret glanced at him and could see his jaw was set. He drove stiffly, with the bottle in his lap, between his legs.

*Does she know,* he thought, *how much grief I took from my parents? They almost disowned me for getting engaged to you.*

A dirt road appeared on the left that ran south across the island. With a slight screech from the tires on the pavement, William swerved the car down it.

"Slow down," said Margaret.

"Don't tell me to do anything," he said. "Don't tell me to do anything at all." He tugged a drink from the bottle.

Margaret smiled. "I'm not sure where you're going, but this isn't the way to the O'Sullivans'."

"Just shut up."

"I'm only trying to help you."

William laughed. "I don't think you ever help anyone. I don't know what you care about. I don't think it's me, and I guess it's not Brendan, because you're engaged to me."

William pulled the car over. No houses were in sight. The crescent moon cast a dull light on the fence alongside the road and the fields on both sides but did little to light the swath of trees just a short distance from the car.

"William, look at me."

He turned to face her.

*He looks smaller now*, she thought. *Defeated and drunk.*

"I do care, William. I do. If you want me to say that I don't love Brendan, I have to apologize. I can't say that.

"You love him? You could have had everything my family offers. Why would you tell me that?"

"You really think that's why I was going to marry you?"

William paused. "Yeah, I did." He shifted in his seat and his face darkened. "Why would you tell me that?"

"Well, you're a fool," she said.

"I *am* a fool for proposing to you."

"You're a drunken ass."

"Well . . . you're a whore."

"To hell with you, William!"

With that, she got out of the car and started walking.

William fumbled with his door handle, got out, and followed her.

"Where do you think you're going?"

"Anywhere where you aren't," she said.

"Get back here!" He stood by the car and watched her walk away.

"No, I won't! Not a chance of that. We're done, William!"

"We're done when I say we're done!" he replied.

"You don't want to marry a whore!"

"Go find your lover man!"

"I will, and he's twice the man you are!"

William's anger rose as he watched her disappear into the night.

He reached through the open window of the car, pulled out the bottle of whisky, and took a drink.

"Get your ass back here! Now!"

Margaret continued to walk. She concentrated on moving at an ambling pace and not acknowledging him in any way.

"I said get back here now. You will marry me and you will obey me!"

He sprinted up the road, grabbed her by the back of her hair, and began pulling her towards the car.

Margaret was shocked and almost lost her footing. When she stumbled, he grabbed her by the arm and held her up while still pulling her to the car.

"That's enough of this shit! You're getting in that car and we're going home!"

Margaret turned to face him, pulled him to her, and quickly raised her knee to his crotch while tears streamed down her face.

He doubled over and let her go.

"Take your goddamn hands off me. I was never going to marry you. How could I when I'm pregnant with Brendan's baby!"

She was weeping and kicking gravel at him. William rolled around on the ground and moaned.

Margaret hopped over the ditch at the roadside and began making her way through a field to the grove of trees ahead of her. *I just need to be alone. I need to be away from him, away from everyone.* She was halfway to the trees when she heard William.

"Whore! Whore! Whore!"

She shook her head and kept moving.

William was standing at the side of the road. "I knew you were a whore! Get back here!"

About fifty feet from the trees, she began to run.

"I'll burn this goddamn island down! Margaret!"

He lost sight of her.

"Get back here! Get out here!"

He went back to the car. He grabbed the keys from the ignition, went to the rear of the vehicle, and opened the trunk. The gas can he kept for emergencies was full. He checked his pocket and realized his cigarettes and lighter were in the car. He went back, opened the door and grabbed the lighter. With the gas can and lighter, he began a steady walk towards the woods.

He kept silent until he reached the woods. "Get out here, Margaret. We both said some things we didn't mean."

He couldn't see her.

He dropped the gas can on the ground and returned to the car. When he'd taken another drink, he came back, bringing the bottle with him.

"So, you're telling me you're pregnant with Brendan's baby and you love him?" he hollered.

"Yes!"

"Get out here, then. Let me see that tummy of yours." William started laughing. "What a goddamn mess you've made."

*Why did I do this?* Margaret wondered. *Why would I get engaged? Standing in these woods, watching this madman, I know I just want to feel like I could be somebody that somebody else would want to marry. I just want to be seen as worthy.*

"I guess I have to clean it up. I'll clean it up, Margaret, but you have to come on out and go home."

"I'm not going anywhere with you."

"Margaret, you are coming with me, whether you like it or not."

"No, I'm not. I'll never love you, William. Never."

"Get out here, Margaret. I'm not gonna chase you."

"No."

"Now!"

"Never."

"Okay, then."

William took another swig, then put down the bottle and picked up the container of gas. He began to circle the grove of trees with it, laying down a trail of gasoline.

"You're gonna come out, Margaret," he told her, as he circled her hiding place. "I'll just wait for you here."

*He's so calm now*, she thought. *I don't like this sort of calm. It's like the moment the wind stops before the storm breaks. Everything goes quiet. The birds, the insects, the wind . . .*

"Margaret! Get out here, Margaret."

She didn't respond. *I feel hunted*, she thought.

"I need a drink anyway," he said. "I'm parched from all that work." His head was swimming.

Margaret had seen what he had done. "Go home, William!" she shouted.

He took another slug from the bottle. It was empty now, and he decided to throw it at Margaret. Not knowing her exact location in the woods, he missed her by several feet.

In the process of throwing the bottle, he tripped over the gas can at his feet. The liquid spilled on the grass and he fell to the ground, wetting his feet and lower legs.

He struggled to his feet and responded to Margaret. "Not without you, my love."

"I'm not your love."

"You will be. Get. Your. Ass. Out. Here."

"Never."

"Okay, then. I'll get you out here."

She saw a small flame appear as he sparked his lighter.

The little light grew into a circle around the trees where she was hiding.

The air crackled and smoked. The ground was dry. The leaves in front of her rustled, and the ones near the field began to burn. The fire grew in front of her, and when she looked around, she saw it was on all sides.

"Coming now?"

"No."

"Goddamn you, woman!"

He picked up the gas can and ran towards the fire. When he got to it, he could see her moving away on the other side.

"I will douse you and burn you, woman! I'm going to leave you out here."

"Do it!"

He took another two steps and the flames caught his gas-soaked pants. He began screeching and fell to the ground.

"Oh my God!" Margaret screamed.

She stepped towards the flames and knew the same fate awaited her if she tried to help him. She could hear him yowling and crying.

"William!" she screamed.

His cries grew weaker.

Margaret began to weep. She fell to her knees, still saying his name. "William, William . . ."

The fire burned, and she was surprised to find that now she was the only one making any noise. She closed her eyes but then forced herself to open them and stare past the flames to where William lay on the ground.

She spoke aloud to herself. "Look at this. Look at what you've done, you malignant wench. Look. Don't you dare look away."

# 9. A Sculptor

December 19, 1959—New York City, New York


Brendan woke early with a start.

*It keeps happening. That goddamn dream. I see the chain disappearing down into the black waters, but then I am the chain, and I look up from beneath the cold lake and see the hole in the ice and the sun on the other side. I don't want to be down here. I don't want to die. It's like I have to keep making that decision or I'm hounded by death. But I'm so far down here now, desperate to get back to the air and light, I can feel the icy fluid filling my lungs. And I wake up, nearly jumping out of my goddamn bed. Covered in sweat. It just makes me not want to sleep.*

He'd had a small apartment in New York for almost a year, near the corner of West Forty-Seventh Street and Tenth Avenue. Hell's Kitchen. When he arrived in the city, the woman at the boarding house told him that was where many of the Irish found work and homes. With only $180 in his pocket, he knew he needed to get to work pretty quickly.

It was his third visit to Malone's Bar, on Thirty-Ninth Street, when he met the owner, Archie Malone, which led to a job.

"You're not from Ireland, but I can still hear the lilt in your voice. Where are you from? Boston or something?"

"No, no. Farther. Canada."

"Right, then. They've got a good number of us up there too. What kind of work do you do?"

"Well, I was a mechanic."

"There's always work for those."

"I hope so."

A few days later, Archie connected Brendan with a garage in the neighbourhood that was servicing some of the cabs in Manhattan. In a week, Brendan had a job.

The city was a wonder to him. The din of it. The flow and the impossible number of people. The island of Manhattan was actually a little smaller than Grand Island, he was surprised to find out, but it couldn't have been more different.

Brendan missed the natural world. So, when we took his walks in the morning and evening, he gravitated to the east or west side of the island to see the water. It led to twinges of homesickness for the great open water of the lake, but it also offered a sense of peace he couldn't find anywhere else. When he had the time and energy, he would walk or take the 1 train to the Battery. The park and walking paths at the bottom of the island gave a wider vista of the waters, lands beyond Manhattan, and the Statue of Liberty.

Despite the early hour this morning, he wasn't going back to sleep. *So, I have the day off. I can't get back to sleep now. Not after that dream. I never can after that one.*

He sighed and got up from his bed, washed his face, cleaned his teeth, dressed, and went down the three flights of stairs and out to West Forty-Seventh Street. It was just before seven, and the city was awake and moving. He stopped at the local corner store, which also made a bit of food, for his regular breakfast—coffee and a slice of buttered toast. With this breakfast in hand, he continued walking.

*Where am I supposed to go? I guess I could walk through Central Park or down to the Battery. It's a walk, but I could use it. The city is at its quietest. I can check out the new artworks in the gallery windows in SoHo, and if I'm tired take the train home.*

He started his trek.

*Maybe I'll pick up a book at Explorer today. I could read it on a bench.*

The second-hand bookstore was along the way, just a few blocks from his apartment. It was one of the few luxuries he granted himself—novels.

He stepped in, and the owner, Charlie, gave him a nod. He liked some of the Hemingway books Charlie was always pushing him to buy.

He picked up *The Dharma Bums*, by Jack Kerouac, and the description on the back cover piqued his interest. The idea of two young guys searching for enlightenment in the far west and Mexico resonated with him.

It was a small book that he could slip into the pocket of his peacoat.

"That's a wild one," Charlie said.

"Well, that sounds like that will suit me just fine."

"Enjoy, then"

"Thanks again"

"No problem. And Brendan, if I don't see you, have a great Christmas."

"Right, that's coming, isn't it?"

"It's less than a week away now."

"And all the best to you and your family, Charlie."

*It was a week before Christmas that I made my walk across the ice. Or at least tried to make it. You didn't make it, did you? I guess it's an anniversary of sorts. But that's nothing I want to celebrate. I had better get a letter off today to the family for Christmas. Maybe give Mom a call. Let her know I can't make it. I'm sure I can get the time—I just don't feel ready to go back there, and they need to understand that. It will take a long time for Dad to understand. He was never one for the city, or really anywhere other than the island, the lake, maybe Kingston the odd night.*

Brendan was distracted by these thoughts and didn't stop to look at any of the windows in SoHo. He made his way down Trinity Place and could see the trees of the Battery in the distance and the open sky.

*Funny to see crowds down here at the park. Usually, it's quiet.*

It had been a little colder than usual for early December, and sheets of ice were piling up along the breaker wall. They stood out of the waters below at varying angles.

It was a sight to see. He'd grown up seeing ice like that, but many of the New Yorkers there wouldn't have. As he approached, he saw one sheet was quite tall, taller than the rest. He could just see the top of it. He felt drawn to the glowing, frozen water. The sun had turned the big slab of ice into a translucent blue wonder. He was transfixed as he moved closer, and what was most striking was that in the midst of this thirty-foot milky azure shard was a great chain. Its links snaked up and down, twice, to form the outline of a body with a head, looped out to delineate legs below and arms raised above it. Was this person raising its arms in jubilation or defeat? The figure stood nearly as tall as the shard of ice that housed it and seemed to move a little in the light and the shifting water.

It spoke to Brendan of loss, hope, love, despair, and jubilation. All in one moment. So much so that he grew weak in his legs. Tears streamed from his face and he grabbed the handrail beside him. He spoke aloud.

"My God, is that our chain?"

*Could unseen hands have ensured it would find me? But what are the chances? Chance doesn't matter for something like this. This is fate, this is the hand of God or what have you. It has to be.*

Brendan's head grew hot, and he found himself sweating in the chill December morning. He hid his face in his hands and wept. He wanted to climb the barrier and touch the ice, be close to the chain. He stayed and watched others come to gaze upon the figure before them in the bay. He did not know what else to do.

By midday, a new feeling was growing in him.

*Something like this rarely happens to a person. To some, it never happens at all. I need to figure out what it means. What I'm supposed to do about it. Just calm down, it will come. Just wait.*

Brendan was chilled and hungry. Hours passed, but his gaze rarely left the chain. The sun was falling in the west and darkness was creeping into the day. He felt a little desperate for an answer.

Just as the lights on the pier flickered and turned on, it struck him. He stood up and took one final look at the marvel before he raised his arms in response and released a great joyous laugh.

"Fine, then," he hollered, and continued laughing.

He arrived at work early on Monday, when he knew only Gus, the owner, would be at the shop. He approached the subject with trepidation but knew he had to do it.

Gus grimaced and said, "So you want scrap then?"

"Well, not really scrap. I want chains of any and all types. Any sort of metal linked things . . ."

"Yeah, a metal linked thing is a chain. Couldn't you just go and buy some? You can go to any number of hardware stores or bike shops."

"I know, I know, and this probably sounds crazy to you, but—"

"It does."

"But I need chains that are old, used. Ya know."

"You want old chains."

"That I do."

"It's none of my business, but this isn't gonna come back on me in some way, is it?"

"No, no. It's not like that. I'm just making something."

"Well, yeah, that's a strange order and a bit tough to get. But if you go around the construction sites and some of the wreckers maybe, maybe the tow companies. . . Do you mind if they're broken?"

"No. Ideally, I would love to see broken chains."

"Okay, kid, I'll give you a list here of some places to take a look at with some addresses. Whatever you do in your free time is none of my business."

"Thanks, Gus."

"It's all right."

It was three days later that he brought home his first collection of chains from Samson and Sons Auto Wreckers. He laid them out on the floor of his apartment, took a chair, sat in it, lit a cigarette, and stared at them. And then, in his mind, the links formed a picture. And with a small welding torch he'd also just purchased, he recreated the image with the pieces of metal. For this first one, it was a profile of a man, mouth agape, and the head tilted upward. He worked all night on it, and as the sun rose the next morning, he held it in a shaft of light and smiled at it, then quickly prepared for work.

Brendan continued like this. He would go to work in the mornings and by late afternoon was scouting the city for chains. As part of his travels, he would head back to Battery Park to see the chain entrapped in ice. It still held him, and he had to pull himself away to work on his sculptures.

For months, his life had a new and engaging rhythm. He would search for links, take them home, sit with them, move around them to look at the metal from various angles and in altering light, and then the form of a sculpture would appear in his head. His apartment was filled with them. He never thought about what to do with the finished work. He just needed to create it.

It was the gleaming bright chain, almost new, delineating a figure with a raised arm holding a stick or baton above a kneeling form that drew attention to him. It haunted him throughout the process of making it and after it was done. He'd seen violence. The violence here in America was different. Not only was it more common, but it was also more accepted as part of life. Most troubling for Brendan was that violence towards certain groups was deemed acceptable: wives, children, Blacks, and the Irish, Italians, and Jews. He heard the talk at work, in the streets and newspapers, and about once a week or so he'd see it.

It was having watched the arrest of a young Black musician that brought the image to his mind when he gazed on the chain lying on his floor. The man had stepped out of a club in Greenwich Village after playing there that night. A few people thanked him, and one offered him a joint. He passed on it and lit a cigarette. Brendan was going by at this moment. Two police officers, walking the beat, were coming in the opposite direction at the same time. They smelled the drugs. They turned to the only Black man in the crowd and demanded he put out his joint and come with them. He laughed and said it was just a cigarette. The bigger of the two policemen stepped back, pulled out his baton, and struck him in the stomach. The musician fell to his knees. The crowd quickly dispersed.

"Are ya done talking now!" the cop growled, standing over the gasping young man.

The musician looked at the officer, defiant, and remained silent.

Brendan was surprised to hear his own voice. "Hey! Come on now!"

Both officers looked at him. It occurred to Brendan that he could outrun these men. He was probably ten years younger than them.

"Bastards!" he yelled, as one of them stepped towards him, and he took off running.

Half a block away, he looked back. The cops weren't chasing him, but he also saw the musician was running too. In the opposite direction. The two officers stood in the street, yelling at the young man. Brendan smiled and kept going.

Brendan fell to work. He'd worked until 1 a.m., slept, woken, studied the emerging sculpture, and then gone to his job at the garage. He hurried home that night with his dinner in a bag. He sat it on the small table in his kitchen and then returned to the sculpture. It only took a few hours to finish it: a figure towered over another, which had one arm raised in defence. It was clearly an act of violence, and the outline of the standing figure's cap made it clear that this was a police officer.

Brendan loved the finished work. He had to think where to store it. His small apartment was already crowded. He had two windows looking onto Forty-Seventh Street and placed the piece on one of the sills.

And then it all happened so quickly. A local newspaper, *The Kitchen News*, wrote an article about the statue in the tenement window in the neighbourhood. Passersby had been stopping to look at it, and then people had started bringing their friends to see it. Finally, Brendan was approached by a gallery owner.

"Do you have any more?" Simon asked, after shaking Brendan's hand. He stood in the doorway and tried to peer past him. He had shown up at the building, got hold of the superintendent, and found Brendan's apartment. He owned Gallery 114, on Chambers Street.

"Yeah, yeah, I have some more," Brendan replied. He stepped aside so Simon could look into the apartment.

"You do, don't you? Okay. That one I saw was a magnificent piece of work. And a brilliant idea leaving it in your window. What a statement."

Brendan didn't know what to say. He shrugged and laughed. "I'll be honest with you, I just sat it there because I had run out of room."

"Police brutality, and state brutality generally, is a real hot problem. I'm afraid it's only gonna get worse."

"It seems that way, doesn't it?"

"Sure does. And many people will admire your take on it. Where did you train, Brendan?"

"Train?"

"As an artist. Which college?"

"No. I'm a mechanic."

"Isn't that amazing? Pure talent and instinct."

"I don't know about that. I just always worked with metal, I guess."

"Oh, as a mechanic?"

"Yeah, well, I mean back in Canada my family worked on the lake, and I did that, but I also liked toying around with engines."

"Oh, you're Canadian."

"Yeah."

"That's exotic. Kind of, I guess."

Brendan laughed. "I never thought of myself as exotic."

"I'd like to come in and take a look at what you have, and maybe we can do an exhibition."

"That would be amazing."

Brendan stepped aside, and Simon took over and launched his career.

The show was set for April. In the weeks leading up to it, Brendan was nervous, not just about the show but about the chain.

All through the winter, he visited it, encased in ice at Battery Park. But spring had arrived and the ice had started to melt and retreat into the Upper Bay.

*I need to get it back. It's bad enough I lost it, but I can't let it happen twice.*

Brendan watched the forecast and visited the chain three or four times a week. A blizzard had struck in March and the temperature stayed near the freezing point. In early April, the temperature had risen and great rainfalls had melted much of the ice. The metal head of the figure now hung limply at the top of the melted ice, the feet dangling below. As more of the chain became free, he visited it more regularly, waiting for the day he could jump the barricade and retrieve it.

It was late, just before eleven, when Brendan did just that. About half of the chain was still encased in ice. He hopped over the barrier fence and down to the concrete ledge beneath it, just above the water. He started pulling at the parts that were free and loosed another few feet of it. He was breathless. Working hard and fast to get it. Then he took a crowbar he had borrowed from the garage and began frantically to chip at the ice.

Two officers, walking through the park and clearing it of the homeless and teenagers, caught sight of Brendan.

"What are you at?"

Brendan said nothing.

"Get out of there, boy!"

*If I don't get this done now, I may lose it before I can get back. I've got to get it.*

Brendan wedged the crowbar beneath the chain, near to where the last few feet of it were still encased in ice.

"I said get down from there!"

He heaved on the crowbar. A few more inches of the iron links popped free.

"Come on, now!" the second police officer shouted.

Brendan looked over and saw the first officer pull out his club. He turned back to his work. He positioned the crowbar once more beneath the chain and used all of his weight to lever it out. He groaned, as did the ice, and he and the chain fell.

"Whaddya doin' with that chain?" the first officer hollered, jumping the fence.

Brendan had fallen just a few feet from the water. He grabbed the chain as the officer coming at him was reaching for his nightstick.

Instinctively, Brendan swung the end of the chain hard at the cop's head. The metal connected with flesh with a jangling thud, and the officer fell backward on the lip of the concrete breakwater.

"Son of a bitch!" the second officer shouted. He jumped the fence and met the same fate as his partner.

Brendan quickly wrapped the chain over his shoulder and began to run. After a few steps, he looked back. The first police officer, still dazed, was sliding into the water below him. Brendan sighed, ran to him, grabbed the man under both arms and hauled him up against the wall of the breakwater. "There ya go, ya bastard."

With the chain gathered to himself, he hurried home as quickly as he could under its weight. He was breathless when he closed the door behind him and dropped the links on his floor.

He slid down the door until he was sitting on the ground. He stared at the chain, and memories and longing for home surfaced. Its presence brought him comfort but also sadness. It was no longer lost, but it reminded him of all that had slipped from his grasp in his first twenty-four years of life: Margaret, his family, his home. Tears welled up in his eyes. He fought them back and lay down beside the chain, looking at it until he fell asleep beside it.

A new installation came to mind. If he worked hard, he could finish it for the exhibition. He had gone to construction sites and collected metal shavings from the contractors. Tiny gleaming pieces of steel that felt surprisingly delicate in Brendan's hands. Like feathers, he thought.

He bought a mirror and hung it in his apartment so that he could see his face in it when he sat at the dining table he had moved into the middle of the room for work. He took a large canvas and glued it to a black magnetic sheet of metal, six feet by five feet and a quarter-inch thick. He painted the canvas black and started arranging the small shards of metal on it. At times, he would pause, raise his head, and study the reflection in the mirror. He even tried letting his hands work as he looked at the image of himself. He continued until a man's profile formed itself from the metal shards. The outer edge of the image had intermittent pieces, and the missing sections appeared to be pulled or falling into the blackness of the canvas background, leaving the figure distorted and giving it a surrealistic quality.

Brendan finished this piece, *Self Portrait #1*, and with the help of Simon ensured all of the artworks were delivered and installed at the gallery in time for the opening. Media attention grew, as did the number of visitors over the first three weeks. The reviews by art critics were positive, and by the end of the month all of the pieces had been sold.

*Self Portrait #1* was referred to in an article in *The New York Times* as "a stunning statement by a bold new voice, capturing the sadness, alienation, and longing of modern man." The writer was Mary O'Donnell.

Mary was intrigued by this artist with no pretense or ambition. "Just talent and vision," as she said to friends. After her first interview with Brendan, before her article was complete, she appeared at the garage and asked him if he would have a drink with her. He had liked her from the moment they met. She was tiny, only a few inches over five feet, and had auburn hair that reflected her bright energy. He felt clumsy and at a loss for words in her presence, but to be in her company he was willing to set his pride aside. He tried to open up to her but found her so quick in conversation he was like an inarticulate fool. He did find he could speak about his work, and she seemed to like it.

Brendan had never met a professional woman in Canada. He sat across the table from her at a cocktail bar and felt his admiration for her grow. *It couldn't be easy,* he thought, *if you grew up in Boston in a Catholic family, to move to New York and be a reporter.*

Her appreciation of his work raised his confidence. And he was surprised to find his sense of inadequacy receding the longer he was with her. It wasn't long before the two were living in a studio in Greenwich Village, where Brendan worked full-time as an artist. Mary continued to write for newspapers and magazines and became the voice and face of Brendan's work in the city's galleries.

# 10. A Prisoner

May 11, 1961—Collins Bay Penitentiary, Kingston, Ontario


*It feels different in my lungs,* Joseph O'Sullivan thought, as he stepped through the gates of the prison and took a deep breath of air. *It just does. I'm not sure why. But it does.*

He started walking up the long driveway towards Bath Road. *Who knows? Maybe it's just the taste of freedom in the air. Freedom. I'm going to go home and hear about it from Dad and Granddad. And then back to the grind. Doesn't feel like freedom. And God knows when I'll see my brother again. Brendan. In the city. New York no less.*

He touched the wallet in his back pocket. It was weird to have it again. And the cash. It was a nice start. Everyone got a ticket to go back to wherever home was, and in his case he only needed a cab fare.

*I can use the cash to grab a drink. I could use a drink before I go back to the island. They're going to be pissed I didn't let them know my release date. But I just need a second. I don't want lectures and I don't want a party. I just want to ease back into it. Is that too much to ask?*

It would be enough to be at the bar. He could hear them: "Joe O'Sullivan, back at the scene of the crime." He had spent a lot of time thinking about what it would be like to be on the outside. That name. O'Sullivan. It had always felt like his father's name, not his own. Or his grandfather's. And then Joe. Joseph O'Sullivan. Best friend and partner of his dad, the veteran and great smuggler. Besides the news reports and the books, there were all the local tales of Joe Haggerty and Colin O'Sullivan. He'd never felt he lived up to it. The daring exploits, parties, and tragedy. It was strange to feel that way. And to know that Joe Haggerty had died before he was born.

It never made him angry or sad, but it felt like a promise he needed to live up to somehow. He would have to do something about it eventually. It was a kind of calling, a feeling that had only grown in him, leading up to that night. And now? He didn't know. He supposed he was living it.

He continued along Bath Road east towards the core of the city.

*It's only been six months. But I feel older and tired. Yeah, tired. And was the city always this loud? I guess it's just the cars. I'm not used to them. But I'm going to get one. I guess I'm walking to the King George. Yeah, a walk will be good.*

Joe stopped in his tracks. Memories of that night flooded his mind. Along with feelings of regret, anger, and shame. *Goddamn it. I was fine with all of this. It's not like I didn't think about it in prison. Why now?*

*. . . I guess, doing it, being out here, is different than thinking about it. Take a deep breath.*

*Kevin Glendon was on a mission, wasn't he? He just wanted to take me down. And because he felt that way, in his mind, it had to happen. He was entitled to it. The little prick couldn't get it done in the alleyway so he had to do it in the court. I know, I know, he lost his brother. That was a real tragedy. No wonder he was pissed off. And so was I. My brother was gone too. My only brother. We thought he was dead and then we got a letter from New York. And we haven't seen him since. Might as well be dead to me. He left me here. Maybe I'm dead to him. I guess the point is that we were both angry. Kevin and I. We have that in common. It's strange to think . . .*

Joe turned right down Princess Street. It was busier with pedestrians. He avoided making eye contact as much as possible and simply nodded his head when someone said hello.

He wondered if he'd see anyone he knew. Just a few blocks over was the courthouse. He hated that building. He hadn't stood much of a chance. The judge was a friend of the Glendon family. Some had said he was a distant cousin. And Kevin had his father's cash to get a lawyer from Ottawa who specialized in assault cases.

It all ended over a shrug. The lawyer had him after that.

"A shrug Mr. O'Sullivan? Attacking the defenceless with a weapon doesn't make you feel bad?"

The judge told Joe he had to answer. So he did.

"If a guy gets aggressive with you in a bar, so you leave, and he comes around the corner behind you with two of his friends and there is a piece of lumber on the ground, wouldn't you swing it?"

Joe's lawyer just shook his head. Joe knew straight away he'd lost, so he thought he might as well make his last stand.

He loved playing that speech back in his brain at night. It still made him smile.

"It just makes sense, but I guess if it had gone the other way I wouldn't be here today. There would be no court case. Mostly because I believe that if a guy's got a problem with you, a big enough one, and it comes to blows, for me it's settled there and then. I don't need to be taking it to a court and hiding in the skirts of the magistrate like a lad in the kitchen with his mom. Which is all we're doing here today. And that's disgusting. No man worth anything would behave like this. Only a wee child, or a man who ain't no man at all."

*Well, I said my piece, didn't I? And I don't regret it. Shame on all of them. Not just the Glendons but the lawyers and the judges. It was all set up for him to win. He couldn't beat me on the street so he had to beat me in court. That's their world. They set it up and it works for them. Especially for them. So at least I got to say my piece. And I'm done with all of this. I don't care anymore about Glendon. If I'm honest, we both paid a price. I lost a few years of my life, but he lost a brother. I got my life back, such as it is, but he'll never have a brother again. He just needs to stay clear of me. And I'll do the same.*

*It's nothing new, is it? With all that time to myself, what else could I do in the clink but read? And that history book on the Irish,* The Great Hunger, *was something. I always wanted to read about it. Granddad always said we were here because of the damn mess and malignancy. And the law then was never on our side. The Penal Laws, they called them. It was written by the Brits for the landlords and to ensure that we were beaten down. No school, no jobs, no lands. Nothing for you if you're Irish Catholic. And then they said we never had any respect for the rule of law. Funny that. Yeah, when a dealer loads the deck, you don't trust the deal, do you?*

Joe was surprised to find himself coming to the end of Princess Street. He was so wrapped up in his thoughts he'd forgotten about his surroundings.

*I need to settle down.* He took a few deep breaths. As the anger drained from his mind and body, sadness crept in. And the feeling that was always waiting for him at the end of the road of these thoughts.

*There's no place for me in this world. There never was one, and I guess I had to find out the hard way. And that means I'll never amount to nothing. That's just the truth.*

He was almost at the King George.

*It's hard to imagine I won't know anyone there. And the papers made such a thing of the trial and all. As soon as people see me, it's the first thing they're going to think about. I know it. So be it.*

He moved through the entrance of the establishment, scanned the room, saw a few regulars at the bar. And someone else.

*I know that sitting posture. Legs braced wide apart like he could move off his stool at any second. The back. I know the back of him well. I was always more comfortable looking at that than at the front. The front of him is a lot.*

He stood still in the room, trying to decide whether to leave or stay. He didn't want to face him.

Colin turned on his stool.

"Take a seat, son. I'm sure you could use a drink."

Joe sighed. "I could."

He sat beside his father, who spoke to the bartender. "Mike, can you get a pint of lager for my son, here?"

"You know I can, Colin. And will you be playing a song?" Mike asked.

"Ah, I'm sorry, Mike, I didn't bring the fiddle with me today."
Joseph shifted in his seat.
"Well, it's our loss, then."
"Ha! Maybe so. I've learned a few new reels."
"You'll have to come back, then, and share 'em."
"That's a deal, then."

Joseph found this part of his father annoying and embarrassing. Colin had become a fiddler when Joe was just a baby. As far as he could remember, his father was always scraping the bow. He'd often find him alone, looking out the window, and playing slow, mournful songs. But the rest of the world knew him as the life of the party, playing jigs and reels with others at gatherings and in bars. It angered him. No one knew about the lonesome songs that filled their house. They only knew the smiling fiddler at the party, quick with a joke. Something about it made him averse to having music around him or in his life. And now, just the thought of it, the thought of his father playing music to dance to while he languished in the penitentiary, made him feel angrier, betrayed. So he fell into deeper silence.

Colin picked up the conversation with his son.
"How's it feel, to be back out?"
"Fine," he said. *But it's not fine. It feels strange. Chaotic. One thing about the pen, you know what to expect. Out here, who knows? I could use that drink to steady myself.*
"Good."
"What are the chances I would find you here?"
"Pretty good. I kept in touch with the prison and they let me know when you would be out. I figured you'd come here."
"Did you?"
Colin shot his son a look.
*I get it,* Joe thought. *You're hurt or angry or something because I didn't tell you.*
"You know, your uncle Pat worked here back in the day. Before he got to working on boats and fishing."
"Right. I think I did know that."
"You could do that. You could change things up. Look at Brendan, off in New York. No one thinks less of ya for what happened. I don't think any man worth a damn would have handled it much differently. You just happened to take down the wrong guy. One with money and malice enough to make a stink about it. And maybe that's your lesson from all of this. Maybe you've learned to discern when it's best to walk away."
"I did walk away. They followed me."
"And then you hit them with a two-by-four."

"Before they beat me." Joe shifted on his stool. "Would you have preferred that? That I just took a shellacking from those assholes?"

"That's not what I'm saying. There are always other options. You have to think. That's all."

"You can't think your way out of everything, Dad."

Colin looked down at the bar. *He's got that anger,* he thought. *Prison will do that. It doesn't make you better. It just turns you worse.*

"Let's have a pint and then head to the island. Your mom and grandparents are waiting on us for dinner."

Joe sighed. The thought of dinner only bothered him. The drink was solace. It gave him focus and steadied him.

"Okay."


Joe moved into the rhythms of his life before his time in prison: fishing with his father, taking tourists out to catch walleye and salmon. But he learned to detest it. He didn't want to make small talk with business owners from Pennsylvania or New York.

*Dad loves talking to the Yanks. Let him do it. He's the storyteller, the entertainer. Not me. Let him pull fish with them.*

The chores on the farm left him alone, and that brought him the closest to contentment. There was a wonder and a beauty to the cycles of nature and the lives of animals. All this living with no words, no recriminations. But within the first few months of being at home, he made a decision to change things.

Jay Truesdale found him at the King George Hotel on a Saturday night a few months later. Joe would come early on Saturdays and take a table near the corner. He wanted to be away from the island and social events, but away from most at the bar too. He could drink in silence.

"I've been wanting to talk to you," Jay said, as he pointed to the chair beside Joe.

Joe nodded for him to take it.

Jay lived a little east of the city, just before Stoneport. He was a mainlander, but a river rat, as they were called—those who spent all their time on the St. Lawrence River engaged either in work or play. His family was known for doing construction on homes on the myriad of islands out there. Before Jay spoke, Joe knew it wasn't about a construction job.

"How are things with you?" Jay asked.

"I'm getting by, Jay. You?"

Jay looked around him and saw the place was pretty quiet. It was still early.

"Well, you know with all the work we do on the river, we're always going into U.S. waters, and the police and such are used to it. No one ever asks much about it.

"Now, I got this guy down in New York that has been moving marijuana. We can make a lot of money if we run it from stateside over here. And he's got a guy from Montreal who meets us over here. We just need someone we can trust to manage it. You know, to meet them in one of our boats on the mainland and run it back here."

"Sounds like risky business, but I'm sure you're gonna make some good money," Joe responded.

"For sure. On both accounts. My problem is that if the old man knew I was doing this, he wouldn't be happy. And I'm still at his side most days. So I need somebody who can do it and that I can trust. If you're in one of our boats, no one's gonna say a word to you. And you know your way around out there. Hell, I'm sure half the cops know you. You would have gone to school with them and the like."

"They may also know my dad."

Jay laughed. "Maybe so. But they would just think you're working for us if you're out in one of our boats."

It was easy enough for Joe. As much as he loved his life as a farmer on the island, something in him needed to do this. He didn't know why, but the urge was undeniable.

So, he told his family he was helping Jay out every now and then with his boat. About once a month, he got a call from Jay, and he would go down the lake, into the St. Lawrence River and the Thousand Islands, pick up a boat from Joe, head to the U.S. side, usually near the small town of Cooper's Bay, and meet the guy an hour later. They'd load the boat with marijuana, and he'd drive back and drop the load on the mainland side just a few miles from Jay's place.

It was a thrill. After each run, when he was making his way home in his boat, his mind would turn to his father.

*Is this what it felt like to him? Did he do it for the same reasons? He rarely spoke about his time as a rum-runner. Maybe it bothered him. It seemed to. It's weird, but it's the only time I feel calm, coming home after making a run. And any of those Kingston business owners or professionals can look down their noses at me all they want because I'm just an ex-con, but I'm making the same money. Maybe more. You can count me out, but I'm pulling cash. The hell with you.*

In the autumn, the runs grew increasingly chilling. He had also taken to smoking marijuana. He found it took the edge off, especially in the evenings.

It was a Sunday evening, after dinner, that things changed. He had been making runs stateside for two months. Colin sat by the fire and played slow, quiet pieces of music on the fiddle. He had just finished playing and singing "Nature Boy." He lay down the fiddle and turned his eyes to Joe and said, "I suppose, with the cold setting in, you won't be running reefer soon enough." He paused, held his gaze on Joe, and then looked back down to his instrument. He picked it up again and began to play

Joe didn't say anything. *Why is he so casual? Not angry. It's so strange.*

Colin played "The Lost Highway," and when he was done, he drifted from the room.

The next morning, Joe was awakened by his father.

"Come on, I need you up with me."

The clock by his bed said it was just after 5 a.m. *What the hell?*

The men drank their tea quietly. Colin at the table. Joe at the kitchen counter. Joe's mother and grandparents were still asleep.

"Done, then?" Colin asked.

"Just about."

Well, let's get going."

"Okay."

Joe didn't want to speak. He didn't want to prompt further conversation.

It was a bright morning for November. The leaves still clung to a few of the maples, oak, and ash in their yard. The air held a chill from the night.

Both men noticed that and felt sad about the coming winter. But neither said anything about it.

Joe began to gather nets for the boat. Colin stopped him. "There'll be no need for nets today."

"Okay," said Joe.

They stepped onto their fishing boat. Colin moved to the wheelhouse and started the engine. Joe stayed on the deck at the stern.

The lake was steaming as they backed out of the boathouse. Colin steered the vessel to the west. There were no other boats in sight. The sun was yet to rise.

When they passed the head of Grand Island, Colin turned the boat towards the southwest and increased the speed. They continued into the open waters of the lake, the land fading into soft forms on the horizon. After about forty minutes, the equally gentle outlines of the Danish Islands appeared over the bow of the boat. Joe had never travelled to them before. He had fished nearby but had not actually anchored or stepped ashore.

When they reached the bay on the west side, Colin turned off the engine. The sun was now peeking above the horizon in the east.

Joe had remained out on the deck for the trip to the island while his dad was at the helm. Now, as the boat bobbed quietly in the light waves, Colin stepped out of the wheelhouse and looked past his son to the bay and the island.

After a long silence, he spoke. "This is where it all happened."

"What's that?"

"Three men died. And I'm to blame for it."

Joe didn't know what to say, so he remained quiet.

"None of it needed to happen, and I could have stopped it all. I should have stopped it all. But I didn't. For no good reason, really. I liked the thrill of it. For a thrill. For my thrill, three men died. I mean, Joe died later, but it was because of this place."

He looked at his son. Joe didn't offer a word or an expression in reply.

"It's a stain on my soul, Joseph. A stain. And there's nothing I can do to get rid of it. I come out here once a year, around the time it happened, to pay my respects, and I hope to find a way to make it right. But there's no way. We've been supporting Joe's wife and children, but that hardly makes it right. And as the years pass, I keep hoping I will receive some sort of path, some way to forgiveness, but I haven't found it. I'm adrift, I'm lost."

Joe saw tears fall down his father's face and looked away.

"It's almost too much to bear at times. Too much. And I wouldn't want this for anyone. I wouldn't wish it on any man. Let alone you, my son." Colin looked to his son with pleading eyes. "Do you understand?"

Joe shifted uncomfortably. *I don't want this. I don't want to know this, to have to hear this. Can you just stop?*

"Will you pray with me, son? For those that we lost here."

Joe nodded. Colin went down on his knees and clasped his hands together.

"Our father who art in heaven, hallowed be thy name." Colin paused. "Say it with me, Joseph."

Joe sighed. "Our father, holy is your name," he began to say.

"'Our father, *hallowed be thy name*' is the correct way now," Colin said.

Joe sighed. "Our father who art in heaven, hallowed thy name."

"*Hallowed be thy name.*"

Joe sighed again.

Colin quickly stood. "I swear to God, if I hear you demonstrate like that with your guffawing and sighing, I'll toss you overboard."

"I wasn't guffawing."

"Ya were!"

Joe shook his head and looked down. Colin caught sight of the anger and dismissal in his son's face.

"Get up!" he hollered.

"What?"

"Get up, I said! I won't have you desecrating this important day with your childish behaviour. It's the most mournful day of the year. The one on which they died."

"This isn't the day he died!" Joe replied, standing to meet his father.

"They did too!"

"They came out here, Vic and Sam, and died in November. But Joseph Haggarty died weeks later with complications from pneumonia! Not this day!"

"Don't begin to tell me what happened!"

The men squared off against each other.

Colin paused. "Get out of my boat."

"What?"

"You heard me. Out. Get out of my boat!"

"No. You're crazy."

"Maybe. But it's still my boat. And you're walking the plank, ya malignant little shit."

Colin grabbed his son and Joe returned the gesture. He was shocked at his father's strength, and knowing it would be a close fight, he relented and was pushed overboard.

Joe bounced his back off the sandy bottom, dropped his feet, and realized they were in only five feet of water. He looked at his father and then turned his back and walked towards the shore. Colin watched him, then started the boat and headed home.

Eva and his parents were clearing the breakfast dishes when he arrived at the house.

"You were at it early," Michael noted, as Colin entered.

"That I was," he replied.

"What were you and Joe doing?" Eva asked.

Colin stopped. *I haven't thought what to tell her. It doesn't matter anyway. I'm gonna hear it.*

"I was trying to make your son into a good man."

"And how did that go?"

"Poorly."

"Where is he?" said Sarah.

"Elsewhere. Thinking about it."

"Colin, where is my son?" Eva said.

"He's the premier resident of a new penal colony."

Michael, Sarah, and Eva looked at Colin, perplexed.

"He's continuing his sentence on the Danish Islands."

"My God, Colin, what have you done?"

"Nothing, Eva. I did nothing to reform the boy. Nothing can be done."

"He'll freeze there."

"No, he won't. He'll be saved by his mother in a few hours and continue running drugs. But he'll not live in this house again. He's lost now. Lost to us. And I don't want to hear any more about it."

Colin went up the stairs to his bedroom. Michael followed behind him. "Later, son. Talk to him later." Colin said nothing and closed the door.

Eva did take the boat to the Danish Islands, where she found her son huddled on the shore. Neither spoke as they returned to Grand Island in the cool late afternoon. Eva took the helm, and Joe sat in the rear of the boat again, this time beneath a blanket his mother bought for him. The anger with his father had drained from him. It had been replaced by a disappointment in this man he had built into something so much greater than himself. And he was resolved to no longer share a roof with him.

Joe moved into a room over the King George Hotel. He took a job bartending in the hotel and continued delivering marijuana from the U.S. to Jay's contacts from Montreal.

After three seasons of moving shipments for Jay, he had saved a large sum of money. As much as he liked being on the water, he knew his days were numbered. He approached Ian Calhoun, the owner of the King George Hotel, and bought it. For $32,900, cash.

He gave up his role as a bartender and turned a few of the rooms upstairs into an apartment and office for himself. As the building stood on the waterfront in the city, facing south, it looked to Grand Island. When he remodelled the rooms, he ensured that his apartment was on that side, the windows looking towards the lake and the island.

His office became an ever-expanding library where he would spend much of his days, when not running the business, reading widely and drinking alone. In time, he became increasingly interested in Irish history and the emerging Troubles in Northern Ireland. He renamed the bar Éirinn go Brách. He hired three sign-makers before it was completed, firing the first two, who he felt were skeptical about the name.

By the late 1960s, he was hosting speakers from Northern Ireland and making donations to the cause of the Provisional Irish Republican Army for the purchase of weapons in their goals for the reunification of Northern Ireland with the Irish Republic. It had all started when he was approached by a few men at the bar who were, they said, from Massachusetts. After confirming that Joseph embraced the Irish cause, they noted that they organized support for it. Joseph was quick to offer a donation, and the men were as quick to accept it.

The men made further visits to the bar to speak to him in the years that followed. It was nearly three years later when they noted a new need.

"You know," one of them said, "where we could use a lot of help is in moving items and people into and out of the States. U.S. laws are a bit tricky when it comes to supporting the cause. But that's not the case up here."

"Right," said Joseph.

The idea of getting out of the bar and back on the water felt good to him. And before long, he was running IRA fundraisers and wanted individuals into the U.S. by boat. And once in a while, he brought large crates, whose contents he did not ask about, from the U.S. side to Canada. He didn't want a lot of information. For their sake and his own.

Over the next three years, he bought the hotel's neighbouring three buildings, in which he established a restaurant and two clothing shops, hiring staff to manage and run them.

Each manager was given a picture of Joe's father and told to let Joe know if the man showed up at the bar. He didn't. But Joseph's mother did appear, and it became a regular occurrence. Every two weeks, she and Joe would have dinner in his apartment. Eva would visit her parents in the city first and then eat with Joseph before returning to the island. Her overtures for her son to return to the island or see his father, which was frequent at first, fell away as time went on. Just as her efforts with her husband yielded the same result.

One of the girls who worked at the bar, Sally Clancy, had become a regular visitor in his apartment as well. Joseph had noticed her when she was at the bar with her friends. *She has an assertiveness and lack of self-consciousness I wish I had,* he'd thought. Blond, petit, and outspoken, she took Joe aback, but more by her way than her looks. After she became a waitress at his tavern, he noticed she had no timidity with him. The rest of the staff were deferential to him, and he found it tiring. She was not. She was like ice water or neat whisky. Direct and sure.

Joseph was standing behind the bar early on a Saturday night. He had only come down to survey the scene and get a bottle for himself. The bartender was busy at the other end of the bar. Sally had been working there for about two weeks.

"I need two Tom Collins," she told Joe.

"Right, then," he answered with a smile and got to work.

As he placed the glasses on the bar, Joseph tried to catch a better look at Sally without her noticing. *There's something about her,* he thought. *She acts more like she's ordering the drink for herself than fetching it for someone else.*

Sally caught him looking and smiled. "You're a little overdressed for this kind of job, aren't you?"

"How's that?" asked Joseph.

"I don't know a lot of bartenders or bouncers who wear a suit."

"Well, maybe you should," he said with a slight smile.

"Maybe."

"I'm also not working."

Sally pieced it together and said nothing.

Joseph finished the drinks and set them on the bar. He stepped back to watch her place them on her tray.

"Enjoy," she said, as she turned to leave.

Joseph smiled more broadly as he watched her cross the bar and deliver the drinks. He also watched one of the men slide a hand up the back of her thigh. Sally brushed it away. The man tried again, and Joseph strode to the table, rolling up the sleeve on his right arm. But before he got there, Sally grabbed the man's drink and dumped it in his lap.

"Maybe that will cool you down, ya creepy bastard!"

"Son of a bitch!" he swore.

"You really are a son of a bitch, Warren, aren't you?" Joe interjected.

The man was stunned to see him there.

"Joseph. I didn't know—"

"Don't you talk to him, you miserable bastard!" Sally demanded. "Talk to me! Apologize to me!"

"I didn't know—"

"What didn't you know?" she said.

He fell silent.

"How to be a gentleman?" she continued. "Goddamn right you didn't know. Look at me, you prick! I'll fucking bust this glass and stick ya with it if you don't apologize."

The man looked at Joseph, who just shook his head.

"Quit lookin' at him! Ya gotta deal with me!"

He looked once more at Joseph.

"That's it," she said, and broke the top of the tall glass on the table.

"Jesus Christ," he said. "I'm sorry. I'm goddamn sorry."

"You bet your ass you're sorry." With that, Sally threw the broken glass and what remained of the drink in his lap and made her way back to the bar.

Joseph looked to the two men. "I don't want to see you in here. You understand?"

They nodded, and the one with the dry lap tried to apologize. "Joseph, if I had known—"

"You knew all you needed to know. But you still behaved like bastards, didn't ya?"

Both men were silent.

"Do I need to repeat myself?" he asked.

"We're leaving, Joe."

Joseph turned and strode to the bar, where Sally was standing.

"So, what are you gonna do about it?" she said. " Fuckin' fire me or something?"

Joe shook his head and released a small laugh.

"Can I fix you a drink?" he asked.

She was suspicious. She paused and looked him over. "I suppose."

"What's your poison?"

"If I'm honest, a grasshopper. I know they look kinda fruity, but they're delicious."

"One grasshopper, then."

He quietly made the drink.

*His silence is kinda nice,* Sally thought, *but it also makes me a little uncomfortable. Most guys aren't this quiet. As soon as they're interested in you, they won't shut up. But this one. And he's handsome.*

"Sally, right?" Joe asked as he placed the drink on a cocktail napkin in front of her.

"That's right. Sally Clancy."

"Well, I'm sorry about what happened. I'm Joseph O'Sullivan. I'm not just the bartender. I'm the owner of the place."

"I know that. Everyone does."

"Well, I wouldn't assume—" And then it hit him. When they first spoke, she'd been teasing him.

"You don't strike me as a guy who assumes a lot. You kinda let people reveal themselves, don't you?"

He smiled. *She's all surprise right hooks and uppercuts. You don't see her coming. I don't stand a chance against her.*

Joe stayed at the bar all night talking to Sally. He could feel his defences softening as the hours passed. Sally, for her part, grew more easy about him. *He's the kind of guy who gives you space to breathe,* she thought. *To be who you are. And listens. He actually listens. A hell of a lot more than he talks. And he's a good listener. He asks good questions. But he ain't much for answering questions about himself. That's okay, though. I like him. His heart is good. You can see it. Better than I ever would have expected or anyone would say about him.*

After a few hours passed, he invited her upstairs for a small meal. When they had eaten, he stood, walked around the table to her, and reached out his hand. She accepted it and stood. He instinctively pulled her close and kissed her once gently. He pulled back to look at her, smiled, and Sally grabbed his head and kissed him deeply.

As they found the bedroom, she undressed him. He was startled but allowed her. When they were on the bed, she was surprised at his delicacy with her. She welcomed it for the first few minutes, then rolled him onto his back and climbed on top of him. When it was over, she sensed a dark cloud forming in him. As though a troubling memory was returning.

"A drink?" he asked, as he stood up from the bed.

She could see he was uncomfortable. *Don't push him. Give him room.* "Sure, whatever you're having."

"Whisky it is, then."

Sally continued to see him, always in his apartment, as he generally refused to go out. He didn't know what to do after they had been to bed. He liked her company but wasn't sure of his role as host. And in the beginning, he wasn't even sure he wanted her around at all. Or for her to stay there. Sally sensed it, and in their first encounters, she would leave early in the morning. As time passed, she began to suggest plans for them: going to a party, another bar, or just for a walk. And she could sense his reluctance but polite consideration. She was surprised that he was so polite.

Sally assessed the situation. Joseph was known as the man who had gone to jail for a violent crime and then been involved in some shady business. *Hardly a recipe for a gentle, considerate man,* she thought. *But that's in him. He is both of those things with me. God knows I'm not the most sensitive and delicate woman. . . And the books. So many books. There's more to him than anyone knows. He just seems a little sad and lonely beneath the calm and outward strength. Hard to reach. He seems most content in his apartment, with his whisky and books, staring into the night. So much drinking alone with his books and looking out into the night. It's like he watches over Grand Island. And that melancholy, they call it, is a vein that runs through him. And maybe he's unaware of why he's so sad, or it could be that he just refuses to look at it. But he's let me in. I'm honoured by it.*

# 11. A Missing Person

May 5, 1972—Grand Island, Ontario

It was early May, and the morning was filled with mist. Michael liked this. "It's the other world entering ours. If you wander into the mist, you can feel the pull of the spirits," he announced to no one at all as he looked out the window.

He paused to listen if any of the others were awake.

*They've all got heads this morning, I'm sure, from that party last night. Colin's sixty-fifth. He looked happy, didn't he? Doesn't look sixty. This existence keeps a man young. Physical and calm. Not the madness of the city. But Joseph was not there. That's a terrible thing. A real pain, and if I felt it, I could only imagine poor Colin and Eva. But on his father's birthday. It seems like he has no north star to guide him, that boy, and Colin, well, he's tied to his anger, isn't he? The Murphys are like that. I won't blame his mother, but her family is that way. Hold a grudge like it was a gold bar. A family heirloom. They took pride in their list of those that were not in their favour. That's a terrible thing to carry. Especially for your own son.*

There had, of course, been no expectation that Brendan would be there.

Michael slipped on his boots. *And here I go now, into that great mist. That's all I can do now, I suppose.*

He opened the front door and walked into the yard, touching the dew on the leaves of Sarah's wild rose bush. "Shame you're not in bloom. Nothing prettier, and your fragrance is like none else," he whispered to the plant.

Sarah had just woken. When she saw that Michael was gone from their bed, she drifted downstairs. She called out to him and heard nothing.

As the hours drew on, Sarah, and then Colin and Eva, began to worry about Michael.

"He's nearly eighty now," Colin said.

"I'm aware, son," Sarah replied.

"I'm just worried is all."

"We all are. He's never missed dinner. Not without telling me. If he's not home by dark, I'm making calls."

"Who will you call?"

"Around the island. To see if anyone has seen him."

"And if they haven't?"

"The police, I suppose."

"You're likely right," Eva said.

"I am."

The sun set just west of Kingston a few minutes before nine. Colin, Eva, and Sarah watched it. Sarah stood and went to the phone and began her first call.

"I'll drive around again and stop into the village, talk to a few folks," Colin said, as he made his way to the door.

He could hear his mother on the phone as he left. "Hello, Jean. How are you this evening?"

Colin knew there'd be no news, so he just kept moving.

As he drove the island and spoke to people, the sense of dread grew in him. *He didn't seem like he'd lost his mind. No more than usual, anyway. Drowned is the only thing that makes sense. He must have went under. Walked down to the shore, fell, and slipped down the coast with the current. I have to call the police. They need to send a marine unit. And I need to make the calls. Brendan, Joe. . . I don't even know how to reach Joe. Eva will, though. It's been almost ten years since I've seen him. I'm sure his mom has a way of getting hold of him. I know she stays in touch. She sees him on the mainland and doesn't think I know. If that boy wants to leave it all behind, there's nothing I can do. Dealing drugs. I know he is. At least that's how he's made his money. Maybe he's done with that now. Eva says it's so. He can cover it up by buying that bar in town but the whole affair was paid for with drug money. Shameless.*

Just after dawn, Colin was making tea when he was startled by a knock at the door. He opened it to see two young men. *They're not islanders. I don't know these kids.*

"What can I do for you?"

"We understand that there's a person missing and you could use some help finding them."

"There is, but how do you know about it? Who are you?"

"We've been sent by Mr. O'Sullivan to offer our assistance."

"Mr. O'Sullivan?"

"Yeah."

"I'm Mr. O'Sullivan."

"Sorry, sir, Joe O'Sullivan. From Kingston."

"You mean Joseph. My son. And he's from this very island and house."

"My apologies, sir."

"No need to apologize, but you need to go back to the mainland. If my son has any concern at all for his grandfather, he can come and do something about it. That's all there is to that. I won't have strangers here now."

The two young men shifted.

"Boys, I'm sure you're fine men, but this is a family affair. And you tell my son . . . you tell Mr. O'Sullivan that."

The men stood there uneasily.

"Go on, now. If you hurry, you can catch the next boat back to the mainland."

They turned and made their way to their car while Colin watched.

"That boy. He'll skirt any responsibility, won't he?"

Joe arrived an hour later. His grandmother, Sarah, was cleaning up.

"Who's that now?" she asked. "Michael!"

"It's just me, Grandma. Joe. It's Joseph."

Sarah would occasionally come with Eva to have dinner with him.

"Joseph, you nearly scared me half to death."

"I'm sorry about that."

"Well, come in, now. Don't just stand in the doorway like a salesman."

"Fine."

"Look at you. Where did you get that scar on your cheek."

"It's part of running a bar. You have to be your own bouncer sometimes."

"Bouncer?"

"Security."

"Joseph, that's a terrible line of business. But good for you, for owning your own."

He didn't want to tell her that he enjoyed the work. Days when he felt a growing gloom, he would relieve Max, who was the head of security, and do it himself. He'd drink a few whiskies and head down to the main floor. On weekends, it was easy to find a man who'd drunk too much and he could toss out of the building. He felt disappointed when they didn't resist.

"Thanks," he said to Sarah. "I'm fine. Any news?"

"Well, your grandfather is missing. Have you heard?"

"I have, of course. That's why I'm here."

"Okay, then."

"Your father is down at the dock. He's going out to search for him in the boat. He's been wandering around the last hour looking for him. I'm sure he could use your help."

"I won't be getting into a boat with that man. Not ever again."

"That's true, you two did have a tussle the last time, didn't you?"

"You could say that."

"And that's the last time you spoke, wasn't it?"

"It was."

"Well, no better time than the present to put it behind you to find your grandfather."

"I'll never get in a boat again with that man. I'll not say it again."

"Fine, then. Take the little one. The runabout."

"Fine."

"Fine, then."

Both stood in the kitchen staring at each other.

"Go, then."

"I'm waiting for him to leave."

"My God, the pair of you are like children."

"He's the child. Tossing me overboard, just because I don't agree with him."

"He tossed you overboard because you disrespected him and he was worried about you. He wanted to get the point across to you."

"He didn't toss me anywhere. I got out. I'd never let any man lay his hands on me."

"No, you wouldn't, and you didn't. And where has that got you? Prison. Didn't it? He's your father. Neither of you are right, and both of you are wrong. He's your father, that's all that matters. And we're your family."

Joe fell silent. He turned and left the kitchen and walked down to the dock. *It's been a long time since anyone really challenged me in any way. My God, she's a good woman.*

His father had already left. Joe could see him just fifty yards or so up the coast to the east. He took the bowline from its ring on the dock and hopped into the twelve-foot aluminum boat. After priming the gas line, he gave the small outboard motor a few pulls and it started. He undid the stern line, put the boat in reverse, turned it, throttled down for a moment, then decided to follow in his father's wake.

Colin had the large fishing boat. Joe could see him peering from side to side, looking into the water.

*The poor bastard. Looking for your dad like this. To find him out here would be a devastating moment for sure.*

Colin's engine came to a stop. Joe was shocked to see his father peel off his coat, toss his hat to the side, and jump into the water. Joe turned off his own motor.

"Dad!"

There was no reply. Colin swam in the cold waters along the shore.

*My God, it's just May. He'll freeze. Drown in there when his arms give out.*

"Dad!"

Joe could see now that Colin was making his way toward a large object floating near the shore.

"Oh, Christ," he muttered to himself. He threw the anchor overboard and hopped into the water himself.

When he reached his father, Colin was standing in waist-deep water, holding something. A large piece of driftwood. He clung to it.

"It's just driftwood, Dad."

Colin spun around.

"Joseph?"

"Yeah."

"Joseph, I can't find them. None of them. My father. Your grandfather. None of them. They were just there," he said, pointing further along the coast. "They were just boys, really. I think they wanted to impress us and make a little money. Nothing terrible. I can't find them, Joseph. I just can't find them, and they deserved better than this. It's all just loss. This life is just me losing one person after another. Just boys. I was their senior. And I can't keep anyone safe. And I can't even honour them by taking them home. Lost. They're all lost, Joseph. I'm so sorry, Joseph. I can't find any of them, let alone help them. I'm so sorry, Joseph. And I thought I lost you."

He put his hands on his son's shoulders. "I'm so sorry, son."

Joe wiped his cheeks with the back of his hand. If he wasn't so overwhelmed, he would have realized that it was the first time he'd shed a tear in over ten years.

"I'm right here, Dad. I'm right here."

Joe let his dad hold on to the driftwood while he led him back to the boat, helped him climb in, and took him home. He came back for his own little boat once his father was safely inside.

When Joe returned to the house, he stepped into the kitchen to find Michael at the table, casually talking with his father and drinking tea. Colin had gotten out of his wet clothes and into dry ones and had a blanket wrapped around himself. He was tuning his fiddle while he and Michael chatted. Eva and Sarah were making breakfast.

"There you are, son. Out for a scoot in the boat this morning?" Michael asked.

Joe walked towards him, stunned.

"Will you be having breakfast, Joe?" Sarah asked.

"Where have you been?" Joe asked.

"Oh, in the lighthouse. I should have left a note or something. My apologies for making you worry."

"Breakfast, Joe?" Sarah asked again.

"Look at you now," Michael said. "All wet, like your dad. It's too early and cold for a dip. He needs a breakfast, Sarah. And hot tea."

Sarah nodded. "Have I not been saying the same? Get outta those wet clothes, Joseph."

Eva stepped forward and hugged her son. "Darling boy. It's so nice to have you here. With your brother coming today."

"But what was he doing?"

"I've been in the ol' thing the last day," Michael said, pointing to the window and the lighthouse. I nipped back into the house at night to get a snack and a book. And to use the lavatory. You know, they're going to automate the light. There will be no need for a lighthouse keeper. And I wanted to, you know, spend some time with her before it happened. We've been through some things. We have—"

"And you didn't tell anyone of your plans?" Joe said.

"I did not ask permission to step into my front yard, it's true. Nor will I ever, my boy. Don't wait for it from me, you'll be sorely disappointed."

Colin shook his head and laughed. Joe laughed with him and slapped his father on his back.

"Did you hear Brendan is on his way?" Colin asked.

"With his new bride. I believe she's expecting," Eva added.

"My absence could spur on your presence, I was sure," Michael muttered.

"What's that, now?" Colin said.

"Nothing at all. It's nothing."

Later that day and while the family sat at the table, Brendan and Mary were driving off the ferry. Mary had noticed how quiet Brendan had grown as they approached the island while their baby cooed in the back seat.

"Worried?" she asked.

"Sorry, what's that, now?"

"Worried? Are you worried?"

"Well, yeah, of course."

"When you called, they said he was back home."

"They did. But I don't know what happened."

Mary reached across and placed a hand on his thigh as he drove.

*It looks the same,* Brendan thought. *And it feels the same. Not very different from twelve years ago. There's beauty here, no doubt. It's funny how it feels foreign now. Like a strange place to visit. I'm a stranger now, I suppose, aren't I?*

Brendan looked at Mary and consciously chose to smile.

*I just want to get through this. Just get through this.*

"What a gorgeous spot, Bren. It's like Martha's Vineyard a bit."

"For sure. I'm glad you like it."

When they entered the house, they found Michael sitting by the window with a book. Eva heard them from the kitchen and came to greet them with Sarah.

"Look at you!" she said to Brendan and embraced her son. "And it's a pleasure to meet you, at last, Mary."

"Thanks. I feel the same. It's been too long."

"And look at this little man! May I hold him?"

"Of course you can!" Mary said.

"Bring him here now, won't you?" Michael said loudly from the table.

"Who are you, the pope?" Sarah countered.

"Pope of Grand Island. I like that. I think I may change our mailbox to read just that."

Mary laughed.

Brendan spoke up. "Hi, Grandfather. I'm glad to see you're safe and sound."

"Who's that, now?" Michael said with a smile. "The prodigal son?"

"Settle down, Your Holiness," Eva said.

"It's nice to see you both," said Brendan.

Michael turned in his chair to face Brendan, Mary, and the baby, Devin.

"That's a handsome family. And Mary, thanks for making him come back here."

"I think we may have you to thank for that," Mary offered.

Brendan looked down. He expected this. *There's nothing to do but to take the ribbing. If only they knew this place opens a wound in me that I feel grow as I approach the border and will persist until I see the skyline of New York again. And the city. Does it bring me joy? Not really. Refuge would be a better word. Distraction. The work, though. The making of it feels good. Just the making of it. All the rest is Mary. And now Devin.*

"Brendan? Did you hear me?" Michael asked.

"Sorry, I missed that."

"Show Mary to your father's old room. You can stay there."

Colin and Joe came in as Michael was speaking. They had been in the village getting a few things for dinner.

"I've put my stuff in there," Joe said.

"Well, it's the bigger room, and there's the three of them," Eva said. "You can take the smaller room."

"Sure. I'm used to having to give things up because of Brendan, aren't I?"

"What's that, now?" Colin asked.

"It's the truth. It's fine, you know. But it's the truth," Joe said. He was surprised at himself for saying it, but he felt as though the day opened up something in him. And he wanted to relieve himself of all of his burdens and gripes.

"What are you talking about now?" Michael asked.

Brendan sighed and shifted uneasily. "Hi, Joe, Dad," Brendan offered.

"Give me a hug, now," Colin said.

Brendan complied and then reached a hand to his brother. Joe paused a second and shook it.

"It's been a long time, Joe."

"It has."

The room fell silent.

Michael spoke up again. "Get yourselves settled and we will have dinner, the lot of us. At last."

After the meal, Brendan took Mary on a walk to show her the property and the lighthouse while the baby slept.

When they came back, Michael, Eva, and Sarah had gone to bed. Colin and Joseph were sitting on the porch. Colin was playing the fiddle.

"It's a beautiful spot you have here," Mary told the two men. "Thank you for having us."

"It's a pleasure to see you and your little one. You're always welcome here," Colin said.

"Thank you, Colin."

"Will you have a drink with us, Mary?"

"I need to check on the baby. But Brendan will."

Brendan nodded and sat in silence until he could find words.

"I'm sorry I've been away for the last ten years or so," he said.

"So are we," said his father.

"It's hard to get out of the city," Brendan quickly said, and then regretted it.

"Sure," said Colin.

"It seems easy enough for you to be there and not come back," said Joe.

"No, no. I think about you all the time. I do."

"You don't think we haven't thought of leaving? The thing is, I can't, can I?" said Joe.

"Why's that?"

"I have a record, don't I? You can't leave the country with a criminal record."

"From that little bar fight?"

"It was more than that, Bren," said Colin. "We didn't tell you. It was Kevin Glendon. He went after your brother with a bunch of fellas *because* he was your brother."

"What? What do you mean?"

Colin continued. "After you left, Kevin's brother, William, tried to marry that James girl, and he went after Joseph because people were still talking about the two of you being together."

"Jesus Christ. Is she okay?"

"She is," said Colin. "She's fine. She lives out here now. On the island."

"She has a daughter too," said Joe. "About eleven now, I guess."

Brendan was shaken. He could hear himself swallowing and breathing. His head was pounding. "But she's okay? The two of them. They're okay?"

"Yeah, she's a nurse at the hospital now," said Colin. "She renovated one of the cottages on the south shore so it's fit for winter. She's fine. We check in on her."

"William's brother went after me for the bar fight after all that."

"Jesus Christ. Why didn't anyone tell me?"

"You were gone, son. I didn't know how much you would want to know, and it seemed like a great burden to have this knowledge."

"And that's why you went to jail?"

"'Tis," said Joe.

"I had no idea. I'm so sorry. Look what I've done."

"You're not responsible, though. Everyone makes their choices," Colin said.

"Joseph. I . . . I'm so sorry. It's like all I can do is hurt everyone I give a damn about."

"I know. I'm sorry too. I've been cold with you. Nothing's been right since I got out. It's like I turned to cement on the inside and nothing can crack it, and I don't even know if I want it to be cracked. It's not just the time but how you're seen now. No one around here will let you forget it. And Glendon makes sure of that. That's why I've had . . . alternative forms of income."

"And you're done with that now," Colin said.

"I am. And you know it. I worked in a few bars. And I took the bit of money I made after prison and started one of my own and a few businesses. I've pieced it together well enough."

"You've done fine, son."

"Have I?"

The men fell silent.

Joe spoke after a while. "I've let it go with Glendon. I spent many an hour when I was locked up thinking about what I would do to him. But then I would remember that he lost his brother. He was in grief. And I kind of lost my brother as well. We had that in common. I felt I could understand him. He just wanted somewhere to drop his anger."

His brother and father said nothing. He felt he was laying a burden on them. He owed them a bit more. "I met a girl, though. Sally. She worked at the bar with me. Still does. Maybe I'll ask her to move in with me. She wants that."

"Well, bring her around, son."

"I will. Thanks."

"What can I do?" Brendan asked. "To help."

"It's all been done," said Colin. "Now you have to live with it. We just thought you should know."

"And Margaret has a daughter. About eleven?"

"She does, son."

"You've seen her?"

"I have," said Colin. "At the store and on the boat, and so on."

"Does she . . . Is she . . . " Brendan began to ask.

"No. She won't ask for any help, but we give it anyway," said Colin.

"But the daughter—"

"I know," said Colin.

"Jesus Christ."

"Right. It's a lot, son. It's a lot. I don't know if there's anything for you to do. Margaret is doing fine. So is the girl. Cute."

"Is she?"

Colin and Joe nodded.

Brendan sat with them a little longer and then excused himself when he thought he could leave them without causing an issue.

The next morning, at five, Brendan woke Mary and rushed her to get ready. He hadn't slept.

"We need to go. Now. The boat leaves in less than thirty minutes."

"That's crazy," Mary said. "What?"

"I can't explain it. We have to go."

"This is goddamn crazy."

"It is. Let's go."

Mary was fuming as they drove. Brendan wanted to speak but couldn't find the words.

By the time they reached the Canadian border and he still hadn't explained, she had grown tired of waiting for him.

"Brendan, you need to tell me what's going on. That's no way to leave your family."

Brendan tried hard to summon the words. *I don't know when I felt worse than I do today. . . Wait. Yes, I do. The last time I was here and made the same trip. There are no words for it.*

"I know I owe you an explanation."

They advanced slowly in the line of vehicles and finally reached the U.S. border official.

"What was the nature of your visit to Canada?"

Mary leaned over Brendan, who was driving. "Visiting family."

"Are you Canadian, then? You have New York plates."

"His family is here. He's from Grand Island."

"But you live in New York now?"

"He married me and got his citizenship."

"I'd like to hear from your husband, ma'am."

"So would I," said Mary.

"What are you doing in the U.S., sir?"

Brendan looked at Mary and then the official. He spoke one word. "Exile."

The officer waved them through and signalled for the next vehicle to come forward.

When they reached their home in Manhattan, above Brendan's gallery in SoHo, he had an idea. As he thought about how to speak to Mary about what had happened, an image came to his mind.

For the next two months, he gathered pieces of metal and copper wire and worked exclusively on a new artwork. He worked in secrecy, offering Mary no explanation of what he was creating or why. When it was finally done, almost eight weeks after he began, he woke Mary. It was just after 2 a.m.

"Come with me. Sorry. Sorry for waking you, but I'm done."

"What? You're done what?"

"Come see the new piece."

When Brendan led her into the back room he'd shut himself away in, Mary was shocked. First, by the size of the sculpture. It covered a large wooden table, eight feet long and four feet wide, and spilled over its sides. It was a diorama, depicting islands and various scenes with people. It consisted of steel and iron lands surrounded by blue metal shavings as water. Thin copper filament connected the islands and the people on them. The little figurines were formed of discarded metal parts, bent and welded to form human bodies. Brendan used the same method to create trees, buildings, vehicles, and boats on the water. The metal was cleaned, shined, and often painted, so the objects were like perfect replicas and shone like bright jewels upon the deep grey stone of the land or against the shimmering blue waters.

"It's the first thing I've made that is meant to be handled. Watch."

He gently touched a figure of a woman standing with a child on the largest of the islands. As the figure moved, the blue filaments that formed the lake began to flow like rippling water, the tiny trees swayed as though there was a breeze, the boats rocked, and the people engaged one another in their various locations.

"Whatever you touch moves all the other pieces, but you can't do it too roughly or it will break their ties," said Brendan.

Mary noticed his voice was hoarse and breaking up a little.

"It's beautiful, Bren. It really is."

She was enthralled. She didn't notice that her husband was sitting on the floor now, silently weeping.

"People will love this. It's gorgeous. And the concept is so . . . lovely. Beauty and frailty combined."

Brendan swallowed hard and whispered, "Thank you."

"It's a whole new type of work. The media will love this. Buyers will love it!"

"It's a technique I can use, I suppose."

"Yeah. For sure. Before we sell it, we should invite some media to the gallery and properly display it there, with the right lighting and everything."

Mary noticed how quiet Brendan was.

"I don't want to sell it. I won't, Mary. I need it. It's all I have of home."

He saw a perplexed and mildly annoyed expression on her face. He chose to ignore it. He stood up, walked back to their bedroom, dropped himself on the bed, and immediately fell into a deep sleep.

# 12. A Silversmith

March 25, 1847—Leadmore West Townland, near Kilrush,
County Clare

Peter O'Donnell stood for some time before he could knock on the door of the O'Sullivan family home. He reached into his trouser pocket and felt the money in it.

*Six pounds isn't much to hand over. I wish we could do more for them. Liam is a good man. A good man. I should have stopped him. I know I should have. If I'd thought about it for just a moment, I would have known we wouldn't succeed. No, there's no way to better our lot, let alone take a bit of the power. But a man can only stand so much, can't he? You can only take the beatings for so long until you have to strike back for your own self. And no doubt he's bound for the prison ship. Terrible.*

Before his hand reached the door it opened and Beatrice was coming out, speaking over her shoulder to James.

"I'll just ask down at Doyle's, and—"

She bumped into Peter before she saw him. She stepped back.

"Peter, isn't it?"

"It is."

She studied him.

*Oh, this has to be Liam's wife,* he thought. *Still a beauty at near forty. All of that red hair. She's going to take it hard, isn't she? But she's strong. Just give her the news.*

"You're Liam's wife? Am I right?"

It took her a moment to recognize him. He was a tall and sturdy man, but he looked weak and pale now. They all did. "I am. You're an O'Donnell, I believe."

"I am. Liam got into some trouble and the constabulary came, ya know, and he's now in a cell. I don't imagine they will let him out before there's a trial. And it doesn't look good. Talk of sedition."

"Sedition?"

"Well, he got a slew of fellas riled up buying seed when he heard they raised the price and stormed the offices, he did."

"On his own!"

"No, a few of us were there and followed, but—"

"But you're here and he's not. Is that right?"

Peter fell silent.

"Is it?"

Peter's silence continued.

"The rest of ya got away but he didn't, so. And ya never thought to try and help him?"

"We did, I swear we did, but . . ."

Peter was overwhelmed with dizziness. He began to fall and put a hand on the door frame.

"I'm sorry, Beatrice. I'm not at my best."

Beatrice couldn't stop her instinct to help him.

"Come in by the fire. Sit, have a splash of milk and tell me about it all. Liam's parents are here too."

"Are you sure?"

"I am."

Peter stepped into their house and shared the story of Liam with the family and passed along the money to James.

"He asked me to give it to you."

"He must have sold the one cow, then," James said.

The others nodded in agreement.

"Is there any talk of his trial?" Dennis asked.

"Not yet, as he was just arrested. You know, yesterday."

"Aye," said Dennis. "And the charge?"

"Oh, I don't know for sure. But there was talk, so you know . . . sedition."

"Sedition!" Ellen replied.

"And I'm sorry to say that, you know."

"They will send him off. Van Diemen's Land, to be sure," James said.

"Well, at least they will feed him in the jail," Dennis offered.

Ellen and Beatrice burst into tears. "Is that the best you have to say, Dennis O'Sullivan!" Ellen said. "With our own son in chains? Is it?"

Dennis bowed his head and made no reply.

James pushed past Peter and out the door. He stood outside and stomped the ground. *Useless*, he thought. *That's all I can do, isn't it? Just have a fit, like a child.*

He looked down to the estuary and back to the town. What was there to do? He fingered the money in his pocket from Peter, looked to the house, and heard the sound of Dennis and Genevieve consoling Ellen and Beatrice.

Dennis followed him outside, worried about his grandson. *He's like me, isn't he? Not only does he look like me, he's guided by his thoughts. They take over for him.*

"A fine mess, isn't it?" he said.

"'Tis," replied James.

"I'd be willing to wager that your father lost control of himself. And understandably. That's what's got him into trouble."

"The trouble is all around us, Grandfather. You don't go looking for it, it finds you."

"It is. I know. It is. You have to work harder than ever to avoid it."

James was pacing now. "You know, when I went to town to meet with Vandeleur, I saw enough of what's going on. There's nothing for us here. There's nothing for us in town. Things are worse there. There's no real work program, and your man Vandeleur told me himself we might be able to join the workhouse. What an invitation! But that would mean they would tear down our house. And yours. And it's a rough thing. Let's be honest, it's a prison for the poor. For being poor. Devised by the powers that made sure we turned out that way. Adults and children are dying in there too. Overcrowded, filthy mess it is. And you're right, Grandfather. Father wasn't well, like the rest of us, and at least in the hands of the constabulary he will eat. Fed better than us and those in the workhouse, so."

"It's not a pretty picture," offered Dennis.

"It's worse than that," James said. "I heard new soldiers are on their way from England. As if we had the strength to fight them. Then they act like it's our fault. Why are they like this? Even those that want to help us seem so angry about it. Or maybe just bent on finding a judgment of us in it. They want to find a way to blame us for it."

Dennis wasn't sure how to reply. *He needs the truth without it sending him into a rage that will get him killed like so many of the young men.* "Well, it would require a lot of a person not to feel guilt and maybe shame for their own country's role in treating us this way. And they can't take that in themselves. It's too big. So instead they place that guilt and shame on us. It's easy enough for them. And then some of them think we're terrible. So much less than them. Barely human. So, why would you need to be humane to the Irish if we're not really even human?"

He looked at his grandson. *He looks even more upset now. At twenty-two, he's not old enough to have experienced the fullness of the cruelty that exists in the world. But he can see the injustice. It's in plain sight now, isn't it?*

"But you know, think of the ones who are trying to help us. The Quakers from England. How much they had to overcome. The scorn and ridicule they must face for trying to come to our aid. There's something quite noble in that, don't you think? And for those souls, we must give thanks. Great thanks, really, and protect them in turn, in any way we can."

"I suppose."

"If you can't hold on to the things that will save you, you're doomed in times like these. And you can't let them take that away from you, son. You can't. Especially when it's all you have left."

James tried to hide his tears. "Okay, Grandfather. Okay, now."

"And I will go to town and see what we can do about your father. I'll speak to the constabulary."

"Right, then."

James didn't want to tell his grandfather about the two other parts of his conversation with their landlord, Crofton Vandeleur. The first was that Vandeleur had offered them passage to Canada if they gave up their home. They would all have to go.

*Maybe if we tell him of Liam's troubles, he could put in a word for us with the constabulary. No, he wouldn't do that, even if we promised to clear off the land. That's what he wants. He's responsible for our care, and turning all of this into pasture for the cattle would relieve him of that, wouldn't it? Maybe we have to leave. But if we do, I want to make sure that the lot of us are in the best possible condition.*

Dennis could see himself in his grandson. James had wanted to be a silversmith, which was quite like Dennis's old desire to be a blacksmith. And there was no room for either, was there? No room in this world for their hopes at all.

When he was sixteen, James had apprenticed in Kilrush with Declan Davis to be a silversmith. But when the crop failures began, the money dried up, and he took work as a labourer and on some of the work programs offered by the government. And this led to the second thing Vandeleur had told him.

When James arrived at the big house to see him about seeds, Vandeleur had just finished his afternoon tea. He complained about the quality of the tea set and asked James if he knew anyone who could make him a fine silver set that his wife might like.

"You know, it's quite a task to convince her to visit me here," Vandeleur confided. She calls this house 'the hut in the bog.' But you know, the area has its charms, doesn't it?"

James nodded. He was nervous about this meeting with the landlord, and as he rehearsed his own request, he had a difficult time focusing on the man's words.

"It does have charms, sir."

"Yes, it does. My new struggle is to find a tea set. This one lacks art. There's nothing charming about it at all. A fine tea set is something she appreciates, and it's something that eludes me here. Do you know anyone who would make a nice silver set?"

"Yes, I do. You know that I have experience—"

"Tell me, why are you here today, Liam?"

"Oh, well, it's James. Liam is my father."

"Right you are."

The conversation then moved to a discussion of the seeds, and James couldn't think of a way to bring it back to having Vandeleur commission a tea set from him. But now, with a bit of money in his pocket, he could buy the sheets of silver and present a tea set to him. *It will give me a greater sum than I have now and could set us up to get to America. Vandeleur can talk about Canada, but it's run by the Brits and couldn't be much better than here, could it? It may be a foolish hope but I have to try, don't I?*

So, as James's fuming ended,

the notion of the tea set rose. *I know I can buy sheets of metal from Davis himself. It will be a fine sterling affair. Milk jug and sugar bowl, of course. All laid upon a beautiful tray of silver. That will make him happy. Impress him, really. I'll bet I can double my money.*

James planned to fall to it straight away. The next day, he started out to Kilrush and Davis's workshop. When he reached the end of his laneway, he paused. *I do not like passing the graveyard. They've been burying the dead from the workhouse in there. It's like an open wound. No, I'll go left here on Shanakyle Road to the laneway and up to Pella Road. It's not that much longer. And sure, I feel ill but I'll make it there fine, so. I've got a calling at last. It's fuel, isn't it?*

As he made his way down the road, just before he met the lane that would take him up to Pella Road, he saw something that caught his attention

*What could that be beneath that old tree? I played by that tree as a boy, didn't I? It has to be a person, leaning against it like. It does.*

He continued to make his way towards it, climbing the small wall at the edge of the field, near the road. He was sure now it was a woman.

When he approached, he found that she was dead. She was of thin frame, and thinner with illness. Her skin had a yellow hue.

On the tree was carved the following words:

MOIRA HOGAN

1797–1847

IN CHAINS UNSEEN

The stone she used to carve the message still lay in her hand.

James turned from the scene in tears.

After a few moments, he gathered himself. *I'll let them know to bury her. Her family. She must be one of the Hogans from town. They will at least know her people. There's a number of them in Kilrush and going north. But I hate to leave her here like this. I'll place her nicely beneath the tree. I don't like going near her, but I have to, don't I?*

He put her hands in her lap and laid her out under the tree with her head near the trunk of it. He was glad her eyes were closed. He didn't know if he could have done that.

123

He stood back and took in the scene. He felt terrible about leaving her, and his high spirits from just a few moments before were cast low. He continued on his walk, trying to turn his thoughts to the task before him.

*I just need to buy the sheets of silver. Declan has agreed to allow me to work in the shop for a few more shillings. I'll have everything I need, so. Here I thought I was done with being a silversmith. The few tools I had are gone, but at Davis's I'll have all I need and space to complete the full project, won't I? The plan seems a bit small after seeing that poor woman. And the inscription. "In Chains Unseen." Haunting, isn't it? That's more than the madness brought on by illness. There's something to that. It did look like she had the yellow fever, but those three words. They call forth something. What is it? These wild times. And the famine is just the worst of it. I've heard the stories going back to Cromwell himself. What am I? There it is. I know what to do, don't I?*

After some ninety minutes of walking, James was at Davis's workshop. He summoned the energy to open the door with a flourish. He smelled the air. *I've always loved it, haven't I? The smell. A pungent, aged elm mixed with the hard steel and silver and the smokiness of the turf fire and soldering equipment. It makes me feel grand. Truly. The wood counters for working with bottles of potions and the assortment of different-sized anvils that are almost works of art themselves. And the tools: forming hammers, raising hammers, planishing hammers, and burins. Neatly arranged, aren't they, with the various punches to do the fine work?*

James closed the door so he wouldn't be disturbed and fell to work right away. *They will know the fullness of who we are. We're not weak fools to be used as you wish. He will see our greatness. I will chase a design showing the great Tuatha Dé Danann, as the old folks call them. The gods from so long ago. Brigid herself. It has to be Brigid. Goddess of the smiths and the purveyor of keening. If ever there was a time for lamentation it is today. And the last several. She must adorn the teapot itself, with her flowing locks and that look of love and strength. In equal measure.*

James remembered asking his grandfather Dennis for more and more stories of the Irish gods and heroes when he was a child. Dennis had picked up the stories in his travels, and especially during his involvement with the Society of United Irishmen. The teacher at the hedge school James attended as a boy noted his interest in Irish mythology and history and sent him home with the books he could secure on the matter. James continued to pursue the stories and found them in the weekend edition of *The Limerick Chronicle*. He had to travel into town to get the newspaper, which he would do on Saturdays.

And then through the week he would let the story he had just read play repeatedly in his mind.

Now, in the workshop, he fell to his task, taking the sheets of silver and first drawing on them. The first thing he drew was the shape of the pot itself and then the image that needed to be fashioned into it. He only noticed the passage of time when the light from the window waned. He hurried to keep working as darkness edged in, until he found he was squinting to see. With a sigh, he sat up and searched the room for candles. Once he found them and they were lit and standing on the wooden workbench, he continued his efforts.

He was shocked to find that the portrait of Brigid he hammered into the metal with punches, and made using acids and resists, was nearly identical to that in his mind. He held the teapot up to the eastern window as the sun was rising to get the clear light on it. On the reverse side, he adorned it with a circle of shamrocks.

"Ah, it's grand. It'll do just fine," he said. He was ready to take on the next piece. "But I should get a nip of sleep. The cot here will be fine." Declan had a small bench near the fireplace where he often slept. James added turf to the fire and went to sleep.

After about three hours, he woke up with a start. He sat up quickly, rubbed his eyes, and fell to his work once again. He was hungry but had grown accustomed to ignoring that sensation.

*Now for the Fianna. Those young warriors who protected our community will rise again, I'm sure. You can sense it. Things are bad. But we will rise out of it. When we need to, we can summon it. And right there on the side of the milk jug. It's been our strength, hasn't it, the milk? Seems the right spot for it.*

James continued through the day, drawing, hammering, and etching the silver. On the sugar bowl, he had included a portrait of the hero Cú Chulainn. *He seemed so real with his abilities and struggles, didn't he?*

His final job was the tray itself. On it, he wanted to include an image of the great house Vandeleur called home. *"A hut in a bog." No, sir. We built this mansion for you and maintained it and the gardens. And of course hunted and grew your food before we prepared it, so. And we've done it well. So, yes, you will need to see the hunters stalking game and those of us working in your fields. Having you in our care. I will show the great three storeys of your house with panoramic views of the Shannon, the Twelve Pins, and the Kerry mountains in the distance. You'll get a portion of the eighty-six windows they say the building offers. Did your family build your home, with its thick, high walls, to be a bulwark against the town? It's all straight lines and towering presence. And with the four hundred acres of your demesne and the high walls surrounding the grounds, it seems you made sure we were kept at bay.*

*But now you can present your tea set to your guests, not knowing that you're presenting the glory of Ireland. With just as many heroes as you Brits have. And every right to our independence, so.*

James finished after another night of sleep and doused the silverware in water to clean it and used a little on himself. *Should I go home now and get a better set of clothes? No, I don't really have them, do I? No, no. Just get your wild hair under control.*

The sun hadn't risen, so he assembled the tea set, put another bit of turf on the fire, and waited for it to rise while he gazed with admiration and pride at his work.

James made his way through the town just after seven. The pieces of the tea set were individually wrapped and placed in a cloth bag he found in the workshop. His excitement grew as he reached the gates to the big house, and he said good morning to the gardeners starting their day. After he knocked on the door of the servants' entrance, he fixed his hair and shifted excitedly in his shoes.

"Mr. Vandeleur is just finishing his breakfast and he has agreed to see you in a few moments," a young woman told him.

"Right. Thank you, then."

She nodded. "Follow me into the scullery. You can wait there."

James was too excited to notice her slightly annoyed tone. He waited another twenty minutes before the young woman returned.

"Follow me," she told him, and James did just that. He walked behind her through the kitchen, up the stairs, through the hall and to the dining room, where servants were clearing dishes from breakfast. Crofton Vandeleur was still sitting there, reading the newspaper. He didn't lift his head as James entered.

The young woman and James both waited awkwardly until Vandeleur flipped the page, having finished an article, and the woman announced James's presence.

"Mr. Vandeleur, James O'Sullivan for you."

"Right. Young James. How are you? Have you come to seek passage?"

"No, not really, sir."

"Right, then. What could it be, then?"

"I have something for you. You mentioned you needed a tea set. So I have one here for you. I could set it up for you."

"A tea set?"

"Yes, sir. You mentioned that you wanted to commission a set, sterling silver like."

"I have thought about doing that, you know."

"Yes, sir. So, I have trained as a silversmith and made one. May I show it to you?"

Vandeleur was perplexed. "Fine, then. Let's see your work, Mr. . ."

"O'Sullivan," James replied. "I'll set it on your table, if you'll allow it."

"Fine. Fine, then."

James did so with no words. He wanted his work to speak for itself. He assembled the pieces carefully, first putting down the tray, and then placing the milk jug and sugar bowl on it. Then finally the teapot itself. He stepped back slowly, beaming.

Vandeleur leaned forward, exhaled, and inspected the pieces for a few seconds.

"They seem just fine. And you made them?"

"I did, so."

"Well, that's a talent to be sure. Good for you."

"Thank you. I think they will please your wife."

The man exhaled heavily. "Little does, my boy."

"Perhaps this will be the gift that makes her enjoy Ireland and spend more time here."

"A gift?"

"Yes, you could make it a gift to her."

"And you're making this a gift to me?"

James was surprised by the question.

"It's fine, young man. I'm sure this cost you a great deal."

"It did, sir."

"And it would cost me more. These are difficult times. Money is scarce. I cannot spend it on luxuries like tea sets. No, I can't."

James had not thought about him not wanting it.

"Maybe you can find a buyer in town? And I hope that you and your family will consider the passage to Canada. I believe I offered that to your people some time ago. The offer still stands."

James nodded.

"Thank you for showing your work to me."

James couldn't summon any words and simply tilted his head once more in response.

The young woman, who had stayed, began to collect the pieces of the tea set. James took them from her hands and dropped them into his sack with a loud clang.

"Easy, now, boy, don't be scratching them. You'll never sell them with degradations."

James couldn't bear to look at Vandeleur or anyone else. He wanted to be gone. He shoved the last piece of the set in his sack, turned, and made his way from the room.

Vandeleur had gone back to reading his newspaper.

The young woman raced to get ahead of him and lead him from the house, but he was nearly running. When he reached the servants' door, he opened it himself. He slowed his pace as he walked through the demesne but picked up speed in town when he saw Pat Moloney, a childhood friend, coming down the street. *He's sure to ask what's in the sack.* James took a quick turn down an alley off Frances Street, stepped behind a tree, and waited for him to pass. Then he sprinted down the street to the harbour.

*I'm a fool. I'm sure they're all laughing at me back there. The staff. They must be thinking what sort of idiot does such a thing? There is no room for foolish hope. We're trapped. And that's it. That's all there is to it, so.*

He made his way to the far end of the harbour, where he was sure he could be alone, and with tears finally streaming from his eyes flung the sack and its contents into the water. Drained of hope and thought, he trudged home.

He arrived to find his mother in poor condition. In the days that had followed Liam's arrest, Beatrice had stopped eating and would not leave her bed.

James was left with only one thought. *There's nothing for us here. The best we can do is take up the offer for passage to Canada.*

The days passed slowly as they tried to nurse Beatrice to health, until they lost her. James and Dennis both moaned lowly as they lifted the body of Beatrice onto the small cart for burial. Normally, the work of the funeral services was handled by Jim McMullen and his son, but they were overrun, and James had to arrange the loan of the McMullens' spare cart with the understanding that he would move his mother's body himself.

Ellen and Dennis helped James and Genevieve place the body on the wooden boards, wrapped in the best bolt of cloth Ellen could find. She had saved it. *I needed just one thing of beauty,* she thought. *Just the one. And now it's gone too.*

Ellen was surprised she hadn't cried yet. *She was dear to me. It seems there is a feeling worse than sadness, and it leaves you with no tears. I haven't cried at her quick death. It was all just too much for her. Understandably. And I still don't know where my own son is. Arrested and soon to be convicted, no doubt, and shipped off. Van Diemen's Land, to be sure. Tears come when we have hopes dashed or expectations not met. But maybe I've given up on hope. It started with seeing the local children dead and then my own gone. . . Some of those babies, gone for hours and days, still in the arms of mothers who won't put them down. And now this. My own so far from my reach. And Dennis is barely holding on, so.*

Dennis had gone out to check at the government offices in town to see if there was any work. There was talk of more road building as part of the relief program. They'd accept anyone. Children even. James and Genevieve could do it and make a little money.

As James led the horse walking beside them, Genevieve turned to him. "What do we do now, James?"

"What is there to be done?"

She had no answer. *How do I tell him? He has to know. We are both so weak. And there's less food now than there was when we were well. And the prospects are tough. There's no way around it. They're just tough. I can't keep pulling dulse from the shore to eat. It's not going to get us better.*

# 13. Her Phone Call

## November 21, 1996—Grand Island, Ontario


*I've had enough of it*, Margaret thought. She picked up the phone. Then she put it back down. She picked it up once more. *I need to speak to Patricia. About Kelly. I have to do it. I have to.* She finally began to dial.

"Hi, Mom," Patricia answered.

"Hi, Patricia. How are you?"

"I'm well. Very well, in fact."

"Oh, yeah. Why's that?"

"Because there's no reason not to be happy."

"Really?"

"Really, Mother."

After a brief silence, Margaret said, "Have you thought about it? Do you know what you're going to do? You've got to do something."

Patricia sighed.

"That's not much of a solution," Margaret said.

"She needs help."

"Who's that?"

"Kelly. Your granddaughter."

"Kelly? Kelly needs help?"

"That's what I said. Your granddaughter needs support."

"I heard you. I just wanted to make sure you knew what you were saying."

"I do, Mother."

"Do you? I mean, you do—you're a good mother. You always have been."

"Thanks, Mom. But too soft, right?"

"What do you mean?"

"Don't pretend to be shocked. You think I've been too easy on Kelly."

"I never said that."

"You didn't have to."

"Well, that father of hers. Is he still working as a bouncer and living at the wreck of a place his mother calls a farm?"

Patricia didn't answer.

"Well, it is a mess of a place, Patricia," Margaret said.

"Okay. But what does that have to do with anything?"

"Well, all the parenting fell on you. It's a lot. I know. I've done it."

"I'm aware you've done it. I was there."

"Don't get snippy."

"I'm not snippy."

"Seems like you are."

"Well, I'm not."

"Okay. I'm just saying that Kelly is with a man, and it's getting worse than it ever did for you or me. And I worry about that poor little boy. He's only six."

"Well, I worry more about Kelly. It's Kelly he hit and said terrible things to."

"She can defend herself. She's a grown woman. She doesn't mind telling you off, or me, for that matter. She can tell that bastard to get lost. And she should. You know she should. Peter is good for nothing."

"They're married, Mom. It's not that easy. And you don't know for sure that he hit her."

"But I know him. His type. Miserable bastard."

"He's part of our family. We need to accept him."

"Do we?"

"Yes, we do."

"Well, if she's gonna be stupid enough to stay with him, then we need to do something."

"What do you mean?"

"If he's abusing her, he's going to abuse that child."

There was no response.

"You know he is, Patricia. You can't say that he isn't. You can't."

"Mother, we don't know anything other than they've had some fights. And maybe he's a little strict with Jacob, but he's the boy's father. It's his choice."

"A little strict? He's an abuser. I can see it in him."

"And there's nothing we can do, anyway."

"There's plenty I'm willing to do about it."

"What are you talking about?"

"I know some guys that would talk to him, rough him up a bit."

"Mother!"

"I'm not saying kill the man, just make it clear he can't do that sort of thing. She's your daughter and that's your grandson. I would think you'd care more about them."

"I swear to God . . . Of course I care about them."

"What are you swearing about? There's nothing to swear about except that miserable SOB. He thinks he can just take what he wants and push them around. What a big man, pushing around a little boy and his wife."

"As I said, you don't know if that's true."

"I know people. And you know it. You know he's a prick."

"I don't."

"Yes, you do. Just say it."

"I won't."

"Well, I'm coming down today. I'm taking Jacob for the weekend. That's all there is to it. Can I get him from your house?"

"What do you mean?"

"Tell Kelly I want to take him and she can bring him to your house."

"Why don't you just pick him up?"

"She's mad at me. And I'm not apologizing. I have nothing to apologize for, to her or that son of a bitch she calls a husband."

"What did you do, Mother?"

"I didn't do anything."

"What did you say?"

"Well, she told me she wanted to get Jacob a dog. He's been asking for one. And it's good for a little boy. I get it. And he's got no one there with him. No other siblings or anything. And thank God for that, because it would just be someone else for that bastard to abuse. So a dog would be good for him. But I said she should be careful, because Peter will likely hurt the dog. And of course, she got mad."

"Mother!"

"It's the truth, and you know it."

Patricia sighed.

"Don't get mad at me. It's him you should be mad at."

Patricia sighed again.

"Another sigh? What's wrong with you? Have you got asthma? I hope not. I do. It's a terrible thing. I wouldn't wish it on my worst enemy. Well, maybe I would. If Peter had asthma, he'd get winded when he tried to hit her or the boy."

"Stop it, now. I'm just thinking."

"What's there to think about? He's a prick. There's no way around that. There's nothing to think about. We have to do something. And Kelly does. She has to leave the rotten bastard. Just leave him! My God! You should know this. She's your daughter!"

"She is my daughter, and I know what it's like to be a single mother and to be raised by one. I don't want it for her. I want better."

"You think this is better? And I wasn't such a terrible mother. You're fine. And that miserable dickhead who got you pregnant is useless. At least he had the good sense to just leave. Besides, you didn't have it so bad. We were fine."

"Well, I never knew my father. My entire life."

"It could have been worse. You're fine."

"I'm not, and neither are you. I would like one woman in this family to have a family, not some broken-down mess of one."

"We're not broken. You've had it good. You don't know how bad it can go with a man."

"And you don't know how to stay with one."

"If I found one worth a damn, I would."

"So my father isn't worth a damn?"

"That's different. And I won't talk about it."

"Yes, you will. And you'll leave Kelly alone. You're a bully. You push and push and push. That's all you do."

"I have to. You'd let her raise that kid with a wicked bastard who will beat him."

"He hasn't done that."

"So we should just wait for him to beat them or murder them?"

"Who is talking about murder?"

"I am. I know men. And he's the type."

"You know nothing about men. You've never kept one around long enough to know one."

"I can tell you this. If she doesn't do something about this—and I mean soon—I will."

"What do you mean?"

"I'll call Children's Services."

"You wouldn't."

"I would. If he's not done anything wrong, what's the problem?"

"Kelly would never forgive you. Did you ever think about that?"

"Someone's got to look out for the child. He deserves a chance at life. . . The poor little guy." Margaret let out a sob.

"And Kelly's my child. . . Don't cry."

"You have to do something. Promise me you'll do something."

"I have to go."

"Okay, then."

"Don't cry, Mom."

"It's fine."

"It will be fine. Don't worry. And I'm sorry I upset you. I know that you care."

"I do. I just care about her, and that little boy, and you, Trish. I love you all. I do."

"I know. I know you do."

"And I'm sorry it wasn't easier for you."

"I know, Mom."

"I love you."

"I love you too."

"And I love Jacob and Kelly. I just want the best for them."

"I know you do."

"And that son of a bitch isn't the best thing for them."

"Okay, Mom, I gotta go."

"Okay, then. You'll talk to Kelly about me taking Jacob for the weekend?"

"I will."

"Thanks, honey."

"It's okay. Bye, Mom."

"Bye, honey."

Margaret listened to the dial tone. Still holding the phone to her ear with her shoulder, she pulled out a tissue to wipe her eyes. Then she pressed her thumb into the palm of her other hand and rubbed it, hoping to feel better.

At her home in Kingston, Patricia was dialling a number in New York. She liked hearing her father's voice.

"You've reached Brendan's home. I'm sorry I can't speak to you right now, but please leave a message and I will return your call."

Patricia considered hanging up, but she left a message. "Hi, Brendan . . . Dad. I'm still getting used to saying that. It's different in letters and emails, but to say it out loud . . . it's strange. But nice. Sorry. It's about Mom. She's getting worse. She just is. I don't know what else to say. And I don't know who else to speak to about it. She's just so sad and angry. I don't know if you're ready to speak to her, but if you are, this would be a good time. Okay? Sorry to leave this as a message. Call me when you can. Thanks, Dad. Thanks. Bye."

# 14. His Journey

June 11, 1997—New York City, New York

As Brendan entered Penn Station, he thought about how he loved taking the train.

*It's slower getting there. And I have a night in Montreal before the next train in the morning. But I could use a little time. I always want time, don't I? I thought it was the cure for all that ailed me. But when does time itself become a sort of stain on your life? So much of it was spent away from that place, when all they wanted from me was a bit of my time. Well, maybe more than a bit of it. They just wanted me back there, didn't they? But I'm going now. Going home like a hero, I suppose some would say. Successful. None of them care about that, really. And God bless them for it. Knowing some of the artists who made it, I'm not sure it's a good thing, the company I keep.*

The train moved through the city, and he thought about the homes along the Hudson River, the mountains, and the tiny towns. *I'm alone now. Not just in New York but in making this journey.* His mood became tinged with a feeling of regret.

*I can be made to feel sad so easily. Goddamn trains . . .*

"Porter, is the beverage car open?"

"It is, sir, just two cars to your rear. It also has food."

"But the bar is open?"

The porter stopped and checked his watch. "It is."

"Thanks."

*It's likely foolish to be going, anyway. It's only me who cares about the past. No one else does. They will all have forgotten. But I'm sure they'll still see me as the fool who lost his mind over a girl. They won't let you forget when you fail. We're good that way, aren't we? Memories like a steel trap for failures. . . And who am I to complain? My lord, I own a house in New York City and my own gallery, under my own name. Everything I create is sold. They all want it still, and I'm not a young man. And the young ones working for me see me as a great man. "A great man," she called me. And I know what she wants. Just twenty-five years old. Just leaves you hollow, doesn't it? Feeling like a fool for considering it. Me in my late sixties.*

"Excuse me," Brendan said, when he bumped a woman's elbow as he got up. "My apologies."

*I've never shaken that, have I? The need to apologize, to be polite. For others. For me? Rarely. I'm more apt to punish myself for what I've done rather than show any care for what I want or need when I'm hurt. And I suppose that's no one else's fault but my own. My own damn fault.*

"Good afternoon," he said to the bartender.

"Hello."

"A whiskey, please. Not bourbon. Rye. And a splash of ginger with a bit of ice, if you have it."

"That's no problem."

He reached into his jacket to pull out the letter but stopped himself.

*What with the train, the drink, and all, I can't be sure I won't start to cry. And I don't want to do that here. . . Maybe it's just inevitable with age that you feel regret. You can't go this long without making choices you would regret. Mistakes or not. Choices. And in those choices, certain . . . opportunities are left behind. And people. For chrissake, Brendan, she wasn't an opportunity, she was the love of your life. Just admit it, you fucking coward.*

*The feeling never waned, never diminished. It's stuck with you, haunted you, comforted you, driven you to create. It was only five hundred miles, but she might as well have been on the moon.*

*For all my supposed creativity, I couldn't imagine a way back to her. I could only long for her. But to find a way to her that would let us live together? I couldn't do it. What if Odysseus never knew if Penelope truly missed him and ached for his return to Ithaca? Would he have faced down the odds to get back to their island? No, he would not. There it is, then.*

Brendan dropped an elbow on the bar.

"Another, please."


That same morning, Patricia woke early to prepare her mother's home for their guest. She had woken at six-thirty, made coffee, and begun to clean the house while her mother slept.

*I know she'll be anxious to see him. It's good she's sleeping. It's a big day.*

Just after eight, she could hear her mother moving in her bedroom.

Patricia poured a cup of coffee, climbed the stairs, turned down the hallway to her mother's room, and knocked on the door.

"Yes?"

"Good morning."

"Is it?"

"It is."

"If you say so."

"I do. And it will be a lovely day."

"You're not young enough to feel that hopeful, Patricia."

"Mother!"

"Oh, come on. I'm just kidding."

"You have a terrible sense of humour."

"Or maybe you're too strident to see what's actually funny?"

"I'm not doing this."

"Doing what?"

"Arguing with you."

"Are we arguing? I thought we were playing."

"This is never fun for me."

"You always had a hard time having fun. Maybe it's an allergy. We should get you checked by a specialist."

*Be patient*, Patricia told herself. *She's just worried about today. Nervous. And this is what she does when she's nervous.*

"May I come in? I'm tired of speaking through a door. I brought you some coffee."

"Why didn't you tell me? I would have let you in right away."

Patricia found her mother in a robe and going through her closet. She didn't turn when her daughter entered but reached out a hand behind herself. Patricia shook her head and wrapped her mother's outstretched fingers around the warm mug.

Margaret turned to her daughter, smiled, and tipped her head to one side.

"Thank you, darling."

"I love you, Mom."

"I love you to the moon and back, my Patricia."

Patricia embraced her mother.

"I always loved it when you said that to me as a child. And I still do."

"I know, darling."

"Can I help you pick a dress?"

"No, I've been dressing myself for years. I think I can manage."

"Okay. Well, I'm going to get ready myself, then, so I can catch the next boat."

"You do that, Patricia."

"We'll be back in a couple of hours."

Her mother turned back to her closet, and Patricia watched her for a few moments before throwing a parting thought at her mother.

"We don't choose the wave of history we find ourselves in. When I was younger, I thought life was an ocean for me to travel on, but now I know we're born into rolling waters and we can only do our best to navigate the storms."

Neither woman spoke for a few seconds, and then Patricia closed the door behind her and made her way to her childhood bedroom, where she was staying, to get herself ready.

She boarded the 1 p.m. ferry to the mainland in her Toyota Corolla. She parked her car and stepped out of it after the horn blew to signal the boat's departure.

She sighed as she climbed the stairs to the second-storey deck. *I can always feel myself relaxing on the boat. Since I was a kid. It was maybe more relaxing than being on the island itself. The departure from the mainland and being on the water. It always feels like a relief from something I didn't know was troubling me.*

She was surprised at how easily she recognized him at the train station. She had looked him up online, but it was more than that. It was as though a charge of energy swept through her as soon as she glanced at him. She felt it even before she consciously processed that it was him.

*He moves slowly. Resisting being here maybe. Trepidatious. Maybe that's it. I don't blame him.*

Brendan spotted her too. *She's tall, like Margaret and me, and she has her mother's beauty. But wild hair like me. I shouldn't be so nervous.*

"Hello, Patricia."

She said nothing. This surprised even her.

"Patricia, I'm sorry."

She quickly walked to her father and threw her arms around him.

"You're here! I can't believe you're here. Thank you."

She held his face in her hands and searched it.

Brendan placed a hand on the back of her head. *She's assertive. But more open than Margaret or I could have been at her age.*

"My beautiful girl."

When she released him, he stepped back to look at her. Each could see tears forming in the other's eyes.

*Don't make it strange*, she told herself. *Talk to him.* "How was the trip?"

"It was good. It's a long haul. But pretty. From here to there. The sights make it worthwhile. And a night in Montreal is always fun. It's teeming with life in a way that New York isn't, you know? New York feels more like everyone is busy and they want you to get out of the way, but in Montreal it always feels like a Saturday. As though you might stumble upon a party at any moment and be invited in."

Patricia laughed. *I can see why Mom fell for him. Handsome. He's big. Strong. But there's such kindness in his eyes.*

"Well, can I give you a hand with your bags?"

"No need. No need at all. But thank you."

They made their way out of the station and to Patricia's car.

"So, are you hungry or anything? If not, I guess I could just take you to her house."

"No, I'm fine, thanks. Yes, let's get to the island. I guess that's why I'm here."

Patricia sensed some strain in his voice. "It's going to be fine, Dad. Nothing to worry about."

"Oh, it's not worry. It brings up a lot of issues. Coming back here. And knowing what I know. It's like a jumble of cords behind the TV. They're all mixed up together. Typically, that makes me want to retreat into myself and get away from here. But I can't. I'm being asked to do just the opposite of that, aren't I?"

"I guess you are. It's like she's been shipwrecked on that island. Alone. By choice, mind you, but shipwrecked nonetheless."

She glanced over and saw a cloud passing over the features of his face. *The poor bastard. I was looking forward to this day as a joyful one. And of course it's more complicated for him. Of course it is. I'm a fool for not thinking of that.*

"I'm sorry to come at you with all of this," she said.

"It's okay. I'll be fine." Brendan took a deep breath.

When they arrived at Margaret's house, they found her out front, cutting flowers in the garden. Peonies. She stopped when she saw them. Stood straight from her bent position. A hint of a smile passed over her face.

He caught his breath. To see her standing among the flowers in a dress. Still so tall, formidable, and beautiful. He quickly stepped out of the car.

"Margaret," he said with a sigh. *She seems insecure and defiant. Just like when we were kids. I always felt special for getting past that. And that she let me.*

"Brendan," she responded and cocked her head to the side. "Are you just going to stand there?"

"For a moment, if you'll allow it."

"You look like you've come a distance from the boy courting me with grease beneath his fingernails and a rental on Horsey Bay."

"It is a long way in so many ways, and at times, like this, I still feel like that boy."

"You do?"

"I do. And you?"

"I rarely felt like a girl when I was a girl."

"With many people, you were never a child, were you?"

"I suppose that's fair."

"But with me, at times."

"I suppose."

Brendan didn't want to continue this cautious circling. *She's so guarded. She hasn't offered me a drink or invited me inside.*

Then he remembered the flowers.

"Hold on!" he said, and turned back to the car.

"Okay, come inside when you're ready." She walked to the front door of the house.

He opened the rear passenger door and retrieved the flowers in their wrapping. When he came back, Patricia said, "I'm going into the village. To the restaurant. I'll give you two some time."

"Okay. Thanks, my dear. For everything."

Patricia smiled. It was such an odd pleasure to see her parents together. It made her feel a sort of completeness she never knew she could feel until this moment.

As he entered the house, he announced, "Camellias. They seemed appropriate."

"Why's that?" she asked.

"Oh, you know."

"I don't," she said with a wry smile.

"They're the flowers that symbolize longing."

Margaret looked away. Out the window and across the lake. "I know something about that."

Brendan watched her. *I can look at her now, without recrimination. I want to touch her. Hold her. But I can't. She doesn't want it.*

"Me too."

"Do you?"

He made sure he made eye contact and said, "Yes. Yes, I do."

Margaret looked away.

"Could I get a drink?" he asked.

"Of course. I'm sorry. I'm so distracted."

"It's fine. Don't worry."

"Coffee? Tea? You always liked tea!"

"Maybe something a little stronger?"

"Right."

"Maybe a whisky?"

"I have a bit of Scotch."

"That would be fine. Many thanks."

"How would you like it? "

"With a dash of water, if you don't mind. Will you join me?"

"I will. I've grown to like it as well."

Margaret poured their drinks and Brendan lifted his glass. "To old friends."

She looked at him steadily. He remembered this gaze.

"And Patricia?" Margaret asked.

"She's wonderful, Margaret. You did well."

"I hope so. I worry, of course. All parents do, I suppose."

"That's true."

"And you have a son?"

"I do. Devin."

"Another fine Irish name. You know, my mother told me that her father was Irish. Catholic. I knew he was Irish, but we were always reminded that we were Protestants. He died when I was young. He became a Presbyterian. Reluctantly. It was a constant problem, a tension in their marriage. She felt bad about being so hard on me. . . But you and I never got married."

Brendan sighed. "Well, I would say—"

"I deserted you, Brendan. I just knew—"

He interrupted her. "I did that. I didn't know what else to do. It seemed like the world had no room for the likes of us."

"I need to tell you that very soon after you, I did date someone else. Just to make my parents stop pestering me. And I never explained it to you."

"You don't need to explain anything. I just about died out on the ice, and it put it all in perspective. Not only wasn't this a place for us, it wasn't a place for me. At least that's what I thought back then."

Both fell silent.

Margaret was rubbing the palm of her left hand with her right thumb. Brendan took hold of her hand in his. He held it and then gently rubbed it. "You've been doing that since we were kids. I always thought you looked nervous and wanted to take your hand in mine, but I was too shy."

Margaret smiled. *Let him do it. Let yourself be comforted for once in your life, would you?*

"But *you* did," she said.

"What's that?"

"Get married."

"I did, I suppose."

"There is so much we missed, isn't there?"

"I missed her. Patricia. Along with you. That was a blow to find out."

"I know. I'm sure."

"I've known for a while now. But I didn't know how to come back here. I had a life in the city. I assumed she was mine, but when I never heard from you, I doubted it, or thought you didn't want me around, so I let it go."

"If you had stayed, could we have been happy?"

"I don't know. Do you think we could have been?"

"I didn't think I could leave my family, but I did, didn't I? Maybe I needed to choose it."

"As opposed to just agreeing with me."

"Maybe. I feel terrible saying it. But I'm too old to lie."

"I had convinced myself that if I could be with you, I could be happy, but I would have still wanted to leave. I had plans for us to leave."

"And would I have done it?"

"I don't know. The deck was stacked against us."

"*Then* it was." Margaret stiffened. "And what happened then with your wife? Patricia said it ended a few years ago."

"Honestly? I think she never knew me. And I never made the effort to truly know her. She met me as I was becoming known as an artist. I appeared so . . . well, I appeared as something. And she liked that thing. That apparition."

"The artist."

"The *successful* artist. It meant something to her that it never meant to me. And I felt like that's what she wanted to see. And in fairness, that's all I let her see. I was so guarded."

"Because of what I did to you."

"Not at all. I mean, partly, yes. I wasn't looking for a wife. I had just decided I wasn't."

"Because I hurt you."

"No, that's not—"

"Just say it already, Brendan. Just say it. We're not children anymore. You can just say that I broke your heart. You couldn't trust another because I broke it. I was awful. You can just say it now. Just say it already."

"No, I won't, because—"

"Because you're a decent man. You don't think I've said it to myself for years. I was a coward and I lost you. I was a fool. Just say it."

"Margaret, stop it, now. I won't say it, because it's not true. I didn't want a wife because I already had one. I didn't need a service or scrap of paper to know I was wed to you. Apparently, I didn't even need you by my side. I was your man. I knew it. I could never be another's. Not in that way. Not fully. But Mary wasn't looking for that. And I did care for her. I did. And she was a good mother to Devin. It was a partnership. A friendship. But I was already . . . Margaret, I was already married to you is what I wanted to tell you."

He finally looked at her. He had been concentrating so much on his own words to ensure he got them out right that he hadn't noticed she was crying.

"Don't cry," he said. "Please don't cry. I'm so sorry. I didn't mean to hurt you."

"Hurt me, you fool? It's the most wonderful thing. . . It's the . . . I always loved you, Brendan. I could never marry either. Marry another either, I mean."

She threw her arms around him and pressed herself into his chest.

"I love you, Brendan," she whispered.

"I love you, my wife. . . What a thing to say to you at last."

# 15. Their Departure

## May 6, 1847—Leadmore West Townland, near Kilrush, County Clare

"It's May now," Dennis said to James and Genevieve as soon as he saw them that morning. "We need to be on the next ship to reach Canada before winter sets in there and the rivers freeze up." It was the first week of May. "I've gone into Kilrush and spoken with one of the passage brokers who can be trusted. There will be a ship leaving in four days from now."

Dennis and Ellen had walked down to James and Genevieve's cottage to share their thoughts.

*They need to be on it. There's no way around that,* thought Dennis. *I know something's happened with James. He disappeared for those few days and came back with nothing but silence. He won't speak. He just sits fuming by the fire or wants to be alone down by the sea. It's been hard. With both his parents gone so quickly. They say Liam will be shipped off soon enough. Nothing we can do, they keep telling me.*

Dennis and Ellen had been having heated conversations with James and Genevieve for days, trying to convince them to board a ship, especially now that Genevieve was pregnant. James had heard about Frank Mulligan scraping together whatever money he could find to book passage for himself and his mother only to find he had been duped. The man who took his money had claimed he was a broker, but he was a crook out of Liverpool who wandered the countryside selling tickets to ships that didn't exist. When Frank and his mother reached the docks, they searched for days for the ship, the *Withrow*. That made James distrustful of the brokers.

"The only future you have is on one of those ships, there's no way around it," Ellen said now. "For you two and the wee baby." Both she and Dennis could see how pleadingly Genevieve looked at James.

"So give up, then?" James asked. "That's what they want from us, isn't it? To just give up and die or leave." He searched their faces and could sense he wasn't making much progress. "It's the truth. We're coming on to two years of the plants spoilin' and the fevers, and starvation, and what do they send? Troops. More and more soldiers. Just to keep us under their heel. Like we have much fight in us now. Dead and dying is all we are. And that's what they like."

"Maybe so," his grandfather said. "Maybe so. But what should we do? It's their world. We can't create much in the way of options now for you. I wish we could. I do. But we can't. And as bad as the last year or two has been, it's going to get worse for us. All of us. A ship to Canada is a fresh start. You can find a way down to America there. Free of the Brits. They need us there. To settle the place and so on. There's no future for a silversmith here. But there? Maybe. If we go, Vandeleur said he will help pay the passage."

"Isn't that a thing?" James responded. "Such a benevolent landlord. We're starving, and he's not willing to forgo the rent but will give us a few shillings to go away. A humanitarian, without a doubt."

"It could be worse, and it is for some, son. Trinity College itself, I heard, owns land in Clare and is demanding tenants pay their rent no matter what. Throwing them off the land if they haven't the money. Can you believe that?"

"Sadly, I can."

"James, I'm weaker each week, and the baby needs me to be strong," Genevieve offered. "You know that to be truth. And what will I feed the baby when it arrives? We can't make it here. Maybe we can go down to America. Some have. My cousin has done it herself with her husband."

James said no more, and his grandfather could sense he was accepting the reality of it. *No easy feat,* he thought, *when you're twenty or so. Nor should it be. He has strength and ideas. And he's going to need them.*

Ellen took her husband's hand and the two began to walk back home.

That evening, James appeared at their door and announced they would go to Canada.

When the day arrived, the four of them made their way to the docks at Kilrush. James and Genevieve were so distracted by the journey ahead that they didn't notice Dennis and Ellen were not carrying any belongings.

Dennis had originally booked passage from Limerick, but their landlord, Vandeleur, found it pricey, so he booked them passage from Limerick to Liverpool and from there to Quebec.

When they reached the docks, Dennis took his grandson by the arm and stepped away from the women.

"Take this with you," Dennis said. He handed James a small purple pouch. James opened it to find a necklace with a silver pendant in the form of a shining circle that at the bottom turned into two hands meeting each other. On the reverse of the device, it read "O'Sullivan" in fine script.

James didn't understand what was happening. His grandfather stared into his face as James took the links in his hands.

"I had it made it with Davis himself to remind you, you know, of us, but also yourself, really. Take it with you, son, wear it, and when we're better, and up to making the journey, we will see you in America or wherever you may be."

"Wait, now. What is it you're saying, Grandfather?"

Dennis tilted his head to the side. We're not strong enough, James."

"I won't—"

"You will," his grandfather said. "That's all there is to it. We will get by here and follow you when we can. But neither of us is well enough. And who knows, maybe I can sell a few things and come with a bit of money."

"Really?"

"Yes, it's fine. Off ya go, then. You need to be strong. For all of us. That's all you've got now, son, your wits and your strength for all that lies ahead. So many are relying on you. We don't get to choose the challenges in our lives. More often, they choose us. And this one is yours. Rise to meet it. I know you can."

Ellen knew the conversation that was happening a few feet away. She gripped Genevieve's arm and tried to hold back her tears.

# 16. Three Mornings



JJ was walking along a shore. There was a presence near him. He could feel it. He looked along the water's edge and saw nothing. He looked inland. *Was it Grand Island?* No one was there. He looked out onto the water. A slow fog was rolling over the calm lake. The presence he felt was out there. He was almost sure he could make out a figure in the fog, somehow standing on the water. But the person was leaving. And then he heard a voice break the calm. "JJ!" it screamed. "JJ!" He was pulled into the waking world.

*Where the hell am I?* He sat up on the couch in the small, cramped back office of the bar. It was located off the hallway to the washrooms. His mother was standing in the doorway. "JJ! Get your goddamn ass up and moving! It's nearly eleven. Ya gotta open up, make sure the staff are set for the day, and then get over to the island to see your great-grandfather. You know there's not much time left. You need to be there. Get your ass up and off that goddamn couch!"

"Jesus Christ, Ma, I hear ya."

"Watch your goddamn language with me."

*Mom is pissed. I know we left glasses and ashtrays out on the bar. It's not like she and Dad didn't do the same thing twenty years ago. Hell, that's how Dad met her. She was a fixture on a stool at the end of the bar. No fucking doubt about it. She's just angry. She's been angry as long as I've known her. But she loves me. She does.*

JJ sighed and got up off the couch. He caught sight of himself in the mirror and saw that he looked rough. He had stayed after closing, drinking at the bar with the staff until about five. There was always business late into the night too. But what really kept him up was a conversation he was having with himself. He had to make a difficult decision and didn't want to sit alone while he did it. So he had invited the staff to stay with him while he pondered it.

"Let me get dressed and clean things up a bit. Then I can give the team their marching orders and head over to the island."

Sally was still in the doorway. Fuming. "Fine," she said. "It's a damn mess you left here." She turned to go. "And if I see Kip Muldoon in here, I'm gonna kick your ass. I know he's dealing. Yeah, I know. I know things. Keep that goddamn shit out of the bar, JJ. I fuckin' told ya that." She was already walking away, so he didn't have to answer. He didn't want to anyway.

JJ picked up the Nirvana T-shirt he had been wearing the night before and slipped it over his shoulders. He bent over to put his running shoes on and felt dizzy. He sat up, took a deep breath, and bent over again to finish the job.

When he emerged, he found his mother heading into the kitchen from the bar with a load of glasses. So he found a rag and began to clean the bar top and empty the ashtrays. *Louise and Max will be here in the next twenty minutes. Then I can get cleaned up. I need a fuckin' shower. It will be good to be on the island. It always is. I've grown up in this place but you can't call it home. The island is home, no doubt.*

JJ saw Max approach from across the street and remembered why he'd stayed up late. He had asked Max to come over this morning to give him the orders. His mother was still tidying up. She didn't need to—JJ and his staff could do it—but to say that would invite a storm from her. He opened the door to the street and went out to meet Max, who had trotted to the curb to avoid a car. A small man, with dark hair, Max had been a few years behind JJ in school. His father was from Quebec, and the guys at school liked to remind him that he wasn't one of them. JJ always admired the way Max let it roll off of him. He wasn't a big guy, but you could tell he knew how to handle himself if pushed.

"Hey, JJ. How are ya, now?"

"Good. Fine. Ya know. You?"

"A bit of a hangover, no doubt."

"No doubt. Same. Sally's kickin' around here. So when Muldoon comes around, push him off until she's gone. She knows he's working, and if she sees him in the bar, I'm gonna fuckin' hear about it."

"Shit, okay. She knows he's working for you?"

"No. She just knows he's *working*, so she's pissed he's in the bar. We may have to shift it up a bit. Get someone new and let Kip work the truck stop or something."

"Okay, JJ."

"Thanks, Maxi. I gotta go. Family stuff. But Lou will be here soon to give you a hand."

"No problem."

"All right, then. . . And I need you to get hold of Todd." Todd Spencer was a dealer for JJ who also collected on loans he'd made that were in default. JJ used to do it himself, but after a charge of assault that he barely beat, he'd stepped back.

"Oh, yeah?"

"Yeah. It's Mikey Serson."

"He's into ya?"

"He is."

"For how much?"

"Too much. And for too long. If I let it go on, word will get out and no one will think they gotta pay back their loans. You can get hold of him?"

"For sure."

"Thanks, Maxi."

"No problem. See ya, JJ."

"Thanks again, Maxi."

JJ was about to turn away. "You know what—he deserves one last warning. I don't want it to go further than that. If he gets it from Todd, it will put the fear of God into him."

JJ went upstairs to his apartment to have a shower. Davy Byrne's Tavern stood on the main street of Thayendanegea. Its large upstairs windows looked onto the street, and he had a habit of standing at those windows for periods of time. So when he emerged from the shower, he went into his bedroom, got into some underwear, and picked out a fresh pair of jeans and a black T-shirt to put on in the living room. He dressed slowly as he looked out the window, thinking about everyone, especially his great-grandfather.

A great oak stood a half block down the street. On the corner, in a little parkette. *I always liked that tree*, JJ thought, as he looked at it. *It's nice that the town put a bench beneath it for old guys to meet there and gossip. It's kinda funny how they gossip. So why am I sad when I look at it today? That's fuckin' weird. It ain't going anywhere. It's a fuckin' tree, for chrissake. And Mikey's got it coming.*

And then the images from his dream popped into his head. *The shore. I was alone. But alone in a strange way, like I just lost something. I was sad, wasn't I?*

JJ pulled himself from his thoughts and finished dressing.

June 17, 1998—24 Norman Street, Kingston, Ontario

Patricia was in a rush to get to the island. To pick up the prescriptions for Michael O'Sullivan and catch the eight o'clock ferry, she needed to leave the house by seven, go to the offices for the nursing services to gather the paperwork, then head over to the pharmacy and be at the line-up for the boat by seven forty to be sure she got a spot.

But Kelly called just as she was on the way out the door. And as soon as Patricia answered the phone it started.

"Oh, my God, Mom, she's at it again."

"Who is at what?"

"For fuck's sake, you know who I mean. "Don't you get fuckin' started with me."

"Kelly!"

"What!"

"You know it's just because she's worried. And honey, I've got to head out for work in a few minutes."

"What's she worried about?"

"You and Jacob."

"Really?"

"Of course she is, and you have to remember that she's been through a lot. I'm going to have to go in a minute."

"Well, she stole Scraps."

"What?"

"She took the fuckin' dog. And attacked Peter. I should call the police on her."

"Is the dog missing? Is Peter okay?"

"Yes the dog is missing, Mom. She stole it."

"How do you know that she took it? And Peter is okay?'

"I know she took Scraps. Peter is fine. It's the goddamn dog I'm worried about."

"But how do you know it was her that took Scraps?"

"Trust me, I fuckin' know."

"The dog could have run off."

"No, she did it."

"Kelly, you can't accuse her without—"

"I can."

"I have to get going."

"Okay. I have to deal with Jimmy Swan anyway."

"What?"

"He's here right now. Sleeping."

"Who is he?"

"A guy from Kingston. He played some hockey and now works construction."

"But why is he *there*?"

"Because of your goddamn mother."

"What are you talking about?"

"Your fuckin' mother sent him over here, as he said, to be a sparring partner for Peter."

"Oh, God."

"He's a thug. He got thrown out of the hockey league because of all of the fights he had."

"Okay. And he has the dog?"

"Yeah, it's in his truck. He was paid by your mother to come and get the dog and to beat up Peter if Peter resisted him. And if he didn't, Jimmy should find another reason to pummel him. I fuckin' yelled at him for a full half hour to make sure he left Pete alone, and then the two of them got drunk. He's still asleep on my goddamn couch."

"Oh, my God."

"I had to feed Scraps in the truck. Jimmy said he will knock Peter out if anyone takes Scraps out of the truck, because if he doesn't bring the dog back with him, he won't get paid by your mother. Stupid bastards are still sleeping it off."

"Okay. I'll talk to your grandmother and take care of it."

"Good luck with that."

The line went dead. Patricia looked at her watch, sighed, and prepared to call Margaret. She took a deep breath to calm herself and looked out the window. If she came in hot to talk to her mother, it would only escalate the situation. It was on her, she had decided years ago, to bring calm to these situations.

She noticed a man standing across the street, gesturing to someone to come closer to him. She looked up and down the street and saw no one. He seemed to be looking at her. She looked back at the man and realized it was Michael O'Sullivan. Surprised, she went to her front door, but when she opened it, he was gone.

Patricia stood there for a minute, trying to make sense of the situation, then decided to make her call. The phone rang at Margaret's five times and went to her voicemail. "Hello, this is Margaret James. I can not take your call at this time. If you'd care to leave a message, I will return your call at my earliest convenience."

"Mom, call me back. I can't believe you did that. I mean, I know you are capable of some pretty remarkable behaviour, but sending some thug over there to intimidate family and steal a dog . . . What the hell is wrong with you? My daughter was there. Your granddaughter. What the hell? And Jacob. You say you care so much about Jacob and that dog, and that you don't want them to get hurt, and then you send over a man to attack Jacob's father. You better call this off and get your butt over there or else you're going to lose—" The voicemail system cut her off.

Patricia slammed down the phone and realized she was going to miss her ferry. She sat on her couch, put her head in her hands, and wept.


June 17, 1998—Labasheeda, County Clare


I was unsure about everything. I stood frozen in the living room because the owner of my vacation rental was gardening in the yard. I wanted to go outside but knew I needed to get myself right before I spoke to another human being. Not just my mind but my appearance. My hair was wild, and pyjamas had been creeping into my daily wardrobe. Two nights before, at a pub in Kilrush, I realized I was wearing the flannel bottoms under my jeans.

Of course, there were bigger issues that troubled me: why I was here; the work I was doing; and, most pressing, my next move. Night would arrive in a few hours. And my doubts used the cover of darkness to sneak into my life and begin their larger assault. It would be morning back home. And for me, that was Boston. A call should be coming at any time in response to a speech I had sent my boss, the governor of Massachusetts. The job was still pretty new. It was only a year and a bit since I got it.

I decided to go for a walk. I'll tell you the full story of what happened at work a little later. First, let me tell you about this morning in Boston and this afternoon in Ireland.

I had been holed up in a former schoolhouse on the Shannon Estuary that had been transformed into a rental for travellers and wayward souls like me. I finally summoned the courage to step out of one of the two front doors. This one still had "boys" written above it.

The owner, Mrs. Foley, was working away in the garden. She was one of the few people I spoke to these days, and I did my best to appear sane when I did.

"Hello, Mrs. Foley."

"Oh, good morning, Devin."

I tried to nonchalantly look for the crow. I was sure I was being hunted by the bird. Wherever I went in Ireland, it was there. Squawking at me. I was both drawn to it and loathed its presence.

"You let me know if you need a hand, okay?"

"I will."

"Okay, take care."

"Enjoy your walk, Devin."

I had arrived in Dublin almost two weeks before. My coming here was prompted by a feeling of panic that had been growing in me for days. It felt like it was gaining power and I needed to do something drastic. So I made a call to the governor's office and then went to Logan and bought a ticket for the flight that evening. What were the forces and choices that brought me here? A need for a change, guilt, anger, honesty . . . and one goddamn speech. It only needed to be a few hundred words and a few hours of my time. Instead, I spent countless hours on it and wrote several thousand words.

The insomnia was worsening. I hadn't been sleeping well for a while and couldn't sleep on the plane, no matter how many Jamesons I drank. I arrived in Dublin too early in the day to get a hotel room. I hadn't booked one before I left the U.S. So I made a few phone calls to meet people I had only read about. Namely, historians in Ireland I had found in my research to write the speech for the governor. It should have been a bit of scribbling that would only take a few hours, but it had gone on for a month and was becoming the chosen device for the ruin of my short career in professional politics. And it had taken me back to the place much of my father's family had called home: County Clare, Ireland.

After my first meeting in Dublin with a historian on Irish migration, I checked into my hotel and slept a few hours, then walked the city, ate dinner, and walked home. I stared into some books before walking the streets once more until 3 a.m. Sleep wouldn't come. In a few hours, I would have to drive to Strokestown to meet with historians and tour an estate, so I finished the bottles in my mini-bar, slept for three hours, picked up my rental car, and then became a hazard to all other motorists on the narrow roads of Dublin and the highway to my destination.

Since I was a kid, I've had to silently manage strong intuitive responses to places. I've always been ashamed of my responses, so I keep them to myself. And something about the County Roscommon estate, mixed with a hangover and sleep deprivation, while being bullied by a bird, sent me. I didn't want to give in to it, but I could feel the desperation, loss, terror, and injustice in the air. It was like I was overcome with a case of the shivers that I couldn't shake.

The ruins of a church, the grand buildings of landlords, with grounds that surrounded them to keep the local people at a distance, the tiny entrances and hidden walkways so the owners wouldn't have to mingle with the local Irish, along with the stories filled with numbers of dead, nearly overcame me. I asked to use the bathroom and slapped some water in my face just to break the dark spell of it.

Can places hold psychic energy? I can only say yes, at the risk of sounding the fool.

My days continued like this, with little sleep at night and an inescapable nap in the day. I continued with hazy meetings where my twitching eye had me winking at academics and guides while I tried to feign calm concentration.

There were joys: the people of Ireland, the walks through the beautiful countryside, and writing. I quickly became fond of the place. I felt at home. The speech I was supposed to write had turned into a sprawling series of notes on the history of Irish immigration, politics, literature, botany, mythology, fishing, economics, sailing, and a lyrical description of one man's descent into a light madness. Of course, that man was me.

I was mostly interested in spending time in County Clare to learn about the experiences of my father's family. I had found a loop I liked to walk from the village of Labasheeda, where I was staying, along a small country road that ran parallel to the Shannon Estuary, up through the hills, and back along the main road to my home. I was counting on the northern sun to revive me and the walk to tire me so I could sleep this evening.

My phone rang. I knew who it was. The previous day, I delivered my draft of the speech, and I was sure this was the governor's office calling me to talk about it. I knew they wouldn't be pleased.

"Devin?"

"Yeah."

"It's Bobby." Bobby Veneziano was the chief of staff and, along with the governor, my boss.

"I know. What's up?"

"What happened with the speech?"

"What do you mean?"

"Well, the governor is pissed about it."

I remained silent. I needed to stand my ground.

Bobby continued. "We talked about this. You gotta keep the peace."

"You mean lie."

"It's politics, Devin. You know what I mean."

I could feel my calm drifting away. So I let loose.

"It's a fucking lie—well, it's actually a couple of lies—that denies history. I mean, it could if you didn't check the facts, which is pretty easy to do."

"Devin! Devin!"

"No, Bobby. It's also just bad politics. This is gonna blow up in his face. Lying like this, and it's so easy to get caught."

"But there's room, Devin, for a grey area."

"Come on, Bobby. You know better."

"You know what? Fuck you, Devin. I covered for you when you pulled your little disappearing act a couple of weeks ago, but I'm done with this shit. I'm gonna fix the goddamn speech and you need to think about whether you should even attend the famine memorial opening. I don't think you should."

The line went dead.

I stood on the side of the road for a moment holding the phone. I knew why I was fighting with Bobby, but I was surprised at how much I didn't want to resolve it. I just wanted the fight. It wasn't even a desire to have them agree with me. Everything had changed over the last few weeks. I wanted to burn it all down. This life I had constructed for myself.

I put the phone in my pocket and turned to the wide waters of the estuary and County Limerick on the other side. There, on the near shore, a sole figure waved. Not to me, I thought. The figure paused, then waved again with greater intensity. I tried to focus my eyes. I couldn't make out who it was, but he looked familiar. No one else was out here, so he must have been waving at me. I found a gate a little ahead of me and went through it and walked into the field towards the shore and the figure. He was older. He looked like ... Yeah, it was my great-grandfather, waving to me. Michael O'Sullivan. But how? I blinked a few times, shook my head, and searched the waterside. The man was gone. No one was there. I ran to the spot on the strand where I thought I'd seen him and looked in all directions but saw no one.

My phone rang again. *Goddamn, Bobby*, I thought. I hit the green button to accept the call without looking at the number.

"You know what, Bobby . . . !"

"Who is Bobby?"

It was my father, Brendan.

"Devin?"

"Dad?"

"Yeah."

"Dad?'

"Give me a second, Devin."

I could hear muffled noises.

"Devin."

"Yeah."

"Let me speak for a minute. It's your great-grandfather. I'm sorry. He's ill. . . They don't know how much time he has left. I'm back here now. With Margaret. I know you were tight with him."

"I'll get there."

"You have to come soon."

"Okay. I'll see you soon."

"Okay, Dad."

He had no idea I was in Ireland. And it didn't seem like the moment to tell him.

I put the phone in my pocket and looked both ways along the shore once more. There was no sign of him.

"You're on your way, aren't you?" I said to the light breeze and the gulls. My great-grandfather. He would be one hundred and eight years old that year. What a man. He was an oak. For the first time in a long day, I knew what to do next.

# 17. Two Arrivals

August 9, 1847—Kingston, Ontario

"Where's the baby?"

The words came out as a low murmur. Genevieve's voice, her entire body, was weak.

"Pardon, my dear?" said the young nurse at the door of the fever shed.

"James. Where's James?"

The nurse, Sister Marie Garnier, a nun from the recently established hospital in the city, Hôtel Dieu, had to search for the correct phrase in English. "Your child is here. Sleeping." She pointed to a wooden box lined with blankets where the child slept. Marie picked up the boy and placed him in his mother's arms. Marie had been staying close to the woman and child for hours now.

Genevieve was trying to make sense of where she was. Her body ached, her head swam, and it made thinking difficult. And then memories struck her like heavy blows. *James's illness on the boat. . . The ship a nightmare of suffering. . . That island up the river in Quebec, where he seemed to be better and they let us pass. . . All of us on that barge that brought us here. . . It was so hot, with no cover. . . And this place. It's all water and trees. There's no space. . . And the baby came early. . . Here, in this town. What is this town? And where is James?*

"My husband. Where is my husband? James O'Sullivan is his name."

The young nun's face fell. *The poor woman,* Marie thought. *She doesn't recall. She has no understanding that her husband has died.*

Marie lifted the child from the wooden crate and laid him on Genevieve's chest.

"I am terribly sorry to tell you that your husband passed away two nights ago. With the fever." *I know the English words to describe loss so well now. That is what I have learned here. It sounds so much more rigid than it does in French.*

Genevieve kissed the head of the baby boy and began to weep. *I remember. We decided to call him Patrick.*

After a few minutes, Genevieve struggled to touch her face. *My arms are so long and heavy.* Her cheeks were dry. There were no tears.

"You are ill, so you have no . . . water . . . in your eyes," Marie told her, sensing the confusion.

"I can't even cry?" Genevieve asked. She turned to Marie. "Will you please take the child?"

"Certainly." Marie lifted the child and held him to her chest. *He's such a sweet child. Calm and loving. You can sense it. This is what I will miss most. It's not men and their demands and roughness but having a child of my own. I do not believe anyone considers this about us. We're almost no longer human, are we? Just servants, really, for those without anyone else to care for them.*

Genevieve had rolled over on her side and released cries that sounded more like coughs.

Marie took the child into the warm night air outside the shed. *The poor woman needs privacy. Whatever privacy she can get. All of these Irish in these sad little structures along the waterfront. What a plight these poor souls have faced. Catholics, they say, like us, but they seem so strange. Wild. Their spiritual sense seems tied to their land more than anything else. It's mixed into their sense of Christianity. So strange. Thank heavens for the mayor here. Thomas Kirkpatrick. Irish extraction himself, they say. He and the town councillors have summoned wonderful relief efforts with us. But that poor woman. I'm not sure she will survive it. I hope she will fight to stay alive for her child. This sweet boy deserves it. I will pray for her but she needs to pray herself, doesn't she?*

The baby cooed, and Sister Marie brought him back to Genevieve. "He is hungry. I'll fetch some milk." Marie made her way down to the area where supplies were kept and found some cow's milk and a small wooden spoon. When she returned, Genevieve was asleep. Marie sat the child on her knee, fed him, and looked across the water to the boats and the islands.

*There is beauty here. This is much like the valley and river of my childhood near Quebec. It's nice to find that in this madness. They say it's some two thousand souls arriving here by those open boats each week. Most in terrible condition. Perhaps that's why the Lord sent us here. Just after we arrived, these Irish began to appear. Malnourished, ill, destitute. This must be the Lord's plan for us.*

After a few minutes of feeding, the child fell asleep in her arms. Marie didn't want to leave him in the crate by Genevieve's bed, so she walked with him for a while. As the night darkened, she returned to find Genevieve still sleeping. She sat by the bed with Patrick and after praying fell asleep in the chair.

The chattering birds woke Patrick, and his movements stirred Marie. It was just before sunrise. She smiled to see him looking at her face. She gave him a small kiss on his nose and turned to Genevieve, who was still lying on her side.

Marie placed a hand on Genevieve's shoulder and whispered, "Good morning, madame." There was no reply. There was no sound at all from the woman. Not even the sound of breathing. She placed Patrick in his crate and rolled Genevieve over.

Marie fell to her knees and said a prayer over the woman. "Hail Mary, full of grace . . ."

When she completed it, she stood to find the priest and a doctor but remembered Patrick.

She knelt down, picked up the child, held him to her, and wept. "Your mother is gone, my poor child," she said in French. "As is your father. But I for one will ensure that you are not alone in this world. You have my solemn oath that I will ensure your health and well-being for the years to come."

With that, she kissed Patrick on the top of his head, held him to her chest, and went to find Father Beauchamp and one of the doctors.

# 18. One Funeral

### June 17, 1998–Labasheeda, County Clare

I made my way to my rental in Labasheeda and packed my belongings while ignoring two calls from the governor's office. I found a flight heading out from Dublin the next morning for Toronto. My mind turned to that image of my great-grandfather I saw on the strand. I wasn't shocked by it. Those sorts of things always happened to me. Since I was a kid. I would know what people would say before they spoke. I had those dreams that would come true. I never knew what to do with it. And I never told anyone.

My mind turned to my family. I hadn't seen my father in a while now. Maybe four months. Our relationship seemed to have more gaps than it did time together. Especially as time has passed. As I started the drive alongside the estuary, I thought about him as one of those boats making their way toward the sea. I was standing on the shore and he was slowly departing towards some distant land. It wasn't always like this. As a boy, I remember playing with him quite a bit. As soon as he was home, he would want to spend time with me. Mom took care of the day-to-day business of meals, bedtimes, and appointments, but it was Dad who was the light, the laughter, and a great portion of the love I felt.

But that wasn't the case between the two of them. As a teenager, I began to notice that there were words unsaid between my parents. A language of anger and letdowns was being stifled. And it was then that he quit spending time with me. Maybe he knew I was done playing and now he would have to talk to me. And that's when he started to drift from the shore. It wasn't a surprise that the year after I went to college, I got the phone call about their separation.

I miss him. Yeah, that's what it is. I just miss him. But I don't want to chase him. This was probably the most intimate conversation we'd had in ten years. The letter a year earlier about Margaret and finding out I had a half-sister was a close second. But it wasn't emotional. It was factual. As he said, he owed it to me to tell me. Blood is what you make of it. I don't know her. And nothing's been made of our relationship. I, for one, haven't tried to reach out to her. I know I should.

My phone rang again. *I wish I could go now*, I thought. *I want to leave it behind me, and drive away with a soundtrack playing in the car. Instead, I know they're going to keep calling me. The memorial opens in eleven days. I could just tell them about my great-granddad and they would understand.*

But then a wave of anger rolled over me. *I don't care if they understand. I don't want to do this anymore. It's been a year of this shit. Compromises for no good reason. Bending to pressure and just to build a greater fiefdom for David. He's not a bad guy, but it seems like he contracted that disease unique to politicians. Once they get a smidge of influence, they just want to make sure they keep that power and get more. The aversion to great legislation and change is caused not by greed but fear. The fear of losing what you have now. And that's hardly leadership.*

I pulled over in Portlaoise for gas and to get something to eat. Next door to the restaurant an internet café was still open, so I decided to go in and check my email. And there it was. Titled "Moving Forward."

Dear Devin,
We thank you for your last year of service to the Governor's office. You have been a great speechwriter and social policy adviser. Given the direction you would like to go with your career, we will be hiring a new person to fulfill your post. We wish you all the best in your future endeavors.

Sincerely,
Robert Veneziano

Chief of Staff
Governor David Pearce

*Like so much garbage, I suppose. That's all I am to them. He will step up to the podium and deliver a speech that is built on a lie that is growing faster by the day. And not only is the lie an affront to my family and friends but it's going to be used to stomp others.*

I leaned back in my chair. *Yes, it's tough to hold on to the job with the rise of the Republicans, but goddamn it. What are we actually about— other than winning?*

I got back into the car. But on the passenger side. I opened my laptop. I clicked on the document I had been working on since my arrival in Ireland. Back then I was writing to try and keep myself from losing my mind. *The Boston Globe* would like to know about this, I thought.

An hour slipped by as I clicked away on the keyboard. I paused and thought about my destination and my great-grandfather, typed a few more words, and then stopped.

Once I was back on the road, I felt a sense of urgency.

*I'm running to something and away from something at the same time*, I thought. *I get the second part but not the first. I'm rushing to see my great-grandfather while there's still time. Maybe that's it. He would be so nice to me when I was there in the summer. Teaching me how to fish, showing me the animals and the lighthouse. I always wanted to say longer. But Dad . . . He was so funny about it. Actually, sad. It's strange how close to each other sad and funny seem to be. He never wanted to be there. And it bothered everyone. It's not his fault. I could tell he didn't mean any harm by it.*

After the first good night of sleep in some weeks, I boarded the plane and arrived in Toronto early in the afternoon. I picked up a rental car, grabbed some lunch, and was on my way. I should be there by dinner, I thought. I looked forward to that ferry ride. I had put on a CD and tried to focus on the music. I'd been listening to the Pogues almost exclusively since I'd arrived in Ireland. I was always attracted to Irish music, but lately it was Shane MacGowan's snarling poetic lyrics that hit me. But my mind wandered back to my situation. *What's next for me? It's like there's a change of weather coming—you can feel it in the air but you don't know what it is. God knows I'm done in politics. Word will get out about me. It's funny, when we don't know what will happen, that we assume the worst. So I can't think about what comes next.*

As I waited for the ferry, my mind turned to my great-grandfather. *How do you talk to someone who is to die soon? What do you say? Goodbye, I guess. That's all there is left to say. We've always been good with each other, so there's nothing we need to resolve or say.*

I stepped out of the car as the ferry sounded its horn and began its journey across the water. The sun was setting in the west. The moon was full. I climbed the stairs that led to the deck. The city of Kingston faded and twinkled. I loved seeing the lights of the city. Especially the headlights of cars moving in the night. Travelling through the dark.

It had been a few years since I'd been back to the island. Seven, I think. It was the longest I'd ever been away from the place. Why would I do that? I had always loved it. I'd become quite good at denying myself the things that brought me joy.

I tried to take in the changes on the island as I drove to my family's home. There seemed to be fewer farms. Some of the small roads were so overgrown, they looked like narrow laneways. Sumac and tall grasses had taken over. The barns that remained were mostly falling in upon themselves. A tractor and plow rusted alongside a hand pump standing in one yard, though the house was gone. Only one herd of cows so far. More cottages dotted the shore. The land reclaimed itself, swallowing the rubble of homes. Nature had taken such a firm hold, there was barely room for memory. It blotted out the objects that would awaken recollections for those that had lived here.

A sign for the lighthouse. It was a tourist attraction. *What would strangers think of this place?* I wondered. *What would they truly know? How much did we want known? My Canadian family seems so inclined to resist being understood. Or even seen.*

There were a number of cars in the driveway when I arrived. I counted five. I was surprised at the noise from within the house.

I stepped through the door into the kitchen and a din of voices. A gang of family members was sitting around the table.

"Look who's here! The American!" Joseph exclaimed.

His son, Joseph Junior, or JJ, as everyone called him, chimed in. "What the fuck! Get your skinny white ass over here!" JJ was the closest thing to a brother I had, and I was pleased to see him. We spent our summers together as kids, and as we grew older we would visit each other outside the family events.

I laughed, and so did my father. He was the first to get up from his chair, while Colin, Eva, and Sarah looked on.

"Look at you," my dad said, standing in front of me for a moment and then embracing me. A deeper and longer hug than any I could remember. It was a strange but welcome surprise. I could sense the emotion in it. It had been over five years since he and my mother separated, I thought, as we stepped away from each other.

He had changed. I was initially worried about him after my mother left and tried to talk to him, but he remained tight-lipped about it for some time. Refusing to speak about the details or his feelings. It was clear that Mary left the marriage. Not him. And maybe for someone else. She had also grown distant from me and embraced a new life of parties and other events with her new beau. Frank, the lawyer, was introduced to me only six months or so after she moved out of the house. He didn't like it when I asked if his specialty was divorce. But my mom seemed happier. I never felt at ease in the world she aspired to join on the Upper East Side of the city, but I didn't give her any grief about it. And Frank seemed to be part of the equation that led to her joy.

Brendan whispered, "My son."

I smiled and said, "Hi, Dad."

I watched as my father cleared his throat and rubbed his eyes, but then I was tackled by someone on my left side. I regained my balance, looked down, and found my cousin, JJ, wrapped around my waist.

"Fuck, cuz, you're all pointy corners and shit," JJ announced.

I laughed and said, "Get off me, ya thug."

"Christ, you could call my last girl, Darla, a thug compared to you."

"Get outta here."

Sarah stepped in. "Settle down, JJ. You're like a raccoon in the cupboard, I swear. Let the poor boy breathe."

"Sorry, Grams."

I loved my summers as a kid with JJ. My parents would send me to the island for at least three to four weeks. JJ's parents did the same. And we were quick friends, sharing a love for the outdoors and sports, being on the water, fishing, helping with cows, wandering the property. It was a place of such peace and adventure for me. I remember when my grandfather told me that the island was roughly the same size as Manhattan and how shocked I was. There was nothing about the two places that could be the same, I thought. They were opposites of each other in every way. And although New York had its charms and thrills, it never brought me the joy I could experience here.

JJ was only a year younger. As boys, I was a little bigger than my cousin, but as we reached manhood, I stayed relatively thin while JJ bulked up with weightlifting. I suppose he needed to have a significant presence for the sort of work he started doing. It was clear that we were related, sharing the same pointy chin, thick wavy hair, and large frames.

I figured out what sort of "work" he was doing when he started skipping high school and visiting me in the city with money in his pocket. It was the summer after Grade 11 that I found out he was hustling pool games, loaning money, and dealing. That September, when I went back to school, JJ didn't. He had been making so much money, he didn't see the point of school. And I guess my aunt and uncle accepted it. It always made me sad, because JJ was smart. Not just street smart. He could learn things fast, but no one seemed to care about teaching him.

A part of me knew that JJ's path was close to mine. I had gotten into some trouble as a teenager, and only a couple of choices separated my life from the world he lived in now.

By the time I graduated from university, JJ was a major force in the narcotics trade in the area and had built up his loan business. All from his bar. He must have had a dozen people working for him. Part of me was proud of him for his entrepreneurial acumen, but more than anything I worried about him. And I made sure I knew what he was up to. Just loans, coke, and weed.

From that time onward, I always worried when the phone rang late at night. My mind would turn to him. Was he in trouble? Had he been arrested or worse?

My great-grandmother, Sarah, hugged me. Eva, my grandmother, followed her. As did my grandfather, Colin.

"Well, we're sure pleased to see you," Eva said.

"I'm so glad to see you, and to be here."

"Good boy. You've always been a good boy."

"Thanks, Grandma."

"It's good to see you, Devin," Colin offered.

JJ stepped in. "Drink? You need a drink. I'll make ya a whisky and ginger."

"And eat," said Eva. "Let me make you a plate."

"Thank you both. And it's great to see you too, Grandpa."

"I worry about us all without him. He's our north star," Colin said, and I could see tears forming in his eyes.

We all fell silent, and I put a hand on my grandfather's shoulder.

A voice called from upstairs. "Who's that, now?"

My father spoke up. "I'll tell him that Devin is here."

I had started to follow my dad to the stairs when I heard a knock at the door. A woman, maybe ten years or so older than me, was standing at the door. I could see her through the glass, and she could see me, but no one else could see her. I shrugged and waved her in.

"Hi, I'm Patricia. I'm with home care. To see Mr. O'Sullivan. Michael. I know he hates it when I call him Mr. O'Sullivan."

"I can let my father know. He's just upstairs. He can help you out."

"That would be great, thanks. Sorry, your father?"

"Yeah," I replied. She was trying to say something else, so I paused, and so did she. So I continued making my way up the stairs.

I approached my great-grandfather's bedroom and heard a strange sound. A muffled sob, I thought. I stopped in my tracks. I didn't want to interrupt them.

"It's okay, Brendan, it's okay. It's not your fault," my great-grandfather was saying. "There's an untamed quality to us. And it's good and bad. And neither. As if the crest of the wave could reform the entire great lake. I can see that now. It's what drove your brother. Nothing you did.

"You know that we're here today because I was troubled by voices and dreams, and it moved me to act like a maniac, hauling that lighthouse here myself with one horse and battering myself on the winch just to get it done. I was driven. Mad. Only your grandmother knows that I turned myself into a bloody pulp doing it, and it took me some time to figure out that it was done for us, for our family. Ask your father that story. Ask him why the lighthouse mattered so much. It took me some time to figure it out, and then a little longer to tell him.

"But he's been wrapped in guilt and shame over his choices. And I see the same for you. And you get locked up inside yourself. You think the world is upset with you, but it's not. You need to learn to love life again and show your dad how to do the same. Free him. No one else can do it. We are not a people of forgiveness. We're a people of truths and stubbornness, or character, depending on the day. And we're the worst for not forgiving ourselves.

"Okay. . . Thank you," my father said, his voice uneven.

"You're all right, now. You're all right. Let me see that boy of yours."

I felt terrible for overhearing all of this but relieved to know more about these men. It was the first time I had heard my father cry. It was a strange sound.

I heard him coming to the bedroom door and started walking towards him to make it seem I had just got there.

"Oh, hey, Dad."

"Son . . . why don't you say hello to your great-granddad," he said, clearly still emotional from their exchange.

"Okay, then."

We both stood in the hall, looking away and then at each other. I wanted to say something to comfort him, but to do so would have meant letting on I had overheard something not intended for me. So I simply stood there. Hoping, I suppose, that he would speak to me as he had to his grandfather.

He spoke first. "Right. I'll see ya downstairs." He carried on down the hall to the stairs. I watched him go.

I needed to say something. "See ya. . . And there's a woman down there. I guess she's a nurse or something. She's here to see Grandpa."

He stopped and turned back to me. "There is?"

I was surprised at his tone. *He seems suddenly more solemn*, I thought.

"Yeah, what's the big deal?"

He began to walk towards me. "I don't know how to say this the right way, so I'm just gonna say it. That's your step-sister. She's a nurse. Just like her mother was. Margaret. As I said in the letter, I wanted you to meet her. But not this way."

I was stunned. "Okay, then. Well, I guess I met her. . ."

"Right. I'm sorry, son. After you see your grandfather, you can properly meet her."

"Okay," I said.

I turned towards the room feeling annoyed—with my father but also with so much more. Why hadn't he told me she was coming today? Or that it could happen? Letdowns were becoming more and more a part of my experience. As were the complications. I had this growing feeling that the world was closing in on me. Just a few years before, the world was an open expanse of possibilities, and lately those possibilities seemed to be dwindling, moments of joy and success being replaced by the awkward and mundane. It was as though I was missing out on something but didn't know what it was. And this was just another example. I had finally met my only sibling and didn't even know it. There was no connection or emotion. It couldn't have been less intimate or moving.

But I had to put it behind me. I needed to focus on my great-grandfather.

Before I stepped into my great-grandparents' bedroom, I was surprised to see that my father was still standing at the top of the stairs, watching me.

I sat in the chair by the bed, still warm from my father's body. My great-grandfather looked very similar to how I remembered him. There was still an energy about him. Even as his body was still. You could see the light and ideas dancing in his eyes.

"And there he is, isn't he?" he said.

"Hi, Grandpa."

"Look at you," he said with a smile.

I laughed.

"A full-grown man now, aren't you? And I heard you have quite a job writing for the governor of Massachusetts. Isn't that a thing? Do you like the writing, then?"

"That is one of the parts I liked the most."

"And the governor, is he a good man, then?"

"I don't know . . ."

"You said *liked*. As though it was in the past. Are you done with him, then?"

"Yeah, I think I am."

"Well, there you go. What I know of politics, and it isn't much, is that it's a tough business. The great ones are a rare thing. And by *great*, I mean worth a damn. . . And then they shot the Kennedys."

"That's fair."

"Well, we could use a writer, couldn't we?"

"Who's that?"

"Our family and the like. To tell our tales."

"I would love to hear them."

"Good. I think it helps us. It's a roadmap, having the stories."

"I think I get it. And the stories matter. I want to hear them."

"So would I," he said, and laughed. "But tomorrow. I'm tired now. We will all let loose if we're lucky to become spirit alone. I look forward to it, Devin, I do. I'm so young in here," he said, pointing to his chest. "It's just this old machine I'm in is done. I hope everyone gets what I feel coming. And maybe I will join the spirits that have hounded and comforted me my whole life. Those creatures I told you about as a boy. The sprites on the old mountains that were here. Remember? It just came to me. Spirits again. Speaking. I'd enjoy being a mischievous little sprite. I sense them in you, the spirits. And I think it's up to you to keep us together. I've failed a bit. I can't speak to others like you can, Devin. I wish I could, but I can't. It's yours now. I still believe this place is a balm for us all. It's a home for our drifting, searching souls. I believe it's the closing of the circle for us. Of our lives. The end we've been seeking. We need this land and water to temper us, dear son. To make us whole. We're best then and can give so much. But we need to be tempered. And we deserve some peace. The circle closed so we can be made whole. You know it. I know you do. I love you, my boy. I love all of you. . . But I have to rest."

He closed his eyes and I laid a hand on his chest. Then he looked at me again and smiled. I wept as I got up. "My God, we all love you. Rest, Grandpa, and let's speak tomorrow."

He began to fade into sleep. "Rest . . . Yes, rest," he said quietly. "Where there is love there can be rest."

I came slowly down the old wooden stairs, listening to them creak beneath me. I wanted this moment to stay with me. I needed it to last. *It's funny*, I thought, *how I can feel loss and joy at the same moment.*

JJ met me at the bottom of the stairs. "What the fuck's up?"

I was distracted and offered a "Huh?"

"I said what the fuck? You're walking down those stairs so slow you'd think you're on your way to your execution."

"Yeah, just thinking."

"I thought you were the fuckin' smart one, and you can't fucking walk and think at the same time?"

"Fuck you," I said, and laughed.

"Come on, cuz, you just need another drink. Come on, now. You need it. You're having a fuckin' day. I heard you met your sister. Your half-sister, I guess." JJ gestured for me to follow him to the living room.

"Okay. I did meet her."

"He can talk some shit, can't he?"

"Who's that?"

"Gramps, man."

"Yeah, he's an impressive man."

"He keeps telling me to look at my hands and ask them if they're pleased with the work they do, or some shit like that. Ask my hands? Like the fuckin' things are gonna answer me."

JJ turned his hands to face each other and made them into mouths. "'So, are you happy?'" one said to the other. "'I guess so, although I mostly spend my nights strokin' his shaft. How about you?' 'I just hang mostly. I'm pretty damn useless.' I mean, what the fuck? Ask my hands?"

"Jesus Christ, JJ."

"What?"

"You only use one hand? I need two."

"Fuck you."

We both laughed.

"So, what's keeping you busy?" I asked him.

"You know, shit . . . not much."

"Whaddya mean?"

"There ain't nothing left to do here. Just, you know, mischief. All the jobs have left. The fish left." JJ looked out the window. "Lighthouses are all fuckin' automated now. And we don't have much of a fuckin' quota with the government for milk. So, what can anyone do—milk a few cows and draw pogey? There's no jobs left here, unless ya wanna work retail. I guess I could move to the city and work in some bullshit office. But who the hell would want that? . . . Sorry, no offence, cuz. But I got the bar."

I laughed. "Don't worry about it. That's rough, man. I think I'm done with the office myself."

"Shit, really?"

"Yeah, man."

"What happens next?"

"I have no fuckin' clue."

"That's crazy, man. The thing is, with people like us, it's either cops or criminals, priests or poets. Those are the options we were handed. It's just how we're built or been raised or somethin'."

I nodded. I was surprised at his insight.

I could hear the rest of the family speaking to Patricia in the kitchen. She laughed. She sounded like us. Familiar. I didn't want to go into the room. Then she announced she was going to check on my great-grandfather, and I decided to take the opportunity to walk down to the shore and have a few moments to myself.

Before I reached the door, I heard a voice call my name. "Devin. Do you have a second?"

It was my father. I turned and saw Patricia standing beside him. There was an openness and ease about her. It surprised me.

"Devin. What a way to meet," she said.

I smiled. "It's okay, I said."

"So, you know who I am?"

"I guess I do."

My father spoke up. "This is your sister, Patricia." I had to stop myself from correcting him. *Half-sister* nearly slipped from my tongue. And I could feel a growing annoyance in me at my father. Something had changed. I was clearly an outsider now. He had been spending a lot of time on the island, staying with Margaret, and obviously seeing Patricia.

And she had been taking care of my great-grandfather. And now, here I was. Back on the island after years away without the familiarity that Patricia had established with them. I knew it wasn't her fault, but I didn't like this new dynamic.

I nodded at my father. "Yes, I figured it out. Patricia, it's nice to meet you. And I'm sorry my family didn't prepare either of us for this moment."

"It's okay," she said. "I knew you were coming. They talk about you all the time."

*Damn you, Patricia,* I thought. *Why do you have to be so charming and kind?* "Ah, well, I'm glad they prepared *you.*"

"Devin," my father said, with an equal mixture of annoyance and pleading in his voice. But I had no patience for it. I knew I needed to step away for a few moments before I made a difficult situation far worse.

"Patricia, it's great to meet you. And thank you for helping my great-grandfather. I have to step outside."

She smiled at me. And my father spoke up again. "It's her great-grandfather as well, Devin."

"And thank you, Dad, once again, for helping me parse the complexity of family relationships."

Patricia blushed and looked away. Her obvious embarrassment and discomfort should have elicited a response from me, but I had little care for anyone else's feelings at the moment. I knew I wasn't handling this well.

When I got outside, I heard another voice.

"Yeah, Patricia's all right," JJ said. I hadn't known he was behind me until he spoke. "She comes all the way over to help out, you know. I mean, Granddad always checked in on them when they moved over and Patricia was growing up. They only have each other, Patricia and her mom. Well, I guess Patricia has a kid too. Their people turned their backs on them. I don't get it. I mean, I guess I do, but it's still fuckin' bullshit. But you know the island. They were taken in by us and the island. It's good for that, the island, ya know. Taking in lost souls."

I nodded. When we got to the water, I sat down and JJ sat beside me. A silence fell. It was filled with ease, understanding, and recognition of what we faced. I turned and looked back to the house and saw Patricia upstairs in my great-grandfather's room, sorting through pill bottles on the little table by the window. I gave JJ a light punch in the shoulder.

The next couple of days, I stayed at the house with my great-grandparents, grandparents, and father. Joseph had a house on the mainland, just like JJ.

It was on my third evening home, when I was at the bar for dinner with JJ, that we got the call. My great-grandfather, Mícheál O'Sullivan, after striding the planet for a century or so, took his rest. He lay down to sleep and remained so.

JJ issued a long sigh and said, "Fuck me."

The funeral was held just three days later in Kingston, with the aid of Martin's Funeral Home. "Specialists in Catholic funerals," Eva noted. Most of the island was quiet that day while the island's residents attended the funeral at Abraham's Catholic Church in Kingston.

I arrived with my father at the church as friends and family were entering the building. It was a large crowd. *Grandpa would have liked seeing all of these people,* I thought.

I spotted Patricia sitting in a pew with an older woman near the rear of the nave. As did my father. He stopped and whispered, "Margaret, Patricia, will you join us?" Margaret nodded, stood, and took Brendan's outstretched hand. They led the way to the front with Patricia and me following behind them.

This couldn't have been easy for Margaret or Patricia. I offered them a smile and reached out my hand to Margaret. "Thank you for being here. We're really pleased to have you with us." She seemed surprised and gave me a faint smile. Patricia took my hand and offered a larger smile.

The local newspaper had sent a photographer. I was surprised, and JJ pointed out that the mayor of Kingston and the local member of parliament were present as well. Word had gotten out about my father's return, and of course his success in New York had become even grander. The photographer asked to take a picture of him and put a few questions to him after the service. Dad was a little taken aback at being asked to do this at the funeral but was accustomed to these interruptions in his life.

Colin delivered a eulogy about his father that noted his dedication to family and community. That he served as a shining example to all. Much like his lighthouse. The parishioners seemed pleased with the words. The only surprise was after Colin had finished and Father O'Malley took the pulpit once more and made an announcement.

"I would ask the family of Michael O'Sullivan to join me in the rectory now."

Most of the family went there. Thirteen in total. Dad had to convince Margaret and Patricia to join us. There weren't enough seats for us, and Margaret refused to sit, so she, my father, Patricia, JJ, and I stood behind the rest of the family, who were seated in front of the priest's desk.

As we waited for Father O'Malley, JJ spoke up in a whisper.

"What the fuck is this about?"

"Joseph Jr.!" Eva said. "You're in a church."

"Sorry, but I thought I was in the house of the guy who works at the church."

Sally turned back to us. "I swear to God, boy."

"I'm sorry, but am I wrong?"

"You're not wrong, you're just a fuckin' idiot."

"And who's swearing now? Desecrating and such."

Sally got up from her seat, furious.

JJ took a step back. "I'm sorry, I'm sorry. I'll not say another fu— I'll not say another word."

"A welcome change, to be sure," Sally replied, and took her seat.

"That's enough, now," Joseph said. "The pair of you."

Sally grimaced and Father O'Malley entered the room.

"I'm sorry to keep you all waiting here."

"It's not a problem, Father," Sarah replied.

"I know this is strange, but I have a letter delivered to me by Sarah," he continued. "Isn't that right, Sarah?"

"'Tis, father. Michael wrote it nearly a week ago now. He knew the end was coming."

She began to weep, and Colin and Eva comforted her.

"This is unusual, but Michael himself was, so . . . He was clear. I was to read this letter after the service and before the burial, as it's, as he wrote, 'the only time the wild creatures will be in one room together.' Well, then, let me read it.

"'There is no greater pleasure than lying in the room where I have lived my adult life and hearing generations of you laughing and talking in the rooms just down the stairs from me. It's funny, for all of life's offerings and successes, this is what I have always loved the most— hearing you all just a few feet away.

"'I say that, knowing it has been the exception, not the rule. Our bonds are strained and loosed from each other. It's no good. We are not the better for it. And few, if any, of you seem to know it or are even bothered about it. My son Colin will need help with the place. His brothers have shown no interest. Nor their families. So, it's on Brendan and Joseph's children now. I've always said I would never sell the place. And I meant it. It's our home, hard-won. And selling it so you all get a little money is a terrible idea and a disgraceful choice. We have a home and nearly one hundred acres of land along the shore, up through the meadows, and into those enchanted woods. There's room enough for us all.

"'So, I'll tell you this. The house and property need to be passed along to my grandsons or their children or it will be signed over to the Glendon family. Kevin Glendon himself. You all have three weeks to assume ownership or it will be a great gift to a miserable bastard."

Father O'Malley paused before beginning again. "I should add that he's written in brackets here, 'Apologies, Father.' The letter continues as such: 'And it will be home to this family at all times. All are welcome for generations. And if someone takes on this home, they will have papers to sign that ensure it's passed on to a direct relative of ours.

"'We've fought to find a place like this. For generations. Most of you don't know that our family hadn't been able to own land for many generations before. And that has left us adrift. No more, I say. No more. We've something to hold to now, and you need to accept that.

"'I love you all, and this is my last request of you. It's medicine, to be sure. But a portion of the cure we need.'

"And that's it. That's all he wrote," the priest said.

The room was quiet.

I was stunned. And moved. Something in me was stirring.

JJ spoke up. "Well, shit. Ain't that a swift kick to the balls."

Sally hopped from her seat, strode to the back of the room, and slapped her son. JJ was so preoccupied, he didn't notice her approach and was genuinely surprised by the blow.

Quiet conversations between family members created a murmur in the room. We made our way out of the rectory and church without speaking to each other and avoided eye contact.

A party was held on the island, in Elizabethville, at the community hall. Another of my great-grandfather's requests. The room was packed and the bar was busy. Most of the people from the church had travelled to the island for it. There was a low hum of private conversations.

JJ interrupted it. Climbing onto a chair he had pulled towards the centre of the room, he raised a glass of beer. "To my great-grandfather and one of the best sons of bitches any of us will ever know. To Michael Peter O'Sullivan!"

Most of the crowd stopped and raised a glass and echoed his sentiment with a hearty "To Michael!"

In an hour or so, Joseph, Colin, and a few other men went out to their cars and returned with instruments, most of them guitars. After they had formed a semicircle in the corner facing the room, the songs began with "Kern River."

I took a seat near the players. My grandfather, Colin, led the musicians. He was clearly shaken, and as I listened to his rendition of "The Parting Glass," I felt I understood how much songs mattered to him. This was how he grieved. The songs allowed it to escape him, and having players with him, and family near, was his solace. I watched my uncle Joseph. A quiet man, he clearly felt great comfort hearing his father and their friends play the music.

JJ pulled a chair over and wrapped an arm around my shoulders.

"Can you believe that shit today?"

"It's been a day," I said.

"Fuckin' right it has. What are we gonna do, cuz?"

"What do you mean?"

"For fuck's sake, you know it's up to me and you, don't you? We're the only grandchildren here. I mean we're great-grandchildren. But your dad isn't coming back here. He's with Margaret and back and forth to New York. And the goddamn miserable offspring of our great uncle didn't even have the decency to show up. Chrissake, I don't know when they were last back here."

I didn't answer him, but I'd been sitting with the information since it was said aloud by Father O'Malley. I knew I needed to do something. But what? Who was I to lay claim to this house, this land? I was an American. I'd been away most of my life. It wasn't my place.

JJ interrupted my thinking. "For fuck's sake, cuz. I thought you were some sort of big speechwriter. Say something."

"I don't know, man. Do you think Grandpa would really let the place be given away? I mean, we could talk to Grandma."

"What the fuck, man?"

"What?"

"You need to honour the man's goddamn wishes. And it's fuckin' bullshit that I have to tell you that. If you weren't my cousin, I'd tell ya to shut your wet fucking mouth or I'll have it fuckin' bleedin' red."

I was shocked not by the violence of his words but by my cousin's sense of honour and decency that lay beneath them. And I was shocked that I was wrong.

"You're right," I said. "I hate to say it, but you're right. And I'm sorry."

"Damn straight I'm right."

"It's just a lot to think about."

"I get it, I get it, college, but you can't think your way outta this one. It's about doing."

I laughed. "Shut the fuck up already. You're right, I said."

"We are judged not by what we say but what we actually fuckin' do. And this is a moment of mother-fuckin' import."

"Shit, man. Did you just say *import*?"

"Clearly, I'm on a righteous rip."

"Shut up already."

JJ grinned and turned to the musicians. They were finishing a rendition of "Carrickfergus."

"Ain't that a fuckin' song?" he asked them.

The musicians laughed.

"Let me get you boys a round," I offered. "All rye and gingers?"

Allen Jenkins spoke up. "That would be great, Devin. And thanks."

"Thanks to all of you for being here. For honouring my great-grandfather," I replied.

Ken Duffy leaned against his Martin guitar and joined in the conversation. "He was a good man, good man."

"He was," Allen said. "He's left a great hole here."

The others nodded.

JJ dropped his head. I could hear him sniffing. "There won't be another like him, boys, there just won't be another."

"There really won't be," Ken said.

Tom Clarke spoke up. "I remember he liked "Why Me Lord," by Kris Kristofferson. How about I play that one, JJ?"

"That sounds right. Thanks, Tommy."

"You betcha, boys," said Tom.

The men began to play, and Jean Clarke, Tom's wife, joined them in singing the song.

The music continued through the night, with a growing crowd of people joining in the songs. At midnight, they had to close the building.

JJ and I invited those still there back to the family home, where all of us gathered, including Patricia and Margaret. I heard my father telling them he insisted on it.

JJ built a fire and set some drinks on the table in the yard. The city lights shone in the distance. The red light of the lighthouse kept capturing my attention. Its presence only seemed to illuminate my great-grandfather's absence and remind me of what he would want me to do.

As the night carried on, I left the group and climbed up the lighthouse. I remembered doing it with my great-grandfather. He always liked it. He'd sit alone, looking over the waters to the city.

"Goodbye, Grandpa. I hope you're resting in peace. You deserve it. You've only tried to bring peace and love to all who knew you."

I climbed back down after an hour or so and joined JJ, my father, Colin, Joseph, Margaret, and Patricia, along with Allen and Tom and half a dozen other islanders at the fire. They were playing "Make the World Go Away" when I arrived.

I lay on the grass, closed my eyes, and listened to the song.

*I like that I can just be quiet,* I thought. *They don't expect anything from me. They get it. We just need to be here and do what we each need to do.*

Brendan left his chair by the fire and sat on the grass beside me. He leaned back on his elbows. "I already miss him."

"Me too," I said.

"He was more than a grandfather to me. My dad struggled with some stuff, and your great-grandfather filled in the gaps. He was good that way."

"I could see that," I said.

"It's never easy. . . . Fatherhood, I mean. My father, your grandfather, struggled with it."

"I could imagine."

"But you were my light. All the play I could muster in me I shared with you. And your joy was my joy. And it's been my greatest joy, honestly."

"Really? More than your work?"

"I think so. I love making it, but for the longest time, whenever it was done, everything that had to follow just seemed like noise to me. And I knew I had to be grateful and sociable, and it just made me feel like a phony."

I nodded. None of this surprised me.

"I know I haven't been around that much," he continued.

"Yeah, I felt like you sort of faded into the distance."

"I sometimes think that I'm best at a distance."

"Don't think that. It's not true. And I don't mean to upset you, but maybe that's what makes you comfortable but it's not what makes other people happy."

"That's fair. And I hear you. And I'll make you a deal."

"What's that?"

"I won't stay at a distance anymore. I'll be in New York sometimes but here with Margaret much of the time. I will make sure I see you."

"Deal," I said.

And then we sat together in the cool summer night air, listening to the musicians play "Hands on the Wheel." I looked over at my father, who was looking back at me. We both smiled.

It was around five that I noticed the birds had begun to stir and the sky had lightened. The friends had all gone home. Only Colin, Joseph, Dad, JJ, Patricia, and I remained.

JJ spoke up. "Come on, now, a final toast to Michael, the greatest grandfather."

He led us to the sweep, thirty feet above the water. He turned to the right and the sun peeking over the waters and islands to the east.

"To Michael," Colin said. "My father."

"To Michael," the others said.

I was silent.

"Ya aren't going to toast and send your gramp's spirit on its way with love, motherfucker?" JJ said to me.

I looked around the small group and spoke. "I want to stay here. I'll take care of the house. And you're all welcome. Always. I need to know it's the same soil my family walked on and are buried in. I'm tired of being a leaf on the wind. I need to be the tree."

JJ broke the silence. "Motherfucker! Look at you, cousin!"

He wrapped an arm around my neck and pulled me towards him. I pushed him off, stood straight, and looked at him.

"I'll only do it if you'll do it with me. You can come and go as you please, but you gotta move out here and help me keep this place running."

JJ paused. "Okay. Fine. As long as you help me build a house for Patricia too. For her and her family. . . If you want it, of course, Patricia."

He was right. I wished I had said it myself. "Yes!" I replied.

We turned our gaze to her.

Patricia looked stunned. "I'm so touched by this," she said. She looked around to see nods of agreement with what JJ had just said, and tears streamed down her face.

"It sounds to me like the right thing to do," I said, and walked to her with open arms. She nodded, and I finally embraced my sister.

JJ spoke up. "All right, fucker. We've got a shit ton of work. Maybe we can have a lodge and pull some more of those U.S. dollars for fishing trips and shit."

"Not a bad idea, cuz."

"Shit, I got scores of them. You don't even fuckin' know."

"No doubt," I said, and gestured for him to come closer. He joined Patricia and me in another hug.

Patricia laughed. I was weeping. *I guess this is what it feels like to have a brother and a sister,* I thought. I never knew I wanted it so much.

I stepped away from the embrace and spoke again. "To my great-grandfather and his wit, heart, and mighty spirit. You are here with us. You're on the wind, aren't you? In the trees. And we will not forget you. You have been and will continue to be our guiding light. Raise your glasses, boys. And our girl."

"Fuckin' right, cuz," JJ said.

# 19. Two Statues

## June 22, 1998—Grand Island, Ontario

I walked back from the water's edge to the house with a new sense of purpose and clarity. I was going to live here. On an island in Canada, with my cousin and half-sister. It was strange, unexpected, and the first thing that felt right in a long time. The other thing I knew was that I wanted to write. The sun had risen and I should have been exhausted, but instead I felt renewed.

I took my laptop from my bag in my room, and while the others started making their way home or to bed, I went to my great-grandfather's study. He had kept this room, he always said, as a place to do the business of the family, but it was really a sanctuary. At least it felt like that. The books and the photos of friends, ships, and family members. The room smelled of his pipe tobacco. I breathed it in deeply.

I opened my computer and read what I had been writing since I began in Ireland. It was only a few days until the opening of the Irish Famine Memorial in Boston. I had done so much research on the subject and had much to say about it. I began to write again. The words kept coming. I heard someone in the hall and stood up and closed the door. It was nearly noon when I stopped and emerged from the study.

I wandered through the empty rooms while family members slept. I could still sense the buzz from the presence and energy of the people. Then I slept for a few hours on the couch in the study, got up, made some coffee and a sandwich, read the words I'd written, and made a few edits. I saved the document and dropped a copy into the body of an email for Victor Sousa at *The Boston Globe*. A reporter I knew. He was a good guy. He could take it to the editors.

Hi Vic,

I hope you're well.

As you know, the Irish Famine Memorial will be officially opened in a few days. Please consider the following article for publication. It's an odd piece of writing. It's not an article. More of a personal essay with public ramifications. I understand if it's not appropriate for the paper.

Thanks,

Devin

## The Trouble with the Irish Famine Memorial
## by Devin O'Sullivan

### 1. A Splinter in the Soul
*"In humans, the fathers who experienced what is most commonly noted as a trauma with a PTSD response are likely to pass along that same response directly to their children if they have been in direct contact with each other."*

I came across this bit of writing while conducting research online in an old stone schoolhouse with a dodgy internet connection along the banks of the Shannon Estuary in Ireland. I had travelled across the ocean from Boston and then, over the past few weeks, through centuries of Irish history. I was alone with insomnia, an eye twitch, and this desperate need to finally understand the forces that were tossing me around in my own life.

And I was sure I was being stalked by a crow, all the way from Dublin to the far west of the country. I was convinced he was carrying a message that I could surely decipher if I listened intently enough to his coarse caws. I could often be found coaxing the bird to make itself more clear. I did check to make sure no one was around when I spoke to the creature. So I was going mad. But I knew I needed to embrace it. It was the only way to shake off what was keeping me from reaching a better state of being. I needed to travel into that madness.

Both sides of my family are of Irish background. My mother is from Boston and my father is from an island in Lake Ontario, Canada. The Irish communities in those places often married within themselves for the reasons you likely know: religion, for one, but mostly because of limited opportunities to marry outside the Irish Catholic community. To be honest, I've rarely thought about what it meant to be of Irish descent. We always knew we were Irish. I didn't let it mean much, I guess. Until now.

For over a year, I have served as the chief speechwriter and as an adviser on some issues of social policy for David Pearce, the governor of Massachusetts. This week, Governor Pearce will deliver a speech to mark the unveiling of the Irish Famine Memorial in Boston.

My role in this project led to the end of my position in the governor's office and, I'm sure, any place in professional politics.

I've been plagued by questions the last few weeks. Namely, What sort of duty of responsibility do we owe to our ancestors? To our community? And when we find that our history was filled with insults to them and, at times, crimes against them—not just overseas but here in the lands they fled to as refugees—what do we do now?

While doing my research on the Great Hunger in Ireland (the term I have adopted from others who have dealt with the subject and which I will get into a little later) to write the speech for Governor Pearce, I became distracted by my own family names: O'Sullivan, Flynn, and Normile. And as I learned that some of my family left Ireland during the years of the Great Hunger, I was surprised that my search became a bit breathless. I felt desperate for more information. It left me anxious, troubled and deeply saddened. But as with most stories of people pressed into being refugees, there was little in the way of records. At best, a note of a birth here in America or Canada in the 1840s.

So, without much warning to my employer and four weeks before the opening of the famine memorial, I hopped a plane to Dublin. I arrived troubled, searching and burdensome to the historians I tracked down and to other patrons in the pubs. I wanted the truth about what the Irish faced in Ireland during the years that led to their mass exodus.

In Ireland, I wrote. A lot. Here's an excerpt from the speech I wrote for the governor, no part of which I expect will ever be said publicly by him.

> Our fair city of Boston, and the state of Massachusetts, have long been home to the Irish. But not a haven. Over 30 million Americans claim Irish heritage, and I'm sure Massachusetts has the most per capita.
>
> Most of us know the stories of the Great Hunger, the proper term for the Irish famine. My mind turns to the great Irish writer George Bernard Shaw and the lines from one of his plays.
>
> The character Malone states, "My father died of starvation in Ireland in the black 47. Maybe you've heard of it."
>
> A character responds, "The Famine?"
>
> Malone replies with the following. "No, the starvation. When a country is full of food, and exporting it, there can be no famine."
>
> Irish historians I respect call it An Gorta Mór. Which translates to The Great Hunger. We can't call it a famine when there was food in Ireland and the powers that be refused to share it with the starving population.
>
> Here are the details: Ireland was a colony of the English. It was the nearest and most troublesome. The Irish consistently organized rebellions over the hundreds of years of colonial rule. The country was treated like most colonies: as a place for the colonizer to make as much money as possible, regardless of the effect on the colonized. In Ireland, this meant outlawing the native

language, religions and customs, denying property rights, political representation, economic opportunity, education and more.

The potato crop, the cornerstone of the Irish diet, failed for several years, and the ruling British government accomplished little in helping those suffering. The British conquest and colonization of Ireland culminated in a catastrophe where about 1 million people died, and more than a million fled the country as refugees. The British government, throughout the famine, continued exporting food for sale from Ireland while the Irish population starved, faced disease, died and took part in one of the largest flights from a country in recorded human history.

Some didn't even complete the journey in the coffin ships, as many were called, due to deplorable conditions and the high number of deaths in them. Our great American journalist Hugh A. Mulligan recently reported on this for the LA Times. He noted that an emigrant escaping the famine for America was crammed with three others into a 6-foot-square berth. The berths were stacked three high in the holds of sailing ships that took five to seven weeks to cross the Atlantic. Some ships carried 1,200 of these steerage passengers, who were seldom allowed on deck for fresh air and exercise.

Mulligan goes on to state that many didn't survive the journey. Ships noted significant numbers of deaths due to the health of the famine victims and the conditions of the vessels. The records tell the tale. The Queen buried 137 of its 427 passengers at sea, who had died from what was noted as "famine, dropsy and fever." The Larch counted 108 dead of its 440 passengers. The Virginius, carrying 476, had 267 deaths. The Ceylon consigned to the deep 45% of its steerage passengers, the Loosthank 33%.

I share the details, as I need to be able to picture the ships and the losses to understand the impact.

"Stowed away like bales of cotton, and packed like slaves in a slave ship," wrote our great novelist Herman Melville, who was a deckhand on an Irish emigrant ship out of Liverpool in 1849. "We had not been at sea one week, when to hold your head down the hatchway was like holding it down a suddenly opened cesspool."

A dense and dark opening to a speech, I know, but compelling, I hoped. If I'm honest, I know I wanted the listener to feel what my ancestors and others from Ireland had to endure. Re-reading it, my pulse soars and my anger rises.

So when I had to return to the speech, I came at it with a head full of steam. And that boiling sentiment was met by the cool wind of the present status quo that asks us not to dwell on the past. Instead, the past is molded to fit whatever present notion the powerful choose to encourage to reach their own ends.

I was asked to bear false witness. I may sound overwrought in saying that, but it is true. The atrocities of the Great Hunger were man-made, and crimes persisted against the Irish in America and in Canada, where half of my family still lives. And in my position of (limited) power, I was being asked to lie about it. The dead rarely have a voice in politics. And I, the speechwriter for the governor of Massachusetts, could not bear to tell anything other than as much of the truth as I could muster. And it's ugly, dirty and persistent truth. I felt an obligation that I couldn't shake. Especially as I read more about the details of the Greater Hunger and the travails of my family and other families of Irish background that arrived here. And there was another reason I struggled with the speech. I'll explain that a little later.

It troubled me so much that after bothering family members with requests for more information and getting little (especially about the Great Hunger), I hopped the plane to Ireland. I used my title to get meetings with historians and museum administrators and bought rounds at pubs from Dublin to Kilrush and Cork to Donegal.

Often, the people in my family seemed to have a splinter in their souls, an abiding discomfort and pain that was not spoken of but was lodged by unseen hands and robbed them of their ease and joy. It was passed down from one generation to the next. I sensed it in Ireland as well. The Great Hunger was the culmination of over 700 years of British colonization efforts in Ireland that were at turns oppressive, then apologetic, then violent once more. So after that and some 150 years in America and Canada, were we past it?

In seeking to answer that, my mind turns to the next paragraph from my speech for the governor:

Upon arriving in Boston and other cities, the souls in these ships were exhausted, penniless and often ill. And, more often than not, greeted with the rhetoric and violence of anti-immigration and, particularly, anti-Irish sentiment. It formed the basis of the nativist party that burned down buildings, harassed and attacked people and attempted to pass legislation to keep the Irish out of American society.

The same was true in Canada. I would say my generation was the first not to face the persistent racism in America and Canada. Making it a history of over 800 years of wounds of varying degrees and locations. The weight of that sits heavy on my chest. And I see it in my family.

Restlessness, anger and a feeling that, no matter what you do, you may not belong here. Or there. Anywhere, perhaps.

Of course, this speech was too much. Too dark. And it didn't deliver votes. But I fought for it. It's where I was comfortable. Fighting for it. But it was not this portion of the speech that got me fired from the governor's office.

## 2. Cellular Responses in the Father

*"The results of our study were quite astonishing. So much so that we continued the research with a variety of groups of mice. In each case, the lab created trauma in young male mice and found the negative repercussions lasted six generations.*

*"Further, we have studied the genetic structures of groups of men who suffered trauma and have seen the same results: an epigenetic change to their DNA sequence. Meaning, it has brought forward cellular responses in the father that were passed to the son.*

*"The evidence, so far, points to this being passed on through the Y-chromosome, meaning to the sons through the fraternal line. There were symptoms in descendants that were similar to those in the first animals. In the mice, the offspring of traumatized fathers took part in more risk-taking behaviour, like exploring exposed areas of a platform suspended off the ground. When dropped in water, they gave up and stopped swimming sooner than the other mice, an indicator of depressive attributes in mice.*

*"In humans, if there has been no direct contact with a father acting out of trauma—meaning, the genetic response is passed down epigenetically—it's most likely to manifest as depression, anxiety and guilt."*

Was I, and others of my generation with Irish backgrounds, at the conclusion of this saga that played out over generations in our genetic code? The poor souls who suffered during the Great Hunger are separated from you and me by five or six generations.

In the village of Labasheeda, in County Clare, Ireland, where I was staying, there is another American who is one of the most active members of the community. He heard of my presence and took it upon himself to introduce me to the historic buildings. He took great pride in them. He quickly told me of his family's ties to the village and all the work he is doing in the community. Do the locals want people like us there at all? Rekindling the details of a painful history that is a greater burden to them than us. They've been steeping in it. But there are thousands of us that come back each year, searching from Ballyliffin to

Bantry and Dublin to Dingle for some sort of . . . peace, I suppose. And maybe it's not just for us but for all of those we carry within.

The crow that relentlessly cawed at me on my first night in Dublin as I walked the banks of the Liffey at 3 a.m., restless and agitated, offered no discernible wisdom that hinted at calmness to come. No, the bird seemed to be squawking about my need to listen to my own unquiet self. There was a cry inside me that kept me awake and pacing the worn quayside paths along the silent water.

Epigenetics fascinates me. The study of how behaviour or environment affects genes is an area of science that's getting a great deal of attention these days. And understandably. We're learning that epigenetics is telling our bodies how to read our genes and, in response, creating physical changes in our bodies. So, for the men facing trauma, our genes respond, and this response is passed down to sons.

We've known for some time that the children of people with unchecked and untreated mental health issues often act in ways that negatively impact their own children. But now we know that the trauma of our ancestors passes down for generations at a cellular level. In an unseen chain that binds us nonetheless.

My mind turns to that phrase often quoted from the Bible: "The Lord . . . does not leave the guilty unpunished; he punishes the children and their children for the sin of the parents to the third and fourth generation." When I think of crimes committed by members of the Irish community, I wonder how many of them involved men acting out of trauma? And isn't that one of the cruelest aspects of life: those who are suffering have to enter the world with it and are offered no balm to heal it? Instead, the opposite is more often the case: we are troubled and eventually act out in anger, fear or desperation and end up isolated and imprisoned while the trauma continues to flourish.

In the two sculptures that constitute the Irish Famine Memorial in Boston, the subject of my controversial speech for the governor, we have the ravaged victims on one side that soon become the thriving family in the next group. And only the mother of the modern, successful family looks back at the frail refugees they once were. Not the father or the son.

I dislike the ridiculous statues in the Irish Famine Memorial. The damn figures and the tale they weave in no way represent the complexity of the experience of the Irish in America. Or any other group of immigrants. Instead, it's propaganda cast in bronze. A lie meant to deny the Irish issues that persist today and the experience of countless other new Americans.

Too many Irish Americans and Canadians have not received the promise of the country. Between those two statue groups, just a step up from being starving refugees and miles from being successful Americans, is where I see many dwell. Other waves of immigrants have arrived in America, overcome the obstacles here and gone on to various levels of success. But that doesn't feel true with the Irish. Not all of us have been able to move beyond our dispossession.

A friend of mine likes to remind me that Boston has the largest white ghetto in America. And it's Irish. Maybe, as Americans of Irish descent, we've lost our history. It is a troubled story, filled with trauma, and the mind flees these painful memories. But it also defines us. We can't know who we are without understanding it. Instead, we act out of it unconsciously.

I remember being in Grade 4 in PS 27 in Brooklyn, New York, and not having lunch. Instead, I had food stamps in my pocket. My father was an emerging artist, but a few bad deals with galleries and a family to support meant our existence when I was young was precarious. We lived in the old dock workers' houses. A lot of Irish and Italians down on their luck lived there. And the community supported us. Our stay was short, only a few years, as my father's luck changed, thanks in part to the efforts of my mother, but the experience stayed with me.

At school, I thought if I didn't go out for lunch, they wouldn't know that I had food stamps. I decided I'd rather be hungry than humiliated. It was the only reason you were allowed to leave school at the age of 10. So, if I didn't leave, they couldn't make fun of me. But the teachers and administrators knew we were without money, so I was given the "free lunch"— a few lunches donated by a local charity. I wasn't asked if I wanted it. It was placed in front of me while all the other boys stopped to watch me. The little plastic plate. The bologna sandwich still wrapped in shameful cellophane. You could see right through it and me. I was poor. To this day, my shame rises when I conjure the image.

My friends went quiet. They knew about the free lunch, but none of us had it. My best friend, Marty Cohen, spoke up quickly and changed the subject to the last Yankees game. A kind boy who obviously sensed my humiliation. And being Jewish, maybe he knew what it meant to feel like an outsider. None of the three boys around me said a word about it. They were my friends and wanted to protect me. But when we went outside to play, a few of the other guys in our class, who weren't as kind, came at me.

"Was it a good lunch? I guess it tastes better than food stamps?" Vic Lucci asked me. I grew silent. His friends joined in taunting me. Something in me knew how to take the verbal blows. I stood. I let them grow in volume until I struck one of them, the loudest, on the nose with a closed fist. And of course I was the one sent to the principal's office after the teacher separated us in the yard. In fairness to that teacher, it was because I never uttered a word to explain why I punched him. It would only increase my shame to speak about the food stamps to another person.

I was on the verge of becoming a teenager and had little interaction with the distracted adults in our house. My father's growing success distracted him, but his negative feelings were never turned against me. Only himself. My mother, however, was born into a home where slaps, fists and wooden spoons were used freely to administer what she said was justice. But there was so much frustration and anger that I knew, even as a child, that it was not a measured response. She would swing and swing again in anger, screaming, and I would not give her the satisfaction of tears or any show of feeling. I simply stood and took it with outrage and disdain for her. I know she suffered worse at the hands of her mother. But her guilt about it and mental health problems continue to keep us at a distance from each other. I didn't try to bridge the gap because she wasn't ready for it. Maybe someday.

My growing frustration and lack of pocket money made it easy for me to join the guys who were dealing weed, acid and cocaine, partying and generally in charge of mayhem in our neighbourhood in Red Hook. It opened a doorway to a way to express my anger and outrage. But the prize for it was lacking.

I ran hot, got in some altercations, and was suspended from high school after my first week for fighting a bully. And I felt bad about it all. Even when I won a fight with a guy who picked it or was bullying someone, I carried a feeling of unease in the pit of my stomach. I just knew it was wrong. It didn't end until my friend Malcolm Walsh brought it all to a head.

Malcolm and I had grown up together in Red Hook. We got high on a Saturday night and stopped at a local store on the way to a party on the other side of the city. I had the loan of my parents' car. My dad's fortunes had turned, and we were now living in Manhattan, above his gallery. But I kept in touch with Malcolm. He was a year older than me, had finished school, and was just partying while he figured out his next move. His mom was from Jamaica, and his dad was Irish. His skin tone was darker, and that was enough to make growing up in Red Hook rougher for him than it was for the rest of us.

I don't even know what Malcolm wanted at the store. I waited in the car, and then I heard a loud noise. I thought it was fireworks. But when I looked into the store, I saw the cashier was holding a gun and Malcolm was on the floor. He had demanded money from the cashier without even showing a gun or any other weapon and was shot. I tried to run into the store but stopped when I heard a bullet crash through the glass door as I reached for it. The man behind the counter screamed at me and shot again. So I hopped in the car and took off. I still have a hard time admitting I left Malcolm there. He survived but spent the next four years in prison for armed robbery because he had just turned 18 and had been picked up once before for possession of marijuana. He never gave them my name. I offered to testify to make sure he didn't get charged with armed robbery, but he told me he did have a gun on him. He just never pulled it. Neither Malcolm nor anyone else in the neighbourhood would tell them I was there.

It changed me. I was done with messing around and wracked with guilt. I felt awful for not being able to help him. He made sure I was free and clear while his life was pretty close to ruined. My visits to Sing Sing seemed to do little for him. I could only watch as things turned from bad to worse for him. It was like a shadow was growing on him.

I turned to books by the end of high school. I took it as a challenge to defy the low expectations of some of my teachers. And it was art and humanities that stuck with me. Especially language. I still needed to do something with my energy, so I played basketball and volunteered as a tutor for kids from my neighbourhood. I thought that if I helped out in my community, I would feel better. And I did.

I got into Boston College. The first member of my mother's family to attend college. When I told Malcolm, he was happy. He also told me I shouldn't come back to see him anymore. Maybe it was too hard on him to see my life improving, or maybe he wanted to free me of the guilt. He might have thought it was about time. But I knew he meant it. He did get out after three years and has yet to respond to my attempts to reach him. There's a divide between us that I don't think either of us can cross now.

So I was off to college. I loved it. And I was a summer camp counsellor in Dorchester, the Boston neighbourhood my mother's side of the family had called home for generations. I also wrote for the college's student paper, *The Heights*. It felt good. In my last year of college, a friend from the paper, Megan Ferdinand, asked if I wanted to volunteer on a congressional campaign for a young Democrat. I did, and it began my life in politics. It allowed me to fight for something and contribute. And now, a few years later, here we are.

I've been feeling more and more like I didn't know what I was fighting for. I wasn't seeing beyond my need to win. And that old unease in the pit of my stomach was becoming more constant. Through it all, I knew something was missing in my life. There was a disquiet simmering beneath my success. So I had to look at it.

Today, Ireland has one of the highest rates of mental illness in Europe. And the troubles of the Irish have extended to America and the entire Irish diaspora around the world. Depression. Schizophrenia. Suicide. And, of course, that ol' standby, alcoholism, runs rampant in the community. A recent study in Boston shows that rates of depression are highest in Dorchester, home to many people of Irish descent. Yet the rates of treatment for mental health are lower in the area than elsewhere in Boston. People are not seeking help. I should also note that Dorchester is changing, and the new waves of mostly Asian immigrants are showing many of the same signs of mental health issues. The same study goes on to tell us that there is a correlation between the amount of time new Americans spend here and increased rates of mental health problems due to racism.

And then there is that line by Freud that the Irish were the only people (he knew) to be "impervious to psychoanalysis." Ah, what a thought that is. Except it's not true. There is no record of Freud stating it. And most scholars dismiss it. So why does it persist? We, the Irish, have embraced it. It's the Irish who say it the most, in my experience. A formalization of our sense of victimhood. A fatalist stance by the unwell. And it ensures we stay distant from the cure.

I don't feel victimized. Nor should I. I grew up with privileges and a sense of belonging. We overcame our financial woes, and we were successful. Maybe the thriving family in the memorial is a reflection of my mother, father and me. And maybe I don't like it because I feel the guilt of the survivor. I'm troubled that so many from my community still get left behind.

And if I'm honest, I know that the path of feeling that is most accessible to me is one of anger. One of my oldest friends, my Canadian cousin actually, grew serious when I spoke to him about this and said, "Of course you want to feel angry. It's the only thing we're allowed to feel." And anger is only a mirage. If you look closer, you can find the sense of sadness and loss, defeat and hopelessness. But we've been taught not to speak of these feelings. Only to become maddened that we have them. A self-destructive urge that should be followed to . . . no good end.

There is a burden upon us. I sense it. Especially with the men in my family. Those difficult feelings that lie just beneath the surface. And a desire to squash vulnerability, need, love or too much joy. Anger, outrage and violence are the paths laid before us. So it's not surprising that the rates of suicide among men are three times higher than those for women.

It all sits heavily. Especially knowing that this was programmed into us from the moment of our conception. The sins of our fathers will be our burden.

Sleepless in Ireland, I read into the wee hours of the night. And my mind often turned to the mythic Irish hero Cú Chulainn. He is so impressive in his physical prowess as a young man that he is invited to eat with the king. And that evening, Cú Chulainn doesn't just sit at the king's table but also shows his battle skills, and more importantly, his sense of justice and morality. From there, he goes on to be a great warrior. And he receives a mission: to defend his land from those who would overrun it.

Cú Chulainn only dies when he breaks the ancient rules of Ireland. He insults the goddess Morrigán. She transforms from a woman into a blackbird and tells him of his transgression.

And I, for one, feel more like that man. That somewhere along the way, I broke the unwritten laws unknown to me. It wasn't completely conscious. An inherited response, maybe. But I feel lacking. There was no king in our sphere that I aspired to emulate. And those around me, including most of the elders that I looked to, were without one as well. And I'm sure, like most men my age, we have insulted the female gods as they've been dismissed and pummeled for generations. Now their fury is most commonly on offer. Understandably. And the tragedy is that we needed both the female and male monarchs in our sphere to find our balance to become full people . . . but they have withdrawn.

Cú Chulainn's end is marked by a final battle where, moments before his death, Morrigán appears as a crow and stands on his shoulder, whispering to him, I presume, "You've been quick to draw the sword but have you learned to dance? Have you loved gently in the soft midnight? For whom will you dare to be kind?"

The young king then drifts into death while I read this in the black night, falling and falling and falling . . .

## 3. Reversible

*"Evidence also shows that traumatized mice raised in an enriched environment that is consistent and mentally engaging didn't pass the symptoms of trauma to their offspring. The data suggests life experience can be healing as well as hurtful and epigenetics can act differently. Environmental enrichment at the right time could eventually help correct some of the alterations which are induced by trauma.*

*"This and a few other studies suggest epigenetic response is reversible. We have the potential to change the narrative of doom around the topic. If it's epigenetic, it's responsive to the environment. That means negative environmental effects are likely reversible. With a supportive and consistent environment where the children are allowed to learn and play at their will, we see people overcome the adversity they inherited."*

I can see my relatives and neighbours in Dorchester and Grand Island grimacing at the sound of this. We're proud. We despise pity. But it's not that. It's caring for yourself and others around you.

This leads to the reason you won't hear the speech I wrote and to what caused my lack of employment today. In the remarks I was to prepare for the governor, after pressure from the park's donor and a growing conservative movement in the state, I was told I needed to embrace the false claim that the Irish were, at times in the past, slaves.

It's not only a lie about my ancestors, but it is a lie meant to undermine the grievances of my friends and neighbours whose ancestors were slaves in America. I was being called to first bear false witness to my own ancestors and then to use that lie to the advantage of the governor and undermine the Black population in America. What cause was I serving in doing so? Nothing that would please Morrigán or Cú Chulainn.

Here's a bit more of that speech you won't be hearing.

We need to reconcile ourselves to the truth of our past and our present. And though the Irish plight may have been heartbreaking, and though there were some who entered this country before the Great Hunger as indentured servants and faced humiliations and hardships, they can not be claimed to be slaves. Indentured servants entered a contract of work for a period of time and knew that freedom lay in the future. Slavery is a hopeless condition. Far worse.

Some today would claim that the Irish were nearly equivalent to slaves and that we overcame this. This is not the truth, and the implication to Americans today that have slavery in their lineage is that they should do as we have been told to do: overcome this setback and move on. This is disheartening, disrespectful and dishonest in many ways. We need to end that lie here today.

Before us in the Irish Famine Memorial, there is less than twenty feet between the two groups of people, each with three members, yet they have traversed the distance from ravaged famine victims to prosperous, twentieth-century, Irish-American family.

This is the hope, and it's the promise. And although we may fall short of achieving it at times, it must be the north star that guides us. So that we never cease to rise to do better for one another to achieve the highest goals of this American experiment.

It's true. Not only did I write a speech that didn't include a statement about the Irish being slaves and overcoming it, I wrote the opposite and handed it to the governor. And yes, I did not comment on the trite quality of the monument. I suppose I thought I had pushed this as far as I could and won the more important battle.

I understand the governor's predicament. He faces re-election in two years and fears an opponent from the Republicans who is willing to stoke the fires of anger with dishonesty to win an election. And the fiction is this: the Irish were slaves in America. "We got over it, and so should you!" And he relies upon the Irish of Boston to buy it so he can maintain his position. He can make them feel victorious in their struggles, even if that means undermining another group of Americans. I'm sure he doesn't *want* to do this, but he feels compelled to utter the words.

If politics has taught me anything, it's that words matter. My mother held the language in our house. My father's most confident expressions were formed in iron and steel. He could wrestle the pounds of chains, metal sheets, bolts and filaments into forms that expressed great aspirations, ideas and questions. But it was my mother who put that into words and attracted the attention of the media and buyers of his artworks. As his agent, manager, confidant, lover, and defender, she opened a door to a career he could not have had without her. Both knew it. And in fairness to my father, I think he inspired her in return and gave her a purpose she loved.

I, their only son, sought the same inspiration and wished for my creations to have three dimensions as well. Politics is the means we have to create reality. The material world we live in. I found a calling, and my mother's love of language aided me in convincing others to share in my vision to use politics as a means to mold the world into something a little better. Yes, I was young and naive about the shortcomings of politics in America today. I only saw it as a way to form a better place to live. I refused to accept that it had any other purpose. And, of course, I was built for the fight to achieve it.

The problem, for me, is that I just didn't want to do this anymore: be the governor's voice. The great and obvious issue is that the park is being used by some to dismiss the horrors of slavery and racism in America. That alone was reason enough for me to put my career on the line. And it should be. And it undermined the truth of the experience of the Irish in the U.S. At root, one question guided me to do what I did: Could I look my friend Malcolm in the eye and tell him that I wrote a speech that claimed the Irish were slaves in America? No.

But doubt still creeps in, and I worry that maybe none of this matters to you. Maybe I don't matter. We don't matter. The leftovers from a devastated island that fled to the emerging empire. Who cares? Because when we finally speak our truth, can we just be dismissed as fiery micks? But maybe we can stand with others for difference in America. The stern and tidy approach fails us all. Colonization fails us. We can be the defenders of that. And that will, I hope, help you and me, and this sometimes damning and sometimes transcendent experiment known as America.

As I took my walk, the morning after reading about the death of Cú Chulainn, I stepped into the late morning sun alone to walk the road along the Shannon in Ireland. There was no crow to be found. I suppose its work was done. And the old rolling green hills stood majestic in the morning light.

Ireland deserves to be unburdened by history and the small troubles of people like me. I came to confirm my suffering but found myself alone. I've been too long alone. I was done. Write it, then forget it. Enjoy the myriad of colours before you. The dazzle of today and today and today, you fool.

# 20. The Burial

June 6, 1868—Two miles northwest of Thayendanegea, Ontario

Patrick woke on the day of his wedding with renewed energy. *There isn't much to do now*, he thought.

It had been just two days since he had left his home at the Johnsons' farm near Sydenham to prepare his own small farm just north of the nearby town of Thayendanegea. He had purchased the land nearly two years before and had built a barn and a small home with the assistance of Steven Johnson and a few of the men from the church.

*They've been good to me*, thought Patrick. *The Johnsons. Taking me in as a boy, teaching me letters and skills. Some Irish children never found a home, died on the streets and disappeared into forests—the ones, like me, who lost their parents.*

Patrick couldn't bring himself to use the word *orphan* to describe himself. The label felt like an insult to all those who had shown care for him, and it seemed as though he would be declaring a fate he couldn't accept.

*I avoided death and abandonment*, he thought. *I should be grateful. My parents died trying to bring me to safety. And they took me in at the hospital until the Johnsons did the same on their farm. I was never deserted like some. I was fortunate. I avoided that humiliation— and worse. I don't know my last name, but that's about the hardest thing I've had to endure. It could have been much worse. And it was for most. I'm fortunate. The Johnsons knew I was Irish and Catholic and even connected me with their neighbours, who took me to church and looked in on me. Good fortune found me. And today I wed. Katie Flynn. A beautiful girl. And we have a home. We built it and we own it. And the land it stands on. That's something, isn't it? For an Irish Catholic, it is, to be sure. Lord, they're still killing us. D'Arcy McGee murdered just two months ago. And a member of parliament. I read the news sheets and hear the talk. I understand, but it doesn't raise my hackles as it does for some.*

*It's been years of saving, but I'm here. And we have a small community. There are many Irish out here. Some may not be doing so well, but we have each other. Everyone throws in for each other.*

He rose and walked through the house to see if there was anything he should do to prepare for Katie's arrival.

*The kitchen seems spare. You know what she will like? Flowers. I can pick some and leave them in a jug with a bit of water on the table.*

*Yes, she would enjoy that. The peonies have started to bloom. She'll like the sight of them and their fragrance, I think.*

After he cut them, he pondered the location for the flowers. *On the table? No, on the blanket chest near the window. That's more cheerful.* And then he realized it was time to begin his travels to the church in Hazelton. It would take a half day to get there.

Patrick was distracted at the wedding service. The congregation from St. Anne's had all come, and he recognized them all. Katie's family were members of the same church. *My family now*, thought Patrick. *And the Johnsons here as well. Both of them. Steven and Caroline. Maybe the first time they've set foot in a Catholic church. And that is not a small thing. But that woman behind them, a Catholic sister, it looks like, with the habit. Who is she? Maybe visiting the parish?*

It wasn't until after their dinner on the lawn of the church that Patrick met the woman he'd wondered about. She introduced herself as he sat alone for a few minutes while Katie was preparing to say goodbye to her family.

"May I take this seat?" she asked as she approached.

It was where Katie had been sitting.

"Of course," said Patrick, and he stood to greet the woman. *What's that faint accent she has*, he thought.

"Why, thank you, Patrick."

"You're quite welcome," he replied and sat down with her.

*Her face seems familiar.* The woman looked to be about forty years old, slim, with a slightly olive complexion. He guessed her hair was likely dark.

"First, let me offer my congratulations to you on your marriage. I am so happy for you."

"Why, thank you," Patrick replied. "But I'm afraid I don't know you."

"You do, but there is little chance that you would remember me. There is no way you would. When you were a child, I took care of you in Kingston, at the hospital until the Johnson family brought you to their home."

"Is that so?"

"It is, Patrick."

"Well, I suppose I should thank you, but I don't know your name."

"Sister Marie Garnier."

"Why, thank you, Sister. I did know that the hospital took me in, and that's about it."

"You are quite welcome, Patrick. You were a gentle baby and a kind little boy. And you seem to have grown into a considerate man. Would you like to know more about your family?"

He was stunned. Patrick had assumed his parents had died on the ship to Canada and that he had been delivered to the hospital when the surviving passengers landed in Kingston.

"Well, I suppose I do, if you know anything more about them."

"Yes, yes, I do. I compiled some information over the years so I could tell you when you grew to be a man."

"That's kind of you to do that."

"Your mother passed away with a fever in Kingston. She was a beautiful, kind, and strong woman, named Genevieve. And your father's name was James. He passed away just before arriving in Kingston."

"Genevieve and James."

"Yes. James and Genevieve O'Sullivan."

"O'Sullivan?"

"Oh, yes. . . Did you not know that was your name?"

*I feel foolish for not knowing it. But I don't want to lie to this woman who has clearly done so much for me.* "No, I did not know that. When anyone asked, I would just say Johnson."

"You wouldn't, would you? I never thought of that. You were just four when you went to the Johnsons' farm."

"Right. My only memory is of being at their home. I must have arrived in Canada just before that, but I have no recollection."

"You were just a babe. Born just as you arrived on Canadian shores."

"Is that so?"

"It is."

"And you . . ."

"Yes, I knew you as a baby. I knew your mother and swore to her that I would ensure you were safe. I took care of you until I found a suitable home for you."

"I didn't know any of this."

"How could you?"

"I could have asked the Johnsons, but . . . for some reason I didn't." *As nice as they were to me, I didn't want to bother them. I knew I was Irish Catholic, and that was not welcomed by some. I just needed a home.*

"You were just a boy, Patrick."

"But you took care of me."

"I did."

"Thank you. I don't know what else to say."

"It was a pleasure, and it was an oath I swore. You were such a nice boy. I was saddened to see you go away."

Patrick was surprised to see tears forming in the corners of her eyes. "You are very kind to have taken care of me after my parents died.

I thank you. And for helping me find a family who would take me in and treat me well. And that they did."

"Patrick, you have become the kind man I always knew you could be."

He was startled to find tears forming in his own eyes, and feelings of sadness and gratitude rising in equal measure.

"Thank you," he whispered.

"There is something I have for you. It was among your mother's possessions. I have kept it and wanted to give it to you myself when you were old enough to appreciate it."

She reached beneath her habit and retrieved a silver necklace with a pendant that was a circle with two hands meeting each other at the base of it. On the back of the circle, *O'Sullivan* was engraved in fine script.

When she placed it in Patrick's hand, he felt a surge and the tears were released.

"I believe your people in Ireland must have made this or had it made for them."

He tried to collect himself. "I believe you're correct."

"I should step away and let you enjoy your wedding celebrations. I did not intend to disturb your lovely day."

"No, please, Sister Marie. I would like to introduce you to Katie." He was surprised at how strongly he wanted this woman to remain near him.

"I would like that very much, Patrick."

As Patrick and Marie waited for Katie to return, he made a pact with himself. *This woman will now be in my care. I would not have made it this far without her. I know it. People still talk of all the dead buried at the waterfront. Over a thousand refugees like me and hundreds of local people who tried to help them. They did that. It's good to remember it. And some were nurses like Marie. In return, she will receive my care. The life of these sisters can be difficult. I will soften it.*

And it was true. At least once a month, in the years to come, Patrick would visit her in Kingston, and she would often spend part of her summers on their farm, teaching Patrick and Katie's children.

The rest of the night of the wedding, whenever he was alone, Patrick would remove the metal links from his suit pocket and run his hands over the small engraved hands and trace the word *O'Sullivan* with his finger.

After Katie fell asleep in their bed at the King George Hotel in Kingston that evening, he put on his pants, shirt, and shoes, and quietly made his way out of their room. Before he closed the door, he reached into his pocket to ensure the pendant was there. As he walked down the hall and out of the hotel, he held it in his pocket.

The hospital was only a thirty-minute walk in the warm night air. He had heard the stories of the fever sheds and the mass graves from the elders at the church. What was most disturbing for him was the mass graves. *All of those poor souls dumped into unconsecrated ground . . . and I suppose I now know my family is to be included in that count. My mother.*

The thought stopped him in his tracks. *There she lay. No funeral for her. And she would have only been about my age. Twenty. So young. . . It should have been the beginning of her life, not the end.*

He pushed himself to continue the walk, and eventually he reached the corner of Emily Street and King Street East. He knew from the talk of others in the community that this was where they had buried the dead from the fever sheds. But now, it was just a great swath of grass stretching down to the lake. *It's all so tidy now, isn't it? But beneath that pretty lawn lies my mother among so many others. And nothing at all to mark it. Dumped she was. Like the rest. In unconsecrated dirt without as much as a simple wooden marker. That great black blight that spread upon Ireland, destroying the only thing we had to eat, was a blackness that devoured my whole country, my community, my family. We were blackened out. They sent us into the gloom of history to be forgotten.. Nothing will ever make it right.*

Patrick fell to his knees on the grass and dropped heavy tears onto the ground, near where his mother lay.

*I won't leave you here. No, no I won't.* "None of you!" he screamed.

Patrick pulled at the turf with his hands, ripping the grass away, then dug his fingers into the dark brown earth and rocks beneath it. He dug wildly, tearing his fingernails and cutting his fingers while he wept. He continued for nearly thirty minutes, then, exhausted, covered in dirt, he stared into the hole he had created. It was nearly three feet deep and just as wide.

"How could you do this!"

He fell to the ground beside the pit, rolled over on his back, and stared into the night sky, sobbing. For nearly an hour he sobbed. Patrick finally let out a deep guttural cry and pulled the necklace from his pocket. He got onto his knees over the pit and dropped it into it. *There's nothing I can do for you.* He cried over the metal. "I'm so sorry. I'm so sorry. . ." He angrily pulled at the dirt around him to fill the hole and cover it. As he placed sod back on top of it, his tears abated. He stood, collected himself, and realized how filthy he was.

*I'll get back and clean up while Katie is still asleep. She won't know.*

He began to make his way back to the hotel. He absently reached into his pocket and the realization that it was empty somehow surprised him. Patrick looked back to the green lawn with its one area of disturbance and then continued on. His life suddenly felt small, and a sadness settled into him that he doubted he could easily shake.

197

him. Patrick looked back to the green lawn with its one area of disturbance and then continued on. His life suddenly felt small, and a sadness settled into him that he doubted he could easily shake.

# 21. The Burial Grounds

March 11, 2002—Grand Island, Ontario

Patricia was thinking about a conversation that stuck with her from the day before.

She was surprised when she'd heard Jeanine Miller speaking about the new buildings.

"Yeah, it's going to be good," Jeanine said. "They'll get rid of some of those rough old buildings and put in new ones and a whole new tower."

"Really?" Patricia asked.

"That's what I was told. Why do you look so confused?"

"Nothing. It's something else."

It was two days before she remembered to speak to me about it. I had been taking Irish language classes at the Irish Cultural Institute in the city. Since I had returned to the area, my uncle, Joseph, had begun to share books and engage me in conversations about Irish history. It was Joseph who had been the original benefactor to the institute. That was back in the 1970s. He brought in speakers from Northern Ireland. He had taken some grief in the local media about bringing in members of Sinn Féin, the political party of the republican movement in Northern Ireland. Some had felt that he was secretly funding the Provisional IRA. After the RCMP contacted him a few times, Joseph kept his activities quiet, with fewer speaking events and material support only.

Patricia was unaware of this history. She liked the dancers, and Joseph's father liked the musicians. So Sally and Colin began to organize events with both—music and dance. That evolved to include the Irish language classes. For my part, I had been working my way through Joseph's library of Irish history, poets, and novelists. I did find I liked the creative work more than the history books. Especially the poets and myths. Patrick Kavanagh, and especially Seamus Heaney, resonated with me.

We were at the kitchen table in Patricia's home, preparing a list of materials needed to build a barn near her house, which was down the lane we created from the main house on our property.

"Devin, I meant to ask you about something."

"What's that?" I asked absently.

"You'd mentioned that there was a mass grave beside the hospital. Of Irish refugees."

"Uh-huh."

"Where exactly were they buried?"

She had piqued my interest. I dug into the conversation.

"They buried bodies all around the hospital. It wasn't done with a great deal of thought or care. The number I have is roughly fourteen hundred Irish women, men, and children died and were buried on the hospital's grounds in unmarked graves. And some of the local residents helped when the Irish refugees arrived ill, and about three hundred of them died caring for the sick. Of course, the locals were given the courtesy of being buried in a cemetery. The Irish, though, were dumped into mass graves around the hospital. They never had much use for the Irish here. In life or death. Sorry, I'm going on. You got me started. The whole thing really bothers me."

"No, no, it's fine."

"What's on your mind?"

"Well, I heard this week that they plan to tear down some of the buildings at the hospital and are putting up new ones. I don't know if they would affect the mass graves, but I thought I would ask you about it."

"From what I know, there are bodies buried all around the grounds. I don't know how they could build without disturbing those remains."

"Really?"

"For sure."

I was now engrossed in the conversation. Patricia could see it. I'm sure she could almost hear the whir of my mind's machinery at work.

"The rotten bastards," I said. "It's bad enough that the bodies, some of whom could have easily been our ancestors, were placed in unmarked mass graves, but now they'll try to ignore the fact they are there at all."

"That's rough."

"It is. And it's nothing new. Back in the sixties, they put in a parking lot for the hospital, and the federal government and local historical society claimed to have moved all of the Irish dead to St. Mary's Cemetery. And guess what? They didn't do it. David Conway and the Irish Cultural Institute thought something was fishy and came across this company that can scan the ground to find out if there are remains beneath the surface. And lo and behold, there they were. Beneath the parking lot.

"That's terrible."

"It really is. I remember our great-grandfather used to say the Irish here called Kingston the Londonderry of Canada."

"Sorry. I don't understand. Why's that?"

"From what I understand, it's long been an Anglo-Protestant stronghold in Ireland. Regardless of the fact that the city has a Catholic majority, the city is run by the Protestants after years of making sure the Catholics were kept out of politics, business, and so on."

"Well, it's never been that bad here, has it?"

I paused. "Well, Patti, if the tensions weren't here, it's likely we'd be full siblings, not half. If you know what I mean."

"Right."

"It's more subtle here, and it's been fading away, thank God. But back thirty years ago, it was still a point of contention, and some of the old folks still feel it."

"That's fair. I know what you mean."

"Unless someone makes a fuss, they're going to do the same thing this time."

"That's brutal."

"Yeah. You know, we need to do what we can to make sure the hospital and the city do it right this time."

"I agree. What can I do to help?"

I smiled. *My God, she's got a good heart.*

"I appreciate it. Well, how about we split up the work? I know Conway and the Irish Cultural Institute, so it might make sense if I went to them for their support. We do need to talk to the local politicians about it. I think all three levels of government need to be aware of this and support a plan to move the remains. Because of jurisdiction and ownership of lands and all that, it could involve any or all of them. How do you feel about that?"

"Fine," she said. "As a nurse, I've dealt with every type of person on some of the most intimate issues. I think I can handle this."

"Good point."

"Illness and accidents happen to us all. You can't avoid me."

I laughed, and Patricia did as well.

"Okay, then," I said. "Let me talk to Conway and get ourselves aligned with them and then you can go after the politicians. I'll make sure you have the support of the institute. They do have some sway."

I was surprised at how happy I was to be working on a political issue again. And something about this felt better than the work I had done in the past. Maybe it was collaborating with my sister on an issue that directly affected our family and community.

The next day, I left Patricia a phone message. "Hey, Patti, I just wanted to let you know that I spoke to Conway and the institute is keen to help. He needs to get an endorsement from the board but he said that shouldn't be an issue. He and I will form a committee to get things rolling on this. You should likely be on it as well. Anyway, feel free to start your talks with the politicians. And let me know if you need anything. I hope you're well. And am I right that Kelly is moving out here this weekend? Let me know if you need a hand with it. We should at least celebrate it. Gimme a ring when you can."

Over the next few days, Patricia began making calls to the mayor's office and the provincial and federal MPs for the area and scheduled some meetings. She didn't get to speak to the mayor, Allan Thompson, but one of his staff told her it sounded like a good idea. Of course, they were only supportive after she mentioned the Irish Cultural Institute was supporting the project. The organization did have sway.

The local federal MP, Liberal Shelley Cragg, also staffed out the conversation. Her young constituency assistant said he would like to follow the issue and that Patricia should keep him abreast of the situation.

The provincial MP, Conservative Richard Smythe, and his staff did not return her calls. But reading *The Kingston Telegraph*, Patricia saw that Smythe would be attending a public event to name a street after a local hockey hero. She decided she would attend.

Patricia caught just the end of the speech by Mayor Thompson. They unveiled the new street sign and the stage party began to mix with the crowd. She caught Smythe when he only had one person with him. In his late fifties, Smythe had short brown hair that was clearly dyed.

"Patricia James," she said and offered her hand.

"Richard Smythe," he responded and offered his in return. The other person there just nodded.

He had no clue who she was, and it began to irritate her.

"I've left you a few messages about the plans for the hospital construction."

"Right. You're the woman so concerned about what's in the ground?" he said.

"That's right. I am that woman. And what's in the ground is people."

"You likely don't know that the federal government sets health care spending."

"The management of services and the buildings is the provincial government, correct?"

He grimaced and looked at the man beside him. "Well, I'm not responsible for graveyards. That's a local affair."

"But it's not a graveyard. They were never properly buried."

"And what is it to you?" he responded.

"I'm letting you know that the new buildings for the hospital, which I'm sure you're aware of, will be built upon the unmarked graves of the Irish who fled during the famine. I thought you might want to do something about it."

"I'm not sure what I can do," he replied. "And you'll have to excuse me—I need to get to another event." With that, he turned and was on his way, as was his companion.

Patricia was stunned. When she shared the story with JJ and me, she became even angrier. "How does he get away with that?"

"He's been the MP here for quite a while, and I would imagine he knows who butters his bread. And he knows it isn't you. Or me. And definitely not JJ."

"Fuck you and fuck him," JJ said.

"Fair," I said.

"But what can we do about it?" Patricia asked.

"Well, the way I see it, you can ignore him and get the support you need from the community and the media and move on, or you can use that support to force him to care."

"I like the sound of the second option. He needs his medicine."

"You're a fucking nurse, no doubt," JJ said. "And an O'Sullivan."

Patricia and I laughed.

In the following months, we shored up support in the Irish community and the local government, and at the hospital itself. Funding and support were still needed from the provincial government. Patricia had been keeping an eye out for news in the paper about Smythe and noticed that he was announcing his bid for re-election at a small public event.

She left work early that day and made her way down to the hotel and convention centre on the waterfront. The event was a luncheon for the Kingston Business Improvement Association, and Smythe had just been introduced when Patricia arrived. She stood at the back of the room. His comments were vague, touching on the history of business in the city and how the families responsible for providing employment in the city for generations deserved greater support from the government, which he would ensure was provided. At the end of his remarks, he also stated that this was one of the reasons he would be seeking re-election in the coming months.

When the applause died down and Smythe was leaving the stage, Patricia noticed the local TV station had arrived, just as I had promised her. She waved at them, and the reporter approached her.

"Hi! You must be Patricia, right?"

"I am. Thanks for coming."

"Well, it's an interesting story. I'm Marcia, by the way."

"It's nice to meet you, Marcia. I think it's interesting and vital. You should know that the hospital has a bad history on this issue. About forty years ago, they were in the same position. They wanted to do some construction at the site of the mass graves and promised to move the remains, but they didn't. Well, they moved some."

"Right. There was an article about it."

"Yeah. And this time, if there is public scrutiny and the politicians are on the hook, I think maybe it will go better."

"Okay, then," she said. "Go ask him your questions."

"Oh, you want me to do it?"

"I do. I'll get it on camera."

"Okay."

Patricia wasn't prepared to be on TV and began to grow nervous.

"Ready?"

"As ready as I'll ever be."

The two, followed closely by the camera operator, moved towards Richard Smythe, who was speaking to a few people just to the right of the stage. He quickly noticed the TV camera and turned to meet Marcia. As he did, he caught sight of Patricia and was visibly attempting to recollect how he knew her.

Patricia stuck out her hand. "Mr. Smythe, it's nice to see you again."

"Why, hello, I—"

"You may recall we met a little while ago. I'm concerned that the hospital construction slated for the coming year will not ensure that the remains of the Irish refugees in the mass graves buried beneath the ground of the project site will be moved to a cemetery. Can you ensure that's the case, that they will be moved?"

"Of course. As I've said, we will ensure that's the case."

"As you've said?"

"Sorry?"

"When did you say you would ensure the remains would be moved to another site?"

"Well, we've met before—"

"We did, and you said it wasn't your responsibility."

"If I did, I have obviously looked into the issue and can promise you that we will do this right."

"You promise this?"

"I do. The expansion of the hospital is vital, and we will ensure it's not only a state-of-the-art facility but that any remains in the ground are moved to a new site."

"You mean they will be placed in a cemetery with a marker noting that they are buried there?"

"Right. I do. That's what I said."

"Actually it isn't, but I'm glad you're saying it now."

Richard Smythe cocked his head to the side and stared at Patricia and then turned to Marcia. "I suppose you're here to speak to me about my plans for re-election."

"No. I'm here about the issues this woman has brought forward to you."

"Well, I guess we're done here, then." He was visibly annoyed and turned from the two women to continue speaking to the small group.

"That was great, Patricia!" Maria said, after they had moved away.

"Was it?"

"Yeah, you did a great job, but I don't think you're making any new friends here. You're going to see this on TV tomorrow."

"Will I?

"You will."

"Thank you!"

When Patricia relayed this story to me, she was sparkling with energy. "It just felt so good! Is that how things get done? Really?"

"Sometimes," I said. "At least in my experience."

"That's wild. I think I like politics."

"You do?"

"I do!"

A few days later, I met with the head of the Liberal Party's provincial riding association at his request. Smythe had a long history in the region, and the Liberal who had run against him in the previous election, Michael Springer, had not done well. Smythe had beaten him handily, but Springer was planning to try again. Word had gotten out about my background and my work in the area. The riding association was quick to think that I might want the nomination.

I laughed when they asked me if I would consider it, but Patricia, I thought, would make a great candidate. She had become a bit of a celebrity. Her interview had been replayed locally and regionally, and she had been interviewed by other media outlets. We were clearly on a course not only to get the remains moved to a cemetery but also to have a commemorative plaque and Celtic cross erected on the site. It had all happened fast, and it was largely thanks to Patricia. She had moved the issue forward and gathered more support and resources.

When I broached the idea of running for office, she became quiet.

She cocked her head to the side and looked at me. Her smile grew.

"Yes, I want to do it. But only under one set of circumstances."

"What's that?"

"You do it with me."

"Sure. I'll help get you there, but I won't be joining you if you win. I'll help you find staff."

She thought for a moment. "Fair enough."

"Fair enough," I said.

"If you don't want to be in politics, what are you going to do? I know you don't just want to run fishing charters."

"That's true."

"So?"

"I'm still figuring it out."

"Okay."

"It has to be okay. That's all I know for now."

# 22. Coda

September 7, 2002—Grand Island, Ontario

I had been living in a sort of limbo for months. I felt at ease being on the island but had no clear direction. I accepted that. But I didn't realize how much I cut myself off from feeling anything more than that. This peace was a respite, and I was basking in it. I was afraid any ambition I had might pull me from this place and these people. I wanted to be here with them, but I needed a purpose beyond helping my sister's campaign. I was thirty, with no partner, children, or career. The only thing keeping me here, keeping me attached to anything at all, was a decision I had made to stay. I needed more.

The essay in *The Boston Globe* had caused something of a stir and had been reprinted in *The Atlantic*. I was proud of that. Of course, it was followed by angry calls from Massachusetts that reminded me my career in politics was over. My acceptance of that seemed to outrage my callers further. It not only confirmed my decision but also highlighted the blank space I had created in my life. I had to trust that something new would arise in its place. I could sense it. It was like I could hear the musicians tuning up before a performance.

One day I received a call from Thompson Archaeological Services. Something had been found on a site in Kingston, and since I was an O'Sullivan they knew from the area, I received the call. The next day, JJ and I met them at their construction offices on the waterfront near the hospital.

A woman greeted me and presented me with a small clear plastic bag, a little larger than a Ziploc. I could see a small metal object in it.

"What the hell is it?" JJ asked.

It was a silver necklace with a pendant—a circle with two hands meeting at the bottom, one on each side, nearly touching each other, the fingers outstretched.

"If you turn it over, you'll see the name O'Sullivan. And we've had it cleaned and polished for you," the woman added cheerily.

Even the frail mechanics of the clasp were still in working condition. It could be worn. And I would wear it. But at that time, my attention was drawn to those fingers reaching for each other.

I traced them with my own fingers, inferring the unsaid from the metal.

My mind was also drawn to the aspirations of hands that belonged to one whose ways would be passed on to form my own. Those plans were buried with their body and the myriad of other unnamed dead.

I spied through the air between the hands and heard the opening phrases of a gentle song. And I felt hope begin to hum lowly. At first, I could only hear instruments. Uilleann pipes led the melody line, bodhran and water drums beneath it, with violins, harps, flutes, guitars, and mandolins between the two.

And then singers' voices rose with them.

I turned to the window. The light from the sun fell equally on the grounds of the buried and forgotten and on the waters just north of their place of rest, and on Grand Island in the distance. But as soothing as they were, the beams could not break the surface and reveal what lay beneath.

Could my role be to dig the earth to find what had been buried? Perhaps I could be an honest witness and share what was discarded or hidden so it could finally be known.

I sighed slowly and listened intently to the words of that song playing in my mind as I studied the slight silver device in my hands. Tales of hope and loss, so much sorrow and longing, acts of dedication, failures, doubts, anger, triumphs, and love. These were new songs. Fresh to me, at least. Of stories and characters often overlooked in this land and stretching back to Ireland itself.

And as the song climbed to its resolution, I thought about how Patricia, JJ, and I were the sixth generation on this shore. I hoped our gift to whoever trod here next from our line would be that they would not feel the past overpower their lives. Their troubles could be their own. Their pains would be their own.

Perhaps they would know of their once-overlooked forebears and the fight they threw themselves into so their descendants would have to face nothing of the sort.

JJ approached me as I stood silent and teary. He was unaware of my state.

"Shit, man, that had to belong to one of our relatives."

I just smiled and hugged my cousin while tears streamed down my face.

"Jesus Christ. Don't get so worked up. It's just a bit of metal."

He could tell something strange was at play with me. He pushed me back to look at me.

"Are you okay?" he asked quietly.

"Yeah," I said. "Finally. . . Maybe."

ACKNOWLEDGEMENTS

To go striding through the past, I engaged a few guides, that kindly showed me the way and grabbed my arm when I slipped. I'd like to first thank my friends in Ireland: Morgan Roughan for sharing his great knowledge of the history of the Kilrush area. And Rebecca Brew for being a generous guide. I'd also like to thank the staff at The National Famine Museum for the time they spent, and information they shared with me.

Here in Canada, I'd like to thank Dr. Mark McGowan from the University of Toronto's History & Celtic Studies Department who answered my many questions.

I'm indebted to many books but two especially: 'Simcoe Island An Eves Perspective - A Chronicle of the Island and its People' by Sanford Sydney Eves. And The Great Hunger: Ireland 1845-1849 by Cecil Woodham-Smith.

I enlisted a myriad of friends and family members to be readers of early drafts. Thank you all! I owe many a glass of wine.

I'd like to acknowledge the greatest Editor I've worked with in my life: Alex Schultz. Brilliant, thoughtful and supportive. I'm in your debt, Alex.

Finally, I'd like to thank my family for their support in writing this book.

www.ingramcontent.com/pod-product-compliance
Lightning Source LLC
Chambersburg PA
CBHW060314310726
48976CB00007B/2323